"That settles it. You have to go out with me."

Matt's gaze was unwavering. "Because we'd be good for each other. And because I can't stop thinking about you."

With the pool lights shining down on him, Matt looked as golden as when Jazz had first seen him bathed in sunlight at the park. Now that she'd gotten to know and like him, he was even more handsome. Her heart hammered. "I wish you would."

"Don't you think about me?"

"No," she said instantly.

"Now why do I think you're not telling the truth?" he asked softly.

It made not one whit of difference if she found him appealing. She needed to operate on the assumption that the twins were the children she'd given up. Honestly, she'd be a lot less likely to run into them if she didn't hang around their uncle.

Honestly, as far as Matt was concerned, she didn't think she could stay away.

Dear Reader,

My mother thought she was carrying twins until the moment I was born. "I hear two heartbeats," the doctor had told her. Instead, she got one big baby.

Maybe that's why I'm drawn to stories about twins and why the idea for *Twice the Chance* came to me fully formed. It's about a woman who stumbles across a girl and boy with unusually colored hair whom she thinks may be the twins she gave up for adoption.

The story, however, has a twist. Jazz Lenox doesn't want anyone, especially Matt Caminetti, the man with whom she's falling in love, to know about her suspicions. That's because she has another secret of her own....

Until next time,

Darlene Gardner

P.S. Visit me on the web at www.darlenegardner.com.

Twice the Chance
Darlene Gardner

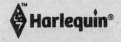

™
Harlequin®

TORONTO NEW YORK LONDON
AMSTERDAM PARIS SYDNEY HAMBURG
STOCKHOLM ATHENS TOKYO MILAN MADRID
PRAGUE WARSAW BUDAPEST AUCKLAND

Recycling programs
for this product may
not exist in your area.

ISBN-13: 978-0-373-71714-9

TWICE THE CHANCE

Copyright © 2011 by Darlene Hrobak Gardner

This is a work of fiction. Names, characters, places and incidents are
either the product of the author's imagination or are used fictitiously,
and any resemblance to actual persons, living or dead, business
establishments, events or locales is entirely coincidental.

This edition published by arrangement with Harlequin Books S.A.

For questions and comments about the quality of this book
please contact us at Customer_eCare@Harlequin.ca.

® and TM are trademarks of the publisher. Trademarks indicated with
® are registered in the United States Patent and Trademark Office, the
Canadian Trade Marks Office and in other countries.

www.Harlequin.com

Printed in U.S.A.

ABOUT THE AUTHOR

While working as a newspaper sportswriter, Darlene Gardner realized she'd rather make up quotes than rely on an athlete to say something interesting. So she quit her job and concentrated on a fiction career that landed her at Harlequin/Silhouette Books, where she wrote for the Temptation, Duets and Intimate Moments lines before finding a home at Superromance. Please visit Darlene on the web at www.darlenegardner.com.

Books by Darlene Gardner

HARLEQUIN SUPERROMANCE

*Return to Indigo Springs

To adoptive mothers
who love their children—and the birth mothers
who gave them the chance.

CHAPTER ONE

THE SOUTH CAROLINA sun bathed the young girl in light, bringing out the unusual color of the long silky hair she wore in a ponytail.

Jazz Lenox forgot about the stitch in her side, the need to watch the packed earth for rocks and exposed roots, and her determination to run two circuits around the trail circling Ashley Greens Park in less than thirty minutes.

The girl was about seven or eight years old and wore black shorts, high blue socks and a bright blue shirt shot through with yellow lightning bolts. She was beneath the crossbar of a soccer net with her back to Jazz, on the balls of her feet, her weight slightly forward. Her ponytail swished back and forth as she moved to catch a ball careening toward her.

Her *dark red* ponytail.

The shade was unusual but not unique. In the three years since Jazz had moved into her one-bedroom apartment in South Carolina, a few miles outside of Charleston, she'd spotted the hair color a dozen times on people of various ages. A middle-aged man. A teenage boy. A toddler girl.

This Sunday morning was the first time Jazz had stumbled across a redhead who appeared to be the right age. Jazz realized, of course, that she could be overreacting. Maybe this child hadn't even been a red-head at birth. It could be a coincidence that the girl's particular shade matched not only the wispy tufts that had been on the newborn, but also Jazz's grandmother's hair.

"Good job! You made the stop!" A man's deep voice cut through the warm August air.

The path of the trail brought Jazz even with the net, which was about thirty feet away. Off to one side of the girl stood a tall man with golden-brown hair wearing a T-shirt and athletic shorts. Probably the girl's father. He clapped his hands.

"Be warned, Robbie," he cried. "The girl in goal is a beast!"

"Boys are beasts, not girls!" The girl was dancing in place, making it appear as though the lightning bolts on her shirt were poised to strike.

"Give me the ball, Brooke." The third voice belonged to a young boy. "I'm scoring on you this time!"

Jazz had been so focused on the girl, she hadn't noticed the boy. Jazz kept running, putting one foot in front of the other by rote, craning her neck as her progress took her past where the boy stood.

He was about the same age as the girl with the exact shade of dark red hair.

The toe of Jazz's running shoe caught on something, and she pitched forward. She reached out her arms to break her fall and slammed down hard on her right side. The breath squeezed out of her and for a moment she couldn't breathe. She sucked at the air, finally feeling it reach her lungs.

Pain seared her shoulder and the forearm that had

taken the brunt of the fall. It was of little consequence. What mattered were the redheaded boy and girl. Were they the twins she sometimes found herself searching for no matter how determined she was to remain out of their lives?

She'd gotten such a brief look at the boy, she could have been mistaken about how old he was. Even if he were roughly the same size as the girl, that didn't mean they were twins.

The ground in front of her yielded no answers.

Praying the children and the man hadn't seen her fall, she got to her feet gingerly. The trio on the soccer field was laughing about something, immersed in their own little world that didn't include Jazz. The man was now standing in goal beside the boy, who gripped the soccer ball with both hands.

Drawing in a deep breath, Jazz wiped at the dirt on her scraped arm and brushed at the twigs and grass on her running clothes. Thankfully nobody had seen her fall. As it got later in the morning and the August temperatures rose, the trail became less populated.

"Go deep, Robbie!" the man yelled, waving his arm to indicate a point roughly even with Jazz. "Brooke's got a good punt."

The man bent his head to say something to the girl, probably instructions. He watched as the girl took three long steps, dropped the ball and punted.

The black-and-white ball arced into the sky and flew down the field. It must have careened off the side of the girl's foot because it didn't travel in a straight line, instead landing and bouncing not far from Jazz.

The redheaded boy was running toward the ball,

arms and legs pumping. Jazz told herself to resume her workout before the boy closed the distance between them but she craved a better look at him. With her heart hammering, she left the trail and headed for the rolling ball. She bent down, picked it up and raised her eyes.

The boy slowed, then stopped. His cheeks were red, she wasn't sure whether from exertion or exposure to the sun. Freckles sprinkled his nose. His expression was open and earnest, something about it striking a note of familiarity she both searched for and feared noticing.

"Can I have that?" the boy asked.

Jazz stared at him, her mind a blank.

He pointed. "The ball."

She looked down at her hands, almost surprised to see what they held. "Oh. Of course."

Jazz tossed him the ball. He caught it easily, but stood his ground. His eyes dipped. "You're bleeding."

She gazed down at herself and saw blood trickling down her right leg from a gash on her knee. "I tripped over a root."

"It looks like it hurts."

"It's nothing." She felt numb to the injury, her entire focus on the boy. Like the girl, he wore long socks that she now saw covered shin guards. Even at his young age, he had an athletic build, and was wiry rather than muscular. As far as Jazz knew, nobody in her family was an athlete. Was that relevant?

"Well, bye." The boy pivoted and dashed away.

She opened her mouth to call him back, then closed it. She shouldn't prolong their encounter. To the boy, she was a stranger who'd happened to retrieve his ball. Maybe that's all she was. She didn't know how old the children were, whether they were twins or if they'd been adopted.

She could probably concoct a story, approach their father and get some answers. But what purpose would that serve? Even though she couldn't help keeping an eye out for redheaded twins wherever she went, she would never consciously search for them. If they were happy, as this boy and girl seemed to be, she had no intention of disrupting their lives.

The boy appeared smaller and smaller as he retreated into the distance, finally stopping next to the man and the girl. The two children were virtually the same size, like twins might be. Jazz's throat thickened. She tried to swallow but couldn't manage it.

The boy said something to the man, then extended his arm and pointed to Jazz. The man patted the boy's shoulder before he took off in a slow jog, heading directly for her. The children followed.

Jazz told herself to move, to rejoin the path and continue her run. Her feet didn't cooperate, remaining as motionless as if they were glued to the grass. The man kept approaching, growing more substantial with every powerful stride. His coloring was nothing like the children's, his hair a sun-lightened medium brown, his skin lightly tanned. He reached her a few seconds before the children.

"Hey, are you okay?" the man asked. "Robbie said you were bleeding."

"She said she fell over a root," Robbie added helpfully. The boy had come up behind him, arriving a few seconds before the girl. Up close, she looked remarkably like the boy.

The girl made a face. "Oh, gross!"

"Blood isn't gross, Brooke," the man said before addressing Jazz. "You look a little pale. You should sit down."

With Brooke's hair pulled back from her face and Robbie's short haircut, it was easy to see their hairlines were identical, down to their widow's peaks. Also the same were their oval faces, their green eyes and the freckles dotting their noses.

"Did you hear me? You're not in shock, are you?" The man was talking again. *To her.* Jazz yanked her gaze from the children and focused on him. She placed him at somewhere around thirty, not much older than she was. With a slightly crooked nose and wide mouth, a combination that worked surprisingly well, he didn't resemble the children facially, either.

"Sorry." Her head was still spinning with possibility but she attempted a smile. "No, I'm not in shock. I'm fine."

He frowned, his brows drawing together. "You should clean that cut so it doesn't get infected."

She attempted to rein in her scattered thoughts. "I will when I get home."

"I have a first-aid kit in my bag," he offered. "It's over there by the goal."

"Oh, no." She immediately shook her head. "Thanks, but I couldn't be a bother."

"No bother," he said. "Name the injury, and I've probably had it. I'm darn near an expert."

She felt herself wavering. If she went with him, she could find out more about the children. What would it hurt to possibly verify these were the twins she'd given up at birth? She'd know for sure they were healthy and happy, all she could wish for.

"I don't want to take time away from your kids," she said, still undecided.

"They're my niece and nephew," he said.

"Uncle Matt's not married," Robbie added. "He doesn't even have a girlfriend."

"Mom says he has lots of girlfriends," Brooke chimed in.

"Nuh-uh," Robbie said. "I never met one."

"Not *serious* girlfriends." Brooke sounded years older than she was.

"Thanks for sharing, kids, but you're not helping," the man said with an exaggerated grimace. He moved close enough to Jazz to extend a hand. "I'm Matt Caminetti. And these blabbermouths are Brooke and Robbie, my sister's children."

"I'm Jazz," she said, deliberately omitting her last name. She had a vague impression of warmth when his hand clasped hers. Her mind whirled even as she greeted the children. Would it be a mistake to spend more time in their presence?

"Come on, Jazz. Let's get that first-aid kit." Matt took the decision out of her hands, turning back toward the grassy field and heading for the soccer goal. Brooke and Robbie skipped along beside him. After a moment's hesitation, Jazz followed.

"Race you!" Robbie called to his sister and took off at a dead run.

"No fair!" Brooke complained even as she raced after him, gaining steadily with every stride.

"Wow," Jazz said to Matt, "she's fast."

"It's tough on Robbie having a sister who's so athletic. She could beat him at just about anything if she tried. Except half the time she lets him win."

Jazz's heart pounded even faster than it had when she was keeping up her seven-minutes-a-mile pace. "They look a lot alike. Are they twins?"

"Yep," he said. "Makes the whole competition thing even harder for Robbie."

She tried to keep her voice from trembling. "How old are they? Seven? Eight?"

"Eight," he said. Jazz's heart squeezed. The twins she'd given away would have been eight last month. "I think," Matt continued. "Or maybe they're seven. I see them all the time but I lose track."

Ahead of them, Brooke put on a burst of speed to draw even with Robbie, then slowed down noticeably. Brother and sister ran alongside each other for a few strides before Robbie stumbled, his arms windmilling as he righted himself. Brooke reached the goal inches ahead of her brother.

"You only won because I tripped!" Robbie cried.

Brooke settled her hands on her slim hips in a pose Jazz had seen females use countless times when dealing with a difficult male. "Whatever."

"Let's go again!"

"No."

"What are you?" Robbie got right in her face. "Chicken?"

"Guys, stop! You'll scare away Jazz," Matt yelled to them good-naturedly, as though he'd heard it all before.

Matt continued walking to an athletic bag lying

behind the goal and crouched down beside it. He looked up at Jazz with eyes that were a light brown instead of green like his niece and nephew's. "Is Jazz short for Jasmine?"

She wanted to ask the questions, specifically whether his sister had adopted Brooke and Robbie and the exact date of their birth. Except she couldn't think of a way to work those topics into the conversation.

"It's just Jazz," she said. "My mother liked the music."

"I like the name." He smiled at her before digging into his bag and pulling out the first-aid kit. "My sister gave this to me for a Christmas present when I started spending lots of time with her kids. She's kind of overprotective."

"Is she a redhead, too?" Jazz ventured, although that wouldn't tell her anything definitive. The gene for red hair was recessive.

"Nope." He opened the kit and pulled out antiseptic and a cotton swab. "Come closer and I'll clean that for you. The bleeding's stopped but this could smart."

She complied, the sting of the antiseptic barely registering while she tried to figure out how to extract more information. Her head started to pound when nothing occurred to her. She'd make a terrible investigative reporter.

"The cut's not too bad, but it needs a bandage." He took one out of his bag, tore off the packaging and positioned it over her skin. "How's the shoulder? You're holding it like it hurts."

She concentrated on his question instead of Brooke and Robbie kicking the soccer ball back and forth a few feet away. The throbbing had subsided to a manageable level. "It's okay."

"You should probably see a doctor," he said. "At the very least, ice it and take some ibuprofen."

"Are you done yet, Uncle Matt?" Robbie called. "You said we'd work on *my* corner kicks next."

"Just a sec," he called, then peered at Jazz. "Do you need a ride home? My car's just over there in the parking lot. It's getting too hot to stay much longer anyway."

She fought the temptation to accept and gestured vaguely to the trail. "Thanks, but I don't live far from here."

He seemed about to protest, but then said, "Okay. Just remember to ice your shoulder. Nice meeting you, Jazz."

"You, too." She drank in the sight of the children who might be hers, assuring herself she was doing all of them a favor by cutting off the acquaintance. "Bye, Brooke, Robbie."

"Bye!" the children said in unison, but Robbie was already picking up the soccer ball and running to his uncle. Brooke was humming a pretty little tune.

Jazz turned away, feeling an ache that had nothing to do with her injuries.

She'd taken maybe ten steps when Matt Caminetti called to her, "Hey, Jazz."

She whirled.

"We'll be here Sunday mornings after church until fall soccer starts and probably even after that, too," he said. "Stop by and say hi."

She raised a hand in acknowledgment before turning

her back and walking out of their lives. She wouldn't accept his invitation no matter how tempting.

Neither would Matt Caminetti have issued it if he'd known Jazz had given birth to redheaded twins while serving a prison sentence for committing a felony.

CHAPTER TWO

MATT SKIMMED the offerings on the lunch menu on a Monday more than two weeks later while breathing in the maple-syrup-scented air. Pancakes with strawberries. Gingerbread pancakes. Cinnamon pumpkin pancakes. German apple pancakes. The list was virtually endless.

"You two ready to order?" A blonde waitress in her mid- to late-twenties with the name *Sadie* written on her name tag stood beside their table, order pad in hand. She had a girlish voice and a figure that was anything but juvenile, shown to advantage by a gold uniform that hugged every curve.

"You go first, Matt." Matt's sixteen-year-old brother Danny spoke without lifting his dark head from the extensive array of pancake choices.

Matt closed his menu and set it down on the table. "I'll have a chicken sandwich and unsweetened iced tea."

Sadie lifted one finely plucked eyebrow. "You sure? We're not named Pancake Palace for nothing."

"I'm sure," Matt said. No point inviting questions by revealing he wasn't overly fond of pancakes.

He hadn't heard of the restaurant until he'd noticed the place advertised on Jazz's T-shirt as the sponsor of a local 10K race. Matt had been at Ashley Greens Park twice with the twins since he'd bandaged her leg, but she hadn't shown up. That was cool with him. Or so he thought until he'd spotted the Pancake Palace sign from the car and suggested he and Danny stop for lunch.

His impulsiveness hadn't paid off. The only other waitress moving about the tables and booths was a shorter, rounder version of his mother.

"Whatever you want, I'm happy to oblige." Sadie held Matt's gaze a few beats longer than necessary before shifting her attention to Danny. "You want me to come back, hon?"

"No, I'm ready. I'll take the wild-blueberry pancakes with a double order of pork sausages, a banana-nut muffin and a large chocolate milk." Danny started to close the menu, then flipped it back open. "And some cinnamon French toast."

"French toast instead of the pancakes?" the waitress asked. Matt felt a smile coming on.

"Nope," Danny said. "I want the pancakes, too."

"Okay." Sadie concentrated on Matt while she leaned forward to take their menus, providing him with an excellent view of her attributes. "Let me know if *you* want anything else."

She left them, her hips swaying from side to side in an exaggerated manner. Danny appeared in danger of straining his neck watching her retreat.

"Did you get a load of that?" Danny asked in a loud whisper. "That waitress was totally coming on to you."

"She was just being nice."

"Yeah, right," Danny drawled. "You gonna get her phone number?"

"No, I'm not, little brother," he said.

"Little?" Danny straightened in his seat, taking offense as Matt had known he would. "I'm almost as tall as you are."

"You'll be a lot wider if you keep eating like a blue whale."

Danny waved him off with a thin arm. "I'm a teenager. I'm supposed to pack it in. Isn't that why you're always feeding me?"

Matt had carved time from his summer schedule at least twice a week to take his much younger brother for driving practice and out to lunch. Finding the time had gotten harder a few weeks ago when Matt had taken over as interim athletic director at Faircrest High. As of tomorrow, the first day of school for students and the start of Danny's sophomore year at Faircrest, it would be tougher still.

"I'm afraid you'd gnaw my arm off if we didn't stop for food," Matt said.

Danny laughed. "Why'd you pick this place, anyway? You don't even like pancakes."

Matt wasn't about to confide in his brother about Jazz, especially because his long shot had misfired. She'd most likely been wearing the T-shirt because she'd run in the race the restaurant sponsored.

"*You* like pancakes," Matt said.

Danny grinned. "I like food."

Danny proved how much when their order came, polishing off his meal in an amazingly short time. Between mouthfuls he kept up a running conversation about family, food and the Faircrest High football team. Practice had started at the beginning of August in preparation for the season opener, which was in a few days.

"I'm busting my butt," Danny said. "I'm the first one at practice and I work the hardest. Dad says that's the way to get noticed."

"Dad knows football." Matt chewed slowly on his chicken sandwich. Their father had played college ball at Florida State and coached the Faircrest football team before becoming the high school's athletic director, the job Matt was currently in. Dad was retired now, which gave him more time to indulge his passion. When he wasn't watching football, he was talking about it.

"I'm getting some time with the first team," Danny said. "I want to be so good Coach Dougherty has to start me."

"That's the attitude," Matt said. "You can't reach goals if you don't set them."

"Dad says that, too." Danny finished his French toast with gusto. "Did he push you to be the best you could be, too?"

Their father had been more interested in trying to persuade Matt that giving up youth football for soccer was a mistake. Never mind that soccer was the world's most popular sport, with billions of fans in all corners of the globe. Or that Matt had gone on to earn a full scholarship on the Clemson soccer team.

"Be the best you can be, huh?" Matt said, avoiding his brother's question. "Seems to me I've heard that on a commercial."

Danny laughed and told him about a senior on the football team who was applying to West Point. By the time Matt paid the bill, his brother had moved on to the subject of the Faircrest High athletic director position.

"So the job's not yours yet?" Danny asked.

"That's what *interim* means," Matt teased. "This is kind of like a tryout."

Danny stood, lanky in his maroon Faircrest High football T-shirt and the baggy black athletic shorts that reached almost to his knees. "You're a lock, man. Things always go your way."

"They go my way for a reason," Matt said when they were outside the restaurant. He'd been a full-time assistant A.D. at Faircrest for six years. It was time he moved on to the top job. "You heard what I said about setting goals. Once I set mine, I go after them hard."

Matt hadn't achieved today's goal of running into Jazz, but she probably wasn't even employed by Pancake Palace. Unless she had the day off, a possibility he had yet to rule out.

"How about meeting me at the car?" he told Danny. "I'll be there in a couple minutes."

Without waiting to see if his brother complied, Matt headed back into the restaurant. He spotted Sadie clearing away the dishes at the table where he'd sat with Danny. The older waitress, who reminded him of his mother, was closer, jotting down an order for a family of four.

Matt intercepted the second waitress beside an empty booth while she was en route to the kitchen. Her name was Helen. "Sorry to bother you, ma'am," he said, "but does a woman named Jazz work here?"

Helen's mouth turned downward at the corners and deep lines formed on her forehead. Up close, she looked nothing like Matt's mother. "Jazz Lenox is one of our short-order cooks."

That explained why Jazz hadn't been waiting tables. "What days does she work?" Matt asked.

"She's in the kitchen now." Helen's eyes narrowed, as though she were making up her mind about something. "I'll tell her you're out here."

"You don't need to do that," Matt said, but he was speaking to the waitress's retreating back.

He breathed in the scent of pancakes and syrup, not sure of his game plan. He was good on the fly, though. When an opportunity presented itself, he could make the most of it.

The interior door leading to the kitchen swung open. A woman emerged with a bandana covering her shoulder-length brown hair. Jazz, looking far different than she had at the park. An apron covered her toned limbs, her forehead was damp and her face flushed from the heat of the kitchen. Yet with her clear gray eyes and the freckles dotting her long nose, she had an appeal Matt couldn't resist.

"Hey, Jazz," Matt said. "Sorry to bother you at work. You look busy."

"I am busy," she confirmed, then went silent.

"You're probably wondering what I'm doing here." He decided to go with blunt honesty. "I'm wondering that same thing myself."

Not a great opening but not bad, either, especially because he couldn't pinpoint why Jazz had made such an impression on him. Unfortunately it didn't seem as though he'd had the same effect on her.

"Matt Caminetti." He introduced himself again. "We met at the park. I was with the twins."

"I remember," she said.

The same curiosity he'd experienced at the park hit him. Jazz was nothing like the chatty females at the high school. Or any of the women he usually came across, for that matter.

"You were wearing a Pancake Palace T-shirt. That's how I found you. Not that I was looking exactly." Matt made a face. "Man, I'm butchering this."

"Butchering what?" Her voice competed with the hum of conversation in the dining room and the clattering of dishes from the kitchen. She lengthened her vowels like a Southerner but her accent didn't sound Charlestonian.

"I think I'm asking you out." He'd checked out her left hand for rings at the park and found none. When she didn't respond, he checked again. Nope. No ring: wedding, engagement or other. But that didn't always tell the full story. "Unless you're dating someone?"

"No," she said. He wasn't sure which question she was responding to.

"I don't mean to be rude, but I need to be getting back to work." She glanced over her right shoulder toward the kitchen and winced.

"Have you seen a doctor about that shoulder?" Matt asked.

"It's fine." She repeated the phrase she'd used at the park, inching backward as she talked. "I really need to go."

"Of course," Matt said, taken aback by how eager she was to get away from him. Even so, he felt compelled to ask another question. "So when you said no, that was to the date?"

She nodded. "But thank you very much for asking."

She disappeared through the swinging kitchen door. He grimaced, feeling as stunned as if the door had hit him in the face. He couldn't remember the last time he'd been so summarily dismissed by a woman, if ever.

The people at the nearby tables weren't paying attention to him. His luck ended there. Danny stood beside the empty hostess stand, his mouth hanging open while he waited for Matt to reach him. "Did you just get shot down?"

Matt frowned at his brother. "Weren't you supposed to wait in the car?"

Danny ignored the question. "Who was that, anyway?"

"Just some woman." Matt walked past his brother out of the restaurant and into the sunny August afternoon, where it became glaringly obvious he hadn't told the truth.

If Jazz Lenox were just another woman, her rejection wouldn't sting so much and Matt's goal wouldn't be to turn her no into a yes.

AN HOUR LATER Jazz slid a plate of chocolate-chip pancakes through the pass-through window, turned back to the griddle and methodically flipped over the apple streusel pancakes arranged in a neat row.

"These are supposed to be cherry, not chocolate chip." Helen Monroe's pinched face appeared through the opening in the window. "And where's the order for table seven? Some of us work for tips, you know."

"Sorry," Jazz muttered, grabbing the plate, annoyed at herself for making the mistake. "Table seven's coming right up, then you'll have your cherry pancakes."

"I can only hope," Helen said before disappearing.

"Don't be nice to her." Carl Rodriguez, the other short-order cook, had also done time in prison. He didn't say much in the course of a shift, but Helen, who had complained to the owner several times about his hiring of ex-cons, was a hot button. "She makes many mistakes."

Jazz set a couple of plates beside the griddle. "That doesn't mean I have to."

"You don't usually." In his thirties with dramatic dark hair and eyes, Carl was of medium height with a slender build. He quirked a black eyebrow at her. "You okay?"

Jazz had been fine until Matt Caminetti made his surprise appearance. More than two weeks had passed since she'd met Matt and the twins at Ashley Greens Park. She'd altered her jogging route and schedule, although she'd nearly convinced herself that they couldn't be her birth children.

Then again, she considered it likely that children were placed for adoption in a different part of the state from where they were born. Jazz had been arrested in Florence and given birth in Columbia.

One thing, however, was certain. If the twins were her biological children, she never wanted them to know they had a mother who'd been locked up.

"I'm kind of tired today." Misleading, but not a lie. Four nights a week Jazz worked as a telemarketer selling magazine subscriptions. Last night she'd finished at

10:00 p.m., which took a toll considering she hadn't been sleeping well and her shift at Pancake Palace started at 5:30 a.m. "It makes it tough to concentrate."

"That's not why you can't concentrate," Sadie Phillips declared. Jazz hadn't even noticed the waitress enter the kitchen. Sadie's lips, painted a deep pink, were smiling. Her hands rested on her curvy hips. "It's because of the hot guy. Who is he?"

Jazz felt heat creep up her neck. "Nobody."

"Oh, come on, Jazz. Stop being so blasted private," Sadie said in her thick Southern drawl. "If a man like that was interested in me, you couldn't get me to shut up about it."

"It's not like that," Jazz said.

"Oh, really? Then why didn't he look twice when I shook my stuff at him?" Sadie demanded.

"You got good stuff," Carl said without glancing up from the potatoes he was slicing.

"Why, thank you, Carl." Sadie sounded pleased by the compliment. "The only reason for a man not to look is if he's interested in other stuff."

Carl chuckled softly. Jazz kept her head down, glad she had the excuse of transferring pancakes to plates. In prison, she'd quickly learned that knowledge was power. She wasn't about to tell Sadie why she had no interest in dating Matt Caminetti. She wouldn't tell anyone.

Jazz got through the rest of her shift without another mention of Matt. When two o'clock arrived, her mind turned to the lonely night ahead. A legion of short-order cooks had come and gone since she'd started at Pancake Palace three years ago, enabling Jazz to choose a shift that allowed her to take a second job. Too bad she hadn't been able to find one that gave her more hours.

"Hey, Jazz." Sadie was waiting for Jazz beside the front door. The waitress's eyes sparkled. "That man who's not interested in you? He's in the parking lot."

Jazz's breath snagged before a logical explanation occurred to her. "He probably has some shopping to do."

Pancake Palace was located in a shopping center a few miles west of historic downtown Charleston, sharing space with a grocery, a drugstore and other assorted businesses.

"We'll soon find out, won't we?" Sadie asked.

The waitress opened the door, stepping aside to let Jazz precede her. Matt Caminetti was leaning against a silver coupe. He immediately straightened and walked toward them.

"Told you so," Sadie said teasingly, her voice a whisper. "I expect to get the whole story on Monday." She headed away from Jazz, waving and calling, "Bye, Jazz."

"Bye, Sadie," Jazz said automatically. She couldn't seem to get her feet unstuck.

She'd been so focused on the twins at the park that Matt had barely made an impression. That wasn't the case today. Matt was the sort of man women looked at, not so much because he was drop-dead handsome but because he had an unmistakable energy. Like someone had thrown on a light switch inside him, causing everything about him to seem more vibrant. Even his slight Southern accent was attractive, smooth instead of twangy.

"I promise I'm not stalking you," Matt said when he stepped onto the sidewalk. He was smiling, his light brown eyes trained on hers. She was five-nine in her bare feet but he was half a head taller. He held out a few sheets of paper along with something red and stretchy. "I brought you some elastic tubing and printouts of isotonic exercises for your shoulder."

She crossed her arms over her chest. "Why?"

"Because this is what my orthopedist said to do when I strained my shoulder back in college." He continued to extend the items to her. One corner of his mouth lifted in a half smile. "I promise I didn't attach any strings."

She uncrossed her arms and took the sheets and the tubing, being very careful not to accidentally touch him. "Thanks."

"You're welcome." He held up a hand in farewell and did a slow jog to his car. Halfway there, he turned back and called, "Notice how I didn't ask you out again?"

"I noticed."

"Out of curiosity, if I had asked, would the answer still be no?"

"Yes," she said.

He jumped on her reply. "Yes? You changed your mind?"

"Yes." She felt her lips curve. "It would still be no."

He snapped his fingers and shook his head. "You can't blame a guy for trying."

She didn't let her smile grow until she got behind the wheel of her car. It was a good thing Matt Caminetti was strictly off-limits. Otherwise, he might tempt her to forget that she couldn't trust her instincts, especially where men were concerned.

THE LARGE BOX SITTING on the carpet in the middle of Jazz's living room floor didn't look like anything special. Slightly battered and made of cardboard that was dirty in places, the box had arrived by UPS almost an hour before.

Jazz hadn't opened it yet because she had the feeling that nothing would be the same once she did. Ridiculous, really, considering she didn't know what was inside.

She had no basis for foreboding except that she seldom got anything delivered to her at all besides bills and junk mail.

The box probably weighed a good thirty pounds or so. If Jazz hadn't been religiously doing the shoulder exercises Matt Caminetti had given her two days ago, she might not have been able to lift it without pain.

She frowned. Thinking about how considerate Matt had been represented a different kind of Pandora's box. It seemed less risky to find out what was inside the package than to open herself to the possibility of dating him.

Jazz got down on her knees beside the box, flipped open her pocketknife, cut through the packing tape and drew back the cardboard flaps. A sheet of white paper lay atop a pile of what looked to be mostly clothes and books.

Jazz picked up the piece of paper, noticing at once the South Carolina Department of Social Services letterhead. She read the few typed paragraphs, then read them again.

It seemed her foster parents had found a box of her belongings in their attic. Instead of trying to find Jazz's current address and mailing her the box themselves, they'd asked DSS to forward it.

Jazz shouldn't be surprised. The last time she'd seen or heard from her foster mother was at a holding cell in the county jail the night Jazz was arrested.

A tear dripped down Jazz's cheek. She angrily dashed it away. She'd learned quickly all those years ago that crying accomplished nothing.

Jazz put the letter aside and turned back to the box, pulling out some skinny jeans and shirts with plunging necklines. The high-heeled black sandals and bangle bracelets she'd been wearing when she was arrested were there, too. So were a black hip-hugging micro miniskirt and a thong bathing suit.

The rest of the box contained more clothes she'd never wear again, a few pieces of cheap costume jewelry, an alarm clock with a dead battery, some Harry Potter paperbacks and a couple of high school yearbooks.

Jazz sat cross-legged on the carpet, her back resting against her love seat, and leafed through the top yearbook. It was from one of the most traumatic times in her life: junior year, after her grandmother died and Jazz was shuffled to foster care. The only image of Jazz was in the class-photo section. She was unsmiling, her hair falling forward in her face, defiance in her eyes.

After flipping her yearbook closed, Jazz picked up the second one. It was black like the first yearbook but the name of the high school on the cover was different.

Jazz ran her fingers over the four embossed numbers that formed the year before Jazz was born.

This was her dead mother's yearbook, not hers.

She'd been so angry at her mother for leaving her the way she did that Jazz had never even looked through it. Jazz had a vague memory of packing the yearbook with the few belongings she'd taken from her grandmother's home. She wasn't exactly sure why she'd kept it except she had nothing else of her mother's.

She held the book without opening it, remembering the chocolate bars her mother would bring when she stopped by every month or so to ask Jazz's grandmother for drug money.

Jazz's gratefulness for those scraps of affection had turned into resentment when her mother died of AIDS, although at nine years old Jazz hadn't fully understood the situation. She still didn't.

Had her mother been on drugs when she got pregnant with Jazz? Is that why her mother claimed not to know who had fathered Jazz?

Jazz stared down at the yearbook, curious if it would shed any light on who her mother had been. She flipped it open to a page that contained a yellowed newspaper clipping and a snapshot. The article was a glowing review of the high school drama department's production of *The Odd Couple,* which heaped praise on Bill Smith, the student who'd played Oscar. Jazz skimmed the article for her mother's name but didn't find it.

She picked up the photo, barely recognizing the young, smiling girl as her mother. Next to her, with his arm around her, was the same handsome, dark-haired boy pictured in the newspaper article.

Jazz leafed through the yearbook but found no other newspaper clippings or snapshots. Why had her mother kept only those?

She turned to the section containing the junior-class photos. Like Jazz, her mother hadn't finished high school. Bill Smith wasn't pictured among the juniors but Marianne Lenox was, smiling almost as widely as she'd been in the snapshot.

Jazz thumbed through the yearbook pages until she reached the senior-photo section, noticing there were no signatures or messages written in the margins with one exception. Something was written in a bold hand under the photo of William Smith.

Thanks for the good times, M. It was signed *Bill.*

The caption underneath his photo read: A Man of Many Talents. Then came a listing of extracurricular activities that included drama, track, honors' society, debate club and jazz band.

Jazz band.

Her heart pounded so hard she could feel the blood pumping in her ears. Jazz stared down at the photo of the dark-haired, dark-eyed Bill Smith, telling herself that what she was thinking was crazy. Jazz saw nothing of herself in him. Why, she looked more like the girl in the photo next to him.

The girl's name jumped out at Jazz: Belinda Smith. Jazz's eyes dipped to the caption under Belinda's name: The Better Half of the Smith Twins.

The page in front of her blurred as Jazz tried to think. She was pretty sure twins ran in families. Jazz didn't know if it was true but she'd even heard it was common for twins to skip a generation.

It no longer seemed like a wild coincidence that her mother had kept an old newspaper clipping and photo of a boy who'd played in a jazz band.

The irony was that in the same month Jazz had stumbled across twins who could be her biological children, she may have identified the man who fathered her.

CHAPTER THREE

JAZZ MIGHT HAVE TO find another form of exercise.

Running had always helped her think more clearly, but in the week and a half since she'd looked through her mother's yearbook she still hadn't decided what to do about Bill Smith.

And now trouble she didn't need was on her heels, because she was nearly convinced that the man behind her on the park's running trail was Matt Caminetti.

She stole another glance over her shoulder. Maybe she was wrong. The man was within thirty or forty yards, far enough away that his features were indistinct but close enough to tell he had a lean build and golden-brown hair.

She'd seen dozens of men over the years while running in Ashley Greens Park who were brown-haired and in shape. Her glimpses of the mystery man had been so fleeting he could be anybody.

Besides, Matt had specified that he came to the park with the twins on Sunday mornings. It was Monday morning, a month after she'd met him and two weeks since he'd stopped by the restaurant. Fearing that she'd bump into him every time she went jogging was crazy.

Except it was Labor Day, when people didn't necessarily stick to their schedules. Jazz would usually be at work on a Monday morning herself, but Pancake Palace was closed for the holiday.

To be on the safe side, she ran faster.

The path left the straightaway to snake through a copse of trees. With her eyes straight ahead, Jazz concentrated on pulling ahead of the man. At the quicker pace, her legs protested, her lungs burned and her breath grew short.

It didn't make a difference. She soon heard the crunching of footsteps gaining on her.

"Hey, Jazz." A familiar voice that didn't even sound winded called from behind her. "I thought that might be you."

Matt was suddenly running abreast of her, matching his pace to hers. Jazz had a notion to speed up and try to lose him but that was extreme, not to mention impossible. She slowed. He did, too.

"I didn't…know…you were…a runner." She could barely catch her breath to form the words.

"I'm not," he said. "But if I'm going to scrimmage with my kids, I need to stay in shape."

"Your kids?" She was sure the twins had said he wasn't married. Was he divorced?

"I coach a youth soccer team of thirteen- and four-teen-year-olds pretty much year-round," Matt said. "They love to try to get the best of me."

In running shorts and a T-shirt that left his legs and arms bare, Matt looked like an athlete, with impressive musculature minus the bulk.

"You must really be into soccer." A rivulet of sweat trickled down the side of her face, but now that she wasn't running as fast it was easier to talk.

"I've played the game almost my whole life." He had a smooth, even stride, and she got the impression he ran the same way he did everything else—effortlessly. Not only wasn't he breathing hard, but he was also barely sweating.

Don't ask about the twins, she told herself.

"Are you trying to turn your niece and nephew into soccer lifers, too?" she heard herself ask.

He laughed. "Robbie's already got the bug. He begged me to help him, not that he had to try too hard."

Change the subject.

"How about Brooke?" She tried not to sound too curious. "Is she into soccer, too?"

"Not like her brother but she's a natural athlete," Matt said. "Once she understands how good she can be, the love will follow."

"What if it doesn't?" Jazz asked.

"It will," Matt said. "That's the way it works."

She took a sidelong glance at him to try to gauge if he found her questions about his niece and nephew suspicious. He wore a pleasant, neutral expression. He'd tell her the date of the twins' birthday if she asked. She could forget the whole thing if it wasn't July twenty-fourth.

But what if it was? Would her resolve be strong enough to stay away from the twins if she knew for certain they were her biological children?

"How about you?" he asked.

She'd forgotten what they were talking about. "Excuse me?"

"You ever play soccer? It's usually the first sport parents sign up their kids for."

Jazz's mother hadn't stuck around long enough to get Jazz involved in anything. The only game Jazz's grandmother had taught her was how to beat the welfare system.

"I'm not very athletic," she said.

"I don't believe that." His eyes swept over her. "You look like you're in great shape."

She'd never exercised regularly until prison, where she'd done legions of sit-ups and push-ups in her cell. During the hour inmates were let outside twice a day, she'd trampled the grass walking laps around the prison yard. Running had only been allowed on the basketball court.

Jazz didn't need a psychologist to tell her that was why she'd taken up jogging. She often hit the trails even after standing on her feet all day. It struck her that Bill Smith's list of high school activities had included track. Could a love of running be hereditary? She shoved the question out of her mind, determined to deal with one problem at a time.

"Thank you," she said, her chance to ask about the twins' birthday gone.

They ran side by side in silence with Jazz watching Matt in her peripheral vision. His skin had a healthy glow, as though he spent a lot of time outdoors. His nose went a little wayward in profile and she guessed it had been broken. The imperfection somehow made him more attractive.

She needed to get a grip. It made not one whit of difference if she found him appealing. She needed to operate on the assumption that the twins were the children she'd given up. She'd be a lot less likely to run into them if she didn't hang around their uncle.

"I need to walk awhile." The perfect excuse to cut their conversation short.

He stopped running, too.

"Is your shoulder bothering you?" He sounded concerned, the way he had at the restaurant. She couldn't say for sure why that touched her.

"My shoulder's fine, thanks." She'd religiously done the exercises he'd given her, a much cheaper alternative than seeking medical attention. She had health care but could barely afford the co-payment for a doctor's visit. "I'm just a little winded."

"Mind if I walk with you?" he asked.

She shrugged instead of stating she'd rather he go ahead without her. What was the matter with her?

"I've got a family picnic later," he said, and she instantly pictured Brooke and Robbie. "How about you? Got any plans?"

"Yes." She swallowed the ache of loneliness in her throat, wondering where it had come from. Her plans involved finding a quiet spot on nearby Folly Beach where she could gaze at the ocean and read a book. "It's nice to have an evening off."

"Don't you work the day shift?"

"I have a second job." Now, why had she told him something even her restaurant coworkers didn't know?

"Does it involve cooking, too?" he asked.

"Telemarketing. I'd love to work for a caterer, but those jobs are hard to come by." She couldn't seem to stop confiding in him. At least she hadn't told him why a caterer would be reluctant to hire her. Or that without two jobs she wouldn't be able to afford her apartment.

He didn't say anything for long moments. "What if *I* offered you a catering job?"

"What?"

"A friend of mine is moving out of state. I'm inviting people to drop by my house Saturday afternoon to say goodbye. I don't know what to feed them."

"How about burgers and hot dogs?"

"The party's in the afternoon and they won't all be coming at the same time. Some of them will be hungry, some won't."

"You could go with finger foods." As the idea took hold, she elaborated. "Mini quiches, stuffed mushrooms, cocktail meatballs. That kind of thing."

"Sounds great," he said. "Then you'll do it?"

She hesitated, and he named a figure double what she earned on any given night at her telemarketing job. "I'll pay for the groceries, of course."

The offer was tantamount to dangling a Godiva in front of a chocoholic. Just the thought of having the freedom to cook something not on the Pancake Palace menu sent her heart beating faster.

Because she wanted to immediately accept, she didn't. She'd learned in prison that opportunities like this one were seldom as good as they seemed. "I hardly know anything about you."

"My players will vouch for me." He slid her a grin. "I don't only coach youth soccer, I coach the Faircrest High boys' team, too."

She hadn't pegged him for a full-time coach. She

would have guessed doctor, lawyer or any of the other professions associated with ambition.

"Is that where Brooke and Robbie will go to high school?" She couldn't seem to stop digging for more information about them.

"Terry—that's my sister—sends them to private school. They don't live in my district, anyway. My brother-in-law inherited a place south of Broad." He named the most prestigious part of peninsular Charleston, an area so rich in history and beauty that it resembled a living museum.

"Is that where you live, too?" Jazz asked.

"My town house is near Magnolia Plantation," he said, referring to a popular tourist attraction nestled along the western banks of the Ashley River. "I bought it because it backs up to green space."

Jazz also lived west of the river but on the less desirable side of Ashley Greens Park, where multi-family housing and strip shopping centers were more common than trendy neighborhoods. Her apartment abutted another apartment.

"Any more questions?" he asked.

Are your niece and nephew my children?

"No," she said.

"You sure? I want you to feel comfortable when you come over," he said. "I swear you can trust me."

She didn't trust anyone.

"Then give me the run of the kitchen and treat me like an employee." She hadn't consciously decided to accept the job until that second.

He saluted her. "Aye aye, captain."

She felt a grin teasing the corners of her mouth. "How do I get in touch with you?"

"Give me your cell number and I'll call you," he said.

"But you don't have your phone with you, do you?"

"Believe me, I'll remember the number." His inflection was jaunty enough that she wouldn't have been surprised had he winked.

She recited her phone number, and he repeated it just as they reached the offshoot of the path that led to her apartment. She pointed. "Home is that way."

"I'll call you," he said before he resumed his run.

She headed home, sure she was making a mistake but equally certain she'd follow through with the job.

"CAN YOU BELIEVE Matt's having a goodbye party for Carter? What, if anything, is he thinking?"

Matt paused at the entrance to the teachers' lounge at Faircrest High School a few days later. The door was ajar, something that volleyball coach and psychology teacher Donna Lee must not have realized, considering the volume of her voice.

Donna sat at the only occupied table, her back to the door. She was flanked by school librarian Fran Van Houten and Tom Dougherty, who'd taught PE and coached football at Faircrest for almost twenty-five years. Fran's body was angled forward, her mouth slightly agape as she focused on Donna. Tom leaned back in his chair, cradling a cup of coffee in his large hands. He met Matt's eyes and rolled his.

"If Carter hadn't given notice," Donna continued,

"the school board would be investigating him as we speak."

Carter Prioleau was leaving Faircrest after eleven successful years as the athletic director. He'd been instrumental in improving the school's athletic facilities and helping to build a stable of winning coaches.

Tom cleared his throat and nodded to where Matt stood. Donna kept talking.

"It makes you wonder if Matt's qualified to run the athletic department," Donna said. "He should be distancing himself from the whole mess."

Tom drew a circle in the air with his finger and pointed at Matt. Donna finally turned, her sleek dark hair swinging with the movement. Her face lost color until it was nearly the shade of the white Formica on the tabletop.

"Good morning, Donna." Matt advanced so he was standing just steps from her. "Am I interrupting?"

She shook her head mutely.

"I thought I heard my name," Matt said.

Donna mumbled something unintelligible, then rose. "I've got to get to class."

"Me, too." Fran got up so fast she bumped her knee on the underside of the table. "Except I'm going to the library. That's where I've got to get to."

The two women hurried off, their heels clicking on the linoleum, leaving Matt alone in the lounge with Tom. The other man was dressed in shorts and a maroon Faircrest High T-shirt, his standard work clothes. At over fifty, with muscle packed onto his short frame, Tom was a walking advertisement for the weight room.

"What was that all about?" Matt asked.

"If you've got a couple minutes, I'll tell you," Tom said.

Matt mentally went over his schedule and determined there was nothing that couldn't wait. He started to pull out a chair and sit down.

"Not here." Tom drained the rest of his coffee. "Somewhere we won't be interrupted."

"That leaves out the athletic office," Matt said. "It's a beautiful morning. Let's go outside."

To get there they needed to navigate a sea of teenagers, most of whom greeted them. When they finally walked through the double doors into the crisp morning air, yellow buses were lining up at the curb. Tom veered around the side of the school building toward a four-hundred-meter running track that Carter had successfully lobbied to have resurfaced.

"It's quiet out here in the morning," Tom said as they stepped onto the springy surface of the deserted track. Beyond it was a thicket of woods that separated the school property from a surrounding neighborhood. "Nobody will overhear us."

"I appreciate that you've got my back, T.D." Matt used the nickname Tom had gotten long ago when his teams started racking up touchdowns. "But I can handle the Donnas of the world."

"That woman's got a bigger mouth than a hippopotamus," Tom said. "But it's not just her. Everybody's talking about Carter and that summer school teacher."

"Carter told me she accused him of sexual harassment." Matt had worked closely with the A.D. since being hired as his assistant. "He said it was blown way out of proportion."

"Not according to the gossips," Tom said. "Donna says it's why Carter resigned before the school year started."

"No way!" Matt's exclamation startled into flight some sparrows foraging for insects in the infield grass.

Tom put up a hand. "Just telling you what I heard."

"But that's bull," Matt said. "Carter had a tough summer, with his marriage breaking up like it did. He's leaving town because he needs a change of scenery."

"You can figure out why people think he's getting a divorce," Tom said.

It didn't take much brain power. If the gossips believed Carter was guilty of sexual harassment, it followed they'd think he cheated on his wife.

"School started two weeks ago," Matt said. "Why didn't these stories come out then?"

"They did," Tom said. "Everybody's talking about it. Teachers. Parents. Students."

"I haven't heard much about it," Matt said.

"That's because everybody knows Carter recommended you to take over his job," Tom said.

"Then why did you tell me?"

"Because your dad and me, we go way back. And because I like you." Tom cleared his throat. "You've got to be smart, Matt."

"What do you mean?"

"That party you're throwing for Carter, you should think about canceling."

"I'm not turning my back on Carter because of

gossip," Matt said. Not to mention he'd lose his excuse to see Jazz again, although he could come up with another reason. He'd been working on a plan when he'd had the good luck of running into her at the park on Labor Day.

"Fair enough," Tom said.

They walked without speaking until they reached the point on the track where they'd started. "You're coming to the party, right?" Matt asked.

"Can't. The wife's got me booked all day." Tom avoided Matt's eyes, telling Matt everything he needed to know.

Tom hadn't only relayed the gossip. He believed it.

JAZZ WHEELED HER grocery cart into a line that was three-deep on Friday afternoon, relieved that for once she didn't have to mentally add the prices of her items.

Crab. Artichoke. Fruit. Ground beef. Sausage. Spinach. Mushrooms. Eggs.

If Matt hadn't dropped off an envelope of cash by Pancake Palace, she wouldn't have had enough money in her checking account to cover the bill.

"Buy whatever you want," he'd told her when he filled her in on the specifics. Guests were dropping by between two and six o'clock on Saturday, so they wouldn't expect a full meal. He was anticipating as few as a dozen people and as many as twenty-five. She should err on the side of too much food rather than too little.

The envelope had contained two crisp one-hundred-dollar bills, which seemed excessive. She wondered why

Matt hadn't bought some party trays from the supermarket's deli department. He could have added precut fruit and veggies and been all set for much less than he was paying her.

"Hey, Jazz!" Sadie came up behind her, still wearing the Pancake Palace waitress uniform that was a size too tight. "Looks like we had the same idea."

The grocery store was two doors down from the restaurant, making it a convenient after-work stop.

Sadie held up a green plastic basket filled with groceries. "Benjy wants sloppy joes for dinner."

Benjy was Sadie's six-year-old son and the reason the waitress didn't work nights. The boy already had a deadbeat dad. Sadie refused to saddle him with an absentee mom even if it meant sharing an apartment and child-care duties with another single mother.

Jazz knew all this because Sadie hung out in the kitchen with her and Carl when business was slow, never seeming bothered that Sadie did almost all the talking.

"What are you making for dinner tonight?" Sadie peered into her buggy before Jazz could block the view. "Ooo. Are you having company?"

"No," Jazz said.

"Then what's the occasion?" Sadie was smiling, making it impossible for Jazz to take offense at her prying.

"A catering job," Jazz said.

"That's great! I didn't know you did that sort of thing! How long have you been at it?"

Jazz swallowed the urge to tell Sadie it wasn't any

of her business. The other woman was just trying to be friendly, the same as always. "Actually, this is my first time."

"How exciting! What kind of job? At a country club? A private party? What?"

"The, um, client is throwing a goodbye party for one of his friends."

"His?" Sadie picked up on the pronoun. "You're dealing with the guy and not his wife?"

"The client's not married," Jazz said.

Sadie placed one hand on her curvy hip. "Then why didn't he just buy a deli tray and some beer?"

Jazz's thoughts exactly. Her doubts resurfaced. "I don't know."

"He probably wants something real nice." Sadie laid a hand on Jazz's upper arm, the deep pink of her fingernails in sharp contrast to Jazz's tan shirt. "I think it's great that he hired you."

A doorbell sounded, loud and urgent. The people in line in front of them looked around to see where the noise was coming from. Sadie giggled, dug in her voluminous purse and pulled out a cell phone. "It's my text message tone. Isn't it funny?"

She pressed a button and read the lines of type. Her face crumbled, all the happiness disappearing. Jazz clamped her mouth shut, reminding herself of her long-term policy not to get involved in problems that weren't hers.

Sadie's eyes teared up. Oh, damn.

"Are you okay, Sadie?" Jazz asked.

"No. It's from Ace." Sadie thrust her cell phone at

Jazz so the text was visible. Ace was the guy Sadie had been dating for the past few weeks.

Sorry, babe. Not feeling it anymore. Later.

Sadie sniffed loudly. "I can't believe he broke up with me by text. What kind of guy does that?"

A guy who isn't worth crying over.

"I'm sorry." Jazz thought of how excited Sadie had been whenever she and Ace had a date planned. "Seems like you really cared about him."

"That's just it. I didn't!" Sadie said. "Ace is a jerk. I mean, he nicknamed himself! And he didn't want to meet Benjy."

"Then why are you crying?"

Sadie dashed away the tears from under her eyes. "Because everybody I date turns out to be a jerk. I wouldn't know a nice guy if he fell from the sky and landed in front of me. I'm a loser magnet!"

"We all make mistakes," Jazz said.

"Have you?" Sadie peered at her through watery blue eyes.

Luke Bennett's face flashed in Jazz's mind. One of his eyebrows was cocked and his grin was coaxing, the way he'd looked when he offered to show Jazz a good time on her eighteenth birthday.

She'd been nervous about becoming a legal adult because her foster parents would only house her until the end of the school year. Luke made the landmark seem like an adventure.

"No more kid stuff," he'd said.

That statement turned out to be prophetic. Since she

was eighteen when the crime was committed, she was charged as an adult.

"Oh, yeah," Jazz said. "I made a whopper."

Sadie's tears stopped. "Is that why you wouldn't go out with that Matt guy?"

"How do you know I wouldn't go out with him?" Jazz hadn't shared any information about Matt. After a while, Sadie had given up asking about him.

"You'd be smiling way more if you were dating someone that hot," Sadie said.

Jazz did smile then. She liked Sadie. The waitress made it impossible not to.

"I'm not looking to date anyone right now," Jazz said.

"Why not?"

Should Jazz tell her? What would it hurt? "I don't trust my instincts."

"You and me both, sister," Sadie exclaimed. "You and me both."

CHAPTER FOUR

JAZZ CRACKED THE Crock-Pot lid Saturday afternoon to check on the meatballs, getting a whiff of the pineapple preserves she'd used to make the sauce.

Excellent.

She transferred bite-sized quiche, stuffed mushrooms and mini crab cakes from plastic containers to a tray she could pop in the oven when guests started to arrive.

All of the hors d'oeuvres had passed her taste test. So had the fresh fruit she'd arranged on skewers, purchased earlier today at the local farmer's market.

"Did you know you're smiling?"

Jazz looked up from her work to find Matt in the kitchen, leaning against the half wall that led to the rest of the town house. He wore khaki shorts that ended a few inches above the knee and a button-down, short-sleeved cream shirt that contrasted with his thick golden-brown hair. He looked fantastic.

"Nothing's more satisfying than cooking." Jazz swept a hand to indicate her surroundings. "Especially in a kitchen like this."

The rest of his town house was nice, with rich, dark-wood furniture and a color scheme that incorporated shades of navy, forest-greens and burgundy. The kitchen was spectacular. Granite countertops with plenty of space. Top-of-the-line stainless steel appliances. Plentiful cabinets with wood inlays. It was a kitchen fit for a gourmet.

"Then you're glad you took the job?" he asked. "I got the impression something was holding you back."

The twins, she thought.

"It was you," she blurted out. Anything to throw him off track. To soften the abruptness of her accusation, she smiled. "I thought the catering thing might be a scam you use on women who refuse to date you."

He threw back his head and laughed, a pleasant, rumbling sound. "Then how do you explain the goodbye party for my friend?"

"Tell me, does this mysterious *friend* have a name?" She injected heavy skepticism into her voice.

Matt was still grinning. "His name is Carter Prioleau."

"A good Charleston name." She stroked her chin, nodding in approval. "I couldn't have made up a better one myself. And why, pray tell, is this Charlestonian leaving God's country?"

Matt's expression turned serious. "I wish I could make up a story, but the truth is he's going through a divorce. It's been pretty hard on him."

The doorbell chimed. Matt checked his watch. "That'll be my proof. Carter's always on time."

"Can't wait to meet your alibi," Jazz said, eager to see his smile again. He didn't disappoint her.

She was also smiling when she turned the oven to preheat. Flirting with Matt had been fun, especially because she could tell he was a good guy. More of a go-getter than she was used to, perhaps. But he wouldn't pursue her if she made it clear she wasn't interested.

Except, didn't being flirtatious convey the opposite message? She took a deep breath. There she went again, worrying for nothing. She was hardly a beauty. Heaven knew she wasn't a catch.

A man as charming, good-natured and—she might as well admit it—*hot* as Matt could have his pick of women. He didn't have to chase an ex-con who really needed to make it clear that nothing would happen between them.

A giggle that didn't sound masculine traveled through the town house.

"It's so nice of you to do this for Carter." The low-pitched female voice preceded Matt and his guests into the kitchen. Its owner had luxurious long black hair and a bra size Jazz guessed was double D, and she was probably no older than thirty. Her pale pink sundress wasn't particularly short or tight but showcased her to voluptuous advantage.

She stood inches away from an average-looking man at least twenty years her senior, his thinning hair parted on the side and swept over his bald spot. The man held his chin high, and a smug smile played about his lips.

Matt's own smile no longer reached his eyes. "Jazz, this is Carter and Kelly."

"Her name's Callie," Carter corrected.

"Spelled with a *C*." The woman formed a semicircle with her thumb and index finger.

"Sorry," Matt said.

"Don't worry about it. I'll answer to anything, even, 'Hey, you!'" Callie laughed again. She was nervous, Jazz realized. She was also pretty definitely not Carter's estranged wife. "I really like *your* name, Jazz."

"Thanks," Jazz said. Matt stood stiffly, saying nothing. "I'm the caterer," Jazz added.

Matt found his voice. "A *friend* who happens to be a caterer."

Was that how Matt thought of her when they'd only known each other a little more than a month? In the three years she'd been out of prison, Jazz had made a number of acquaintances but nobody she'd call a friend, except possibly Sadie.

"A caterer, huh?" Carter released a low whistle and slapped Matt lightly on the back. "I didn't know I rated that high."

"Are you kidding? I owe you." Matt sounded more like his normal self.

"For what?" Carter retorted.

"The job recommendation."

Carter snorted. "Bull. You'll be named A.D. even if I didn't lobby for you."

"A.D.? Isn't that short for *athletic director?*" Jazz had intended to fade into the anonymity of the catering job but couldn't let the comment pass. "I thought Matt was the high school soccer coach."

"He is in the spring. And he's doing wonderful things with the program," Carter said. "But Matt's destined for greater things. Right now he's the interim A.D. but he's the favorite for the top job."

"I learned from the best," Matt said, turning his head to address Jazz. "Carter just resigned as A.D."

"I'm leaving the athletic program in good hands." Carter gave Matt a hearty slap on the back. "Matt's a golden boy who gets things done. He probably even managed to talk some people into showing up today for my party."

An uneasy current ran beneath the smooth words. Callie fidgeted, appearing even more uncomfortable. Jazz wondered what was going on.

"Of course people will come," Matt said.

"People from my golf league," Carter countered. "Good thinking inviting them."

"No problem," Matt said. "If I ever want to join, I'll have an in."

"The league doesn't play in the summer, buddy," Carter said. "If you get the A.D. job, that's the only season you'll have time to breathe."

"Excuse me." Jazz didn't need to stick around and listen to more evidence that Matt was a responsible person. "These hors d'ouevres have to go in the oven."

That was the truth. Once the guests started arriving, her plan was to provide a steady supply of warm appetizers.

"Hey, Matt. Before I forget, can you show me that new putter you got?" Carter asked. "I'm planning to play a lot of golf in Florida."

"Sure," Matt said. "My golf bag's in the shed out back."

"I'll come with you." Carter turned to Callie. "Honey, will you be okay for a few minutes without me?"

"I guess," Callie said.

Carter kissed Callie on the lips before heading with Matt for the French doors that led to the backyard. The town house was situated perfectly for a party, with a deck overlooking a good-sized yard flanked by evergreens. The temperature was in the low seventies and the sun was shining; ideal outdoor weather. Yet Callie stayed in the kitchen with Jazz.

"The food looks great," Callie said in her soft voice when the men were gone. "But if I don't watch, my butt blows up like a hot-air balloon."

Jazz laughed. "I doubt that. But there's fruit, if you want it."

"Not my thing. Unless the fruit's covered in chocolate." Callie sat down on one of the tall stools beside the breakfast bar and Jazz got a whiff of perfume. Callie remained quiet for long moments before drawing an audible breath. "Can I ask you something, Jazz?"

The way Callie phrased the question made Jazz long to say no. She hesitated. "Go ahead."

"Did it seem like Matt didn't know about me?"

Oh, yeah.

Jazz lowered the oven temperature. She wanted the food warm, not overdone. "Why do you ask?"

"Carter's the best boyfriend I ever had." Callie rolled her eyes. "I mean, moving to Florida's not costing me a dime. But I had to fuss up a storm before he'd agree to bring me today."

The doorbell rang again, a timely interruption.

Callie rose from the stool. "I'll get it."

Jazz wasn't about to fight her for the honor. She opened the oven door and removed the cookie sheet. Using a wide spatula, she transferred the food onto the pretty serving trays she'd found at a yard sale, the way she'd acquired most of her better kitchen supplies.

She heard voices, some belonging to children. Brooke and Robbie? *Don't panic,* she told herself. The party was for Matt's friends, not his family. One of the guys from Carter's golf league probably had children.

"Uncle Matt! Look what Dad bought me!" Robbie dashed into the kitchen carrying a soccer ball draped with netting.

Jazz's heart thudded so hard she felt nauseous. Inside the house, Robbie's hair didn't look as red as it had in the sun but his skin appeared more pale, his eyes greener. His coloring reminded Jazz of a photo her grandmother had kept of herself as a child.

The young boy scanned the kitchen. "Where's Uncle Matt?"

Brooke followed her brother into the kitchen, humming an unrecognizable tune and doubling the visual punch. Jazz braced a hand on the counter to steady herself.

"Your uncle's out back with Carter." Callie had reentered the kitchen, although Jazz hadn't noticed until she spoke.

Brooke stayed in the kitchen, peering at Jazz. "Aren't you the lady from the park?"

"What lady?" asked a plump brunette who must have been their mother. Her curly brown hair was pulled back from a round, pretty face. She looked nothing like the children in either coloring or stature.

"I remember you," Robbie said to Jazz. "You're the lady who fell!"

"Hi, I'm Terry. Matt's sister." Terry's dark eyes crinkled at the corners when she smiled, exactly like her brother's. "Matt didn't tell us he was dating anyone."

"We're not dating," Jazz said quickly. "I'm Jazz, the caterer."

"Then you didn't meet Matt at the park?" Terry asked.

"Well, yes," Jazz said.

"After she fell down," Brooke supplied.

"Is that when you told him you were a caterer?" Terry asked.

"You're asking too many questions, darlin'." A man with a wiry build, boyish features and thick blond hair that looked expensively cut joined them. He was dressed in crisp khaki slacks and a shirt with an alligator over the pocket. "I'm Kevin Pinckney, Terry's husband. I'm sorry she's freaking you out."

"I am not," Terry declared. "Jazz, am I freaking you out?"

Kevin held up a hand, but he was laughing. "Enough. Cut the woman a break, will you, Ter?"

"I'm simply trying to figure it all out," Terry said. "So, Jazz, are you into my brother or aren't you?"

Just like that, Callie's problems took a backseat.

Jazz had enough of her own.

MATT WATCHED Carter line up an imaginary putt and slowly pull back the golf club, stroking through the short blades of grass in the backyard.

"Yep, I could do some damage with this baby." Carter tossed the club a foot or so into the air and caught it in the middle of the shaft. "I'll definitely have to get me one."

"You know it," Matt said, his mind still on the woman in the kitchen. Not Jazz this time, Callie. How long had Carter been seeing her? The other man had never mentioned her. "But you're going to do more than golf in Florida. You have a job lined up, right?"

Carter's face changed, his usually affable expression growing dark. "Yeah. As an assistant A.D. at a private school. I would have taken some time off if the bitch wasn't being so vindictive."

"What bitch?" Matt asked.

"Lilly," Carter growled. "She's trying to rob me blind."

Lilly was Carter's soon-to-be ex-wife, a pleasant woman with a great laugh who'd been married to him for twenty-seven years. Matt had never heard Lilly say an unkind word. Even though the backyard was secluded, Matt looked around to make sure nobody had overheard what Carter had called her.

"That's pretty strong, Carter," Matt said.

"Yeah, well, Lilly found out I was seeing Callie before we separated. Except she never uses Callie's name. She always says *that child*. She's jealous, I tell you. Just because I'm fifty doesn't mean my life is over."

Matt remembered the good-natured ribbing and gag gifts the coaches at school had given Carter last spring when he'd hit the milestone. The track coach even had a wheelchair waiting in Carter's office, although Carter hadn't thought that was funny.

"I almost didn't bring Callie along today because I know how things get twisted. Look what happened with that teacher." Carter sounded as though he expected Matt to commiserate with him.

"You never told me the details," Matt reminded him. "You only said the story wasn't true."

"Damn right it's not true." A warm wind blew through the yard, wreaking havoc with Carter's comb-over. "That teacher, who doesn't even work at Faircrest, came on to *me*. She emailed *me* first. Yeah, I emailed back, even met her for a drink. But that was it."

Matt digested the information, which wasn't far removed from the gossip. He suddenly had to know the rest of the story. "Everybody's saying the school board was about to launch an investigation."

Carter's hand tightened on the putter. "Only because of the vindictive bitch. Turns out the teacher—her name's Karen—plays tennis with Lilly. I don't know exactly how it went down but Lilly must've convinced Karen to file a complaint."

The conversation was moving too fast for Matt. "Why would Lilly do that?"

"Because she found out about Callie!"

"But why would it matter if this Karen filed a complaint if there was no evidence?"

"You're forgetting the emails." Carter sounded exasperated. "They came from my work computer. Taken out of context, they don't look so good."

The pieces were starting to fit together in a shape Matt didn't like. "So you did resign because of the investigation?"

"What else could I do?" Carter threw up the hand not holding the putter.

A rabbit dashed across the yard for the woods. Matt wished he could run away too so he didn't have to hear what Carter would spew next.

"I probably should have gotten a lawyer and fought

the whole thing," Carter said. "That job in Florida is a crap job. I better not have much trouble getting a better one."

Motion inside the house caught Matt's eye. He was absurdly grateful to see more guests arriving. Matt had never spent much time with Carter socially. Obviously Matt didn't know the other man as well as he'd thought he did.

"We should be getting back inside," Matt suggested.

They walked in silence for a few steps before Carter asked, "You're not seeing anyone, are you, Matt?"

Matt wondered what that had to do with anything. "Nope."

"Not even the caterer?"

"Not even her," Matt said. Yet.

"Then listen up." Carter sounded like his old self, full of bluster and confidence. "Take a good long look before you leap."

"Excuse me?"

"Make damn sure you don't get involved with the wrong woman."

The French doors opened and Callie stepped outside, the sun shining down on her and highlighting the lines around her eyes. She was older than she'd first appeared, but still substantially younger than Carter.

"Hey, honey." Carter's voice softened. "Miss me?"

Tom Dougherty had been on to something at the track the other day, Matt thought. Fair or not, people who dealt with high school students were held to higher standards than others.

Don't get involved with the wrong woman, Carter had said.

The former A.D. didn't seem to realize which woman in his life that was.

JAZZ CLOSED HER MOUTH, which meant jaws really must drop. She tried to compose an answer to Matt's sister's question about whether she was into Matt.

"Oh, honey. You should see your face." Terry clapped her hands. "You really just need to tell me to mind my own business. Everybody else does."

"I can vouch for that," her husband, Kevin, said.

"My curiosity got the best of me," Terry said. "I've never met one of Matt's girlfriends before."

That was an easier topic for Jazz to address than her opinion of Matt.

"You still haven't. I did meet your brother at the park but I really am the caterer." Jazz indicated the tray of food. "Here. Try something."

Terry picked up a stuffed mushroom, took a bite and fluttered her eyelids as though she were in ecstasy. "Okay. You convinced me. These are divine."

Robbie appeared at his mother's side and wrinkled his nose. "Mushrooms! Yech!"

"Robbie, mind your manners." Kevin flashed Jazz a grin. "Sorry about my boy. If it's not a hot dog or PB and J, he won't touch it."

"Hey, that's not true," Robbie protested. "I like Pop-Tarts and mac and cheese."

Kevin ruffled his son's red hair. Callie had left the kitchen but the room seemed much too small for a caterer and a family of four. Especially *this* family of four.

"I'll take this tray of food onto the deck," Jazz said. "I think that's where Matt wants everybody."

"That must be where Carter is," Kevin said. "I don't care if it is his going-away party, he owes me money."

Terry made a face. "Why do you guys have to bet on the golf course?"

"Why is the sky blue?" Kevin asked with a grin. "Why do you like to shop?"

"Smart aleck," Terry said, but her eyes sparkled with humor.

"I'll take the tray out there for you, Jazz." Kevin picked it up, but not before Terry snagged another stuffed mushroom. She winked at Jazz, then followed her husband out of the town house, their two children flanking them.

"Uncle Matt! There you are!" Robbie yelled before disappearing outside.

Jazz sank onto one of the kitchen stools, the heat from the oven enveloping her. How had it happened that she was catering a party attended by children who were quite possibly hers biologically?

Matt hadn't forced her to accept this job. And it was clear Kevin was in the golf league with Carter, but a part of Jazz must have realized Matt might invite family to a going-away party for a friend. Maybe a chance to see the twins again had even been part of the allure. Jazz's willpower had certainly let her down before.

The French doors opened. Matt entered the kitchen and spotted her sitting down. His brows creased. "Hey, are you okay?"

She got up from the stool so fast she felt light-headed. "Why wouldn't I be?"

"Kevin—that's my brother-in-law—just told me about Terry and all her questions. Sorry about that."

"No problem."

He tilted his head. His eyes were almost the exact shade of golden-brown as his hair. A golden boy, Carter had called him.

"You sure you're okay?" Matt asked. "The way Terry goes on sometimes, I think she misses the interrogation room."

"Excuse me?"

"She used to be a cop until the kids came along. That's how she met Kevin. He's a D.A. They're good people even if Terry can be kind of scary." He paused just as the doorbell rang. "Excuse me. I need to get that."

More guests trickled in over the next few hours, a decent turnout. Jazz kept busy supplying a constant stream of hot finger foods, trying not to think about what Matt had said. It didn't work.

Ironically, the ex-con's children had quite possibly ended up with a district attorney and a former cop for parents.

The kitchen window provided a panoramic view of the backyard, where Brooke and Robbie played. The soccer ball covered with netting appeared to be a training tool with a boomerang effect. The twins took turns kicking it under the supervision of their father and uncle.

Jazz was careful to stand far enough back from the window not to be seen. Through the screen she could hear snippets of conversation about this morning's youth soccer games. She watched Robbie run up to his sister, tag her on the arm and backpedal.

"Bet you can't catch me!" the boy shouted.

"Maybe I don't want to catch you," Brooke retorted just as loudly.

"Chicken!" Robbie taunted.

After a long hesitation, Brooke dropped the soccer ball and dashed after him. Robbie ran in a zigzag pattern, his laughter ringing out. Brooke was about to tag him when she stumbled. She fell down, giggling even before she hit the grass.

Robbie raised both arms to the sky in triumph. "Told you that you couldn't catch me!" he shouted.

"This is scrumptious. What's in it? I think I taste eggplant." Terry walked into the kitchen holding up a cracker slathered with dip.

Jazz slid back from the window, feeling unaccountably guilty. She strived for composure. "Eggplant, sunflower oil, onions, garlic and black pepper," she said. "It's called *vinetta* in Hungarian."

"Sounds like something your mom used to make," Terry said. "Was she a good cook, too?"

"I'm not sure," Jazz answered. "I was mostly raised by my grandma."

"So your grandmother used to make *vinetta?*"

She hadn't, although in a backhanded way Grandma had spurred Jazz's interest in cooking. If Jazz hadn't learned her way around the kitchen, she'd have eaten many more sandwiches for dinner.

"No," Jazz said. "My foster mother did."

"Really, you grew up in foster care? That must have sucked."

"It wasn't so bad." Jazz hadn't realized there were worse things than being a ward of the state until she was housed in a prison cell.

"If everything your foster mother made was as tasty as this dip, that must've helped." Terry licked her lips. "Thank the Lord I can't cook like this. I already snack enough with the kids as it is. Since I quit work, I've gained twenty pounds. But anything would be worth it to stay home with them."

Spoken like a happy stay-at-home mom who was raising well-adjusted kids. If the twins were Jazz's biological children, she couldn't have hoped for a more ideal situation.

Terry finished off the cracker. "Do you have any children, Jazz?"

Two children, Jazz thought. Except they'd never really been hers. How could she answer without being untruthful?

"I've never been married," Jazz said.

"Matt hasn't, either." Terry's comment seemed out of context. Before Jazz could say so, Terry added, "Listen, would you be interested in another catering job? We're having a party for the twins next Sunday in the park. I thought we'd grill but it would be great to have a special cake and some kid-friendly desserts. You do bake, right?"

"I do." Jazz was once again having a hard time keeping up with Terry. The other woman didn't have the leisurely Southern drawl that was so prevalent in the Lowcountry. Terry spoke so quickly, her sentences seemed to run together.

A party, Terry had said without naming the occasion.

With the school year having started only a few weeks ago and no more holidays on the September calendar, the most logical reason for a celebration was a birthday.

Disappointment cut through Jazz, as sharp as it was unexpected. Robbie and Brooke weren't her biological children, after all.

Terry kept talking, naming a time and a place as though Jazz had already agreed. And why shouldn't she now that she no longer needed to avoid Terry, the twins or Matt?

"How does all that sound?" Terry asked.

"Fine." Jazz didn't let on that she'd hardly heard a word. "But it would be better if you wrote it all down."

"You got it." Terry found a pad on top of the microwave and a pen in a holder by the stove.

Matt came into the kitchen, his eyes zeroing in on his sister and narrowing. "You're not bothering Jazz again, are you, Terry?"

"For your information," Terry said haughtily, "I just hired Jazz for the party I'm throwing for the twins."

"Great!" Matt said, his approval out of proportion to the occasion.

"How old will Brooke and Robbie be?" Jazz didn't even tense in preparation for the answer.

Terry glanced up from what she was writing on the pad. "Oh, it's not their birthday. We're having an adoption-day party."

CHAPTER FIVE

CLEANING UP WAS taking too long.

Jazz was desperate to be alone in order to sort out her jumbled thoughts now that she knew the twins were adopted. The party guests were gone, but she couldn't leave until Matt's kitchen was as spotless as it had been when she arrived.

Matt was outside on the deck dumping plastic cups and plates in a trash bag while Jazz wiped down counters and washed serving trays.

She spied her empty Crock-Pot on the kitchen counter. She usually let the dish soak so it would be easier to clean but that would delay her departure even more.

Matt would soon come inside the town house.

He'd smile at her and flirt with her, which would only complicate matters further. She hadn't even told Terry she couldn't work the party for the twins. She'd meant to but an influx of guests had arrived soon after Terry confirmed that Brooke and Robbie had been adopted.

Making up her mind to leave, Jazz balanced the dirty Crock-Pot on top of her serving trays. She picked up the entire stack and took a few steps toward escape.

The door to the deck slid open, and Matt walked into the kitchen carrying a white plastic garbage bag. He looked tall and handsome with his tousled hair shot through with gold and his shirt untucked, a man most women wouldn't dream of fleeing. Most women would run toward him.

"You're not leaving, are you?" he asked. "I still need to write you a check."

How had payment slipped her mind when it had been her main reason to take the job?

"I, uh—" she hoped to think up an excuse "—was just going to take these dishes out to my car."

"Let me pay you first so you don't have to make two trips." Matt tied the garbage bag closed, set it down and picked up a checkbook and a pen from a side table.

He sat down at the kitchen table, wrote out the check and handed it to her. She was forced to put her dishes down on the kitchen counter to take it.

"Thank you." She shoved the check into the pocket of her khaki shorts without checking the amount.

"No. Thank *you*." Matt's shirt was gold, a good color for him. Of course, this was a man who'd look good in anything he wore. "Everything was delicious. You heard Terry and Carter arguing over the leftovers."

Their good-natured quarrel had been music to a caterer's ears. "Does Terry always get her way?"

Matt cocked an eyebrow. "You do remember meeting my sister, right?"

Jazz felt some of the tension leave her body. How did he manage to put her at ease so effortlessly? Especially when she was keenly aware she needed to be on guard around him.

"Terry only let Carter take the rest of the stuffed mushrooms because of Robbie," Matt said.

At the mention of the little boy, Jazz's heart stuttered.

She tried to sound normal. "Robbie must really hate mushrooms."

"Did you hear him say nobody should have to eat fungus?" Matt chuckled. "That proves there's a drawback to teaching a kid new vocabulary words."

They shared a smile.

"Hey, would you like to have a drink with me?" Matt gestured to a bottle of Scotch on the kitchen counter that was three-quarters full and stood up. She hadn't noticed Matt with alcohol during the party, had even wondered if he drank at all.

"I don't drink much," he said as if he'd read her thoughts. "But I could use one."

The touch of melancholy in his voice stopped Jazz from automatically refusing.

"Are you okay?" she asked. An ill-advised question. What possible good would it do to learn more about him?

"I'm fine." He walked around the counter and opened a cabinet door. For the first time, Jazz noticed that his smile seemed strained.

Clamping her lips shut stopped Jazz from talking for only an instant. "Are you sure nothing's bothering you?"

Matt made a face. "You can tell? And here I thought I was the strong, stoic type."

She'd waded this far into the deepening water. She might as well dive in the rest of the way. "Do you want to talk about it?"

"There's not much to tell." He paused. "Let's just say I found out things about a friend I wish I hadn't."

He took two glasses from the cabinet and set them

on the counter before holding up the bottle of Scotch, with an inquiring eyebrow.

"I'll just have ice water." Jazz hadn't touched alcohol since the night of her arrest. She only wished she'd been smart enough to abstain when she was a teenager.

Once Matt filled their glasses, he handed her the ice water and picked up his drink from the kitchen counter. He nodded toward the deck. "It's nice back there this time of night."

She was tempted to gulp her water and head for the door. The knowledge that something wasn't quite right with Matt stopped her. When he slid open the French doors and stepped back, she hesitated only briefly before preceding him onto the deck.

The warm breeze felt silky against her skin and she caught a whiff of jasmine. It wasn't quite seven o'clock and the temperature had dropped to a comfortable level. He indicated that she should sit down on a low-slung mesh chair and he took the matching one. The chairs faced not each other but the backyard.

The silence stretched until it became clear he didn't intend to continue the conversation she'd started in the kitchen.

"This friend," Jazz ventured, "is it Carter?"

He nodded. "How'd you figure that out?"

"Callie," she said. "It was obvious you didn't know about her."

"I didn't." Matt leaned forward, forearms resting on his knees. "I didn't know about a lot of things. I guess I'm…disappointed."

Disappointed was the exact word Jazz's foster mother

had used when she'd visited Jazz in jail after her arrest on that awful night.

"Maybe you were holding Carter to too high a standard," Jazz said softly.

"Maybe," Matt said after a moment. "But Carter should have held himself to a higher standard. Hell, it's even in our contracts."

"I don't understand," Jazz said.

"There's a clause about how the school district can fire you for bringing embarrassment to the school," Matt said. "A few years ago, a teacher was let go for appearing topless in a community-theater production of *Hair*."

Jazz wondered what Carter had done that was so damning but wouldn't ask. No matter how disillusioned he was, Matt seemed reluctant to gossip about his friend.

"Is that even legal?" Jazz asked.

"Doesn't matter if nobody challenges it," Matt said. "Besides, you're not forced to sign the contract."

"But if you don't sign, you won't be hired," Jazz reasoned.

"Exactly," Matt said.

"You don't have a problem with that?"

"Not much of a problem," Matt said. "Oh, I can come up with a scenario that's unfair, like the topless teacher. But we work with kids. We're supposed to set good examples."

"But Carter wasn't a teacher," Jazz said.

"People in the athletic department have to be even stronger role models," Matt said. "Faircrest athletes are expected to stay away from drugs and alcohol and maintain a 2.5 GPA."

Jazz thought back to her own high school days. Never an A student, she'd made mostly Cs and Ds after entering foster care. "Isn't the standard usually 2.0?"

"That's my point," Matt said. "If we expect Faircrest athletes to be better than the average student, we have to strive to be above reproach."

What would Matt think if he knew he was sitting on his deck with an ex-con? Jazz swallowed. "You seem like you *are* above reproach."

Matt laughed. "Terry and Danny wouldn't agree."

"Danny?"

"My younger brother. I'm the middle child. Danny's sixteen. You'll meet him at the party for the twins." Matt talked as though her presence were a given. "He likes to point out my faults, especially to my parents. That way, he says, they won't expect too much from him."

She would have liked to learn about Matt's childhood, but she couldn't justify hanging around the twins for the same reason she hadn't contacted Bill Smith. Her intrusion into their lives would not be welcomed.

"About the party," she said. "I might not cater it."

Matt looked at her blankly. "Of course you will. You told Terry you would."

Spoken like a man who expected others to keep their word, the way he did. Except, there was so much Matt didn't know about her, so much Jazz would rather he not find out. She liked the way he looked at her, as though she were the woman she'd always intended to be.

Jazz got up abruptly, nearly spilling the rest of her

water. She put her glass down on a wicker end table. "I've got to get going."

She went through the French doors, reentered the town house and walked quickly through the kitchen and foyer. She heard footsteps behind her, then Matt's voice. "Wait! You're forgetting your dishes."

She stopped just shy of the door. She didn't have a choice. Matt joined her, handing over the serving platters and Crock-Pot.

"Thank you," she said formally.

He tilted his head at an angle, his expression troubled. "Did I say something to offend you?"

She shook her head, annoyed at herself for not handling the situation with more poise. "Of course not. I just remembered something I need to do."

Her explanation seemed to satisfy him. He smiled, reached out his hand and touched her cheek. A jolt of awareness skittered through her.

"Great," he said. "Because in case you haven't noticed, I'm still trying to make a good impression on you."

Her heart thudded. She stepped back and his hand dropped away. She went through the unlocked door to the porch landing, poise once again in short supply when he followed her.

"What you said about the party, are you really going to cancel?" Matt asked.

She hesitated. Since she'd never tell anyone what she suspected, would it really be so terrible to spend a final afternoon in the company of Matt and the twins? Especially because it could represent her only chance to do something nice for them?

Matt waited for her answer with his gaze steady on her, as though he were trying to take her measure. She realized there was another reason to cater the party.

"I'll be there," she said. "Just like I said I would."

MATT'S HAND TIGHTENED on the receiver as he listened to the man on the other end of the line. Running a hand through his hair, he sat down on the edge of a desk in the deserted athletic office.

He'd been about to leave for home after a very long Monday when he remembered he hadn't returned a call. That was when he'd learned that the father of the girl who was dating Faircrest's quarterback was also a retired military man with a strong sense of duty.

"So this happened on Saturday night?" Matt asked the girl's father, needing to get the facts straight.

"At about midnight," the man said.

Not that many hours after Jazz had fled Matt's town house and the night after the Faircrest football team had kicked a field goal in the final moments to improve its record to 2-1.

"The wife and I went to Savannah to meet friends," the man said. "We were gonna stay the night but decided to drive back. Surprised the hell out of my daughter and her friends."

There had been eight of them in all, with D. J. Huff the only athlete present. According to the man, beer cans and a couple bottles of cheap whiskey littered the basement where the kids were having a party.

"And you're sure D.J. was drinking?" Matt asked.

"The boy was so wrecked he could barely stand," the man said. "He wasn't even one of the kids who tried to

make a break for it when I told them what I was going
to do."

The man had already relayed that part. He'd gotten
on the phone to their parents, then ordered the drunk
teenagers to sit and wait until someone picked them
up.

"I appreciate you telling me this," Matt said, "although I've gotta admit, I'm also surprised you called
me."

The man released an audible breath. "I'll be straight
with you. I'm no D. J. Huff fan. The boy's full of himself. Found my daughter crying over him more than
once."

"I get that," Matt said, "but why talk to me and not
Coach Dougherty?"

"I did talk to Coach Dougherty," the man said. "This
morning. I got him on the phone first try."

That was odd. Tom hadn't said anything about the
situation. Matt hopped off the desk and went to the
window that overlooked the football practice field.

At a solidly built six foot three, D. J. Huff was easy
to spot. A Monday practice after a Friday game was
typically light and this one appeared to be winding
down. D.J. was dressed in the same reversible maroon-
and-black practice jersey as the rest of the squad.

Matt ended the conversation, trying not to jump to
conclusions about how Tom was handling the situation. He left the school building and walked across the
practice field against the flow of players headed for the
locker room.

"You coming to our next game, Mr. Caminetti?"

asked one of the burly linemen. He sounded out of breath, and sweat dripped off his chin.

"Wouldn't miss it," Matt said.

"Valley Field's going down," another player yelled to nobody in particular. The Faircrest team had a bye on Friday but the following Friday they'd take on Valley Field, the defending district champion. "We're on the way to victory, baby!"

"We got it goin' on!" D. J. Huff yelled.

All of the players were grinning, including the trio that trailed the rest of their teammates. One of them was Matt's brother, Danny. He broke away and jogged up to Matt, waiting until his teammates were past him before he spoke.

"I got moved to first team!" Danny whispered, his eyes sparkling.

"I'm proud of you, kid." Matt put out a fist and Danny bumped it with his own fist. Danny beamed at Matt one more time, then ran to join his teammates.

Tom Dougherty was the last guy on the field. He wore shorts, a maroon Faircrest Football T-shirt and a matching ball cap.

"I saw you over there with Danny. He musta told you he's starting the next game." Tom took off his cap, wiped the perspiration from his forehead and put it back on. "He's earned it."

"Danny works hard," Matt said.

"Most of 'em do but few can catch like your little brother," Tom said. "But I've got a feeling you're not here to talk about Danny."

"You're right about that." Matt made a habit of getting straight to the point. "I want to talk about D. J. Huff."

Tom grimaced and wiped a hand over his lower face. "So you heard about that photo on Facebook?" Tom shook his head. "And here I thought you didn't put stock in gossip."

Matt said nothing, unwilling to let on he didn't know what Tom was talking about.

"I've seen the photo," Tom said. "Yeah, D.J.'s only wearing his boxers. That's why everybody's talking about it. But it's damn near impossible to tell anything else."

"You mean, like whether D.J.'s been drinking?" Matt asked. "Because that would be violating team policy."

"Yeah." Tom didn't meet his eyes. "Pictures don't always paint a thousand words."

"But if you got a call from, say, a man who told you he'd seen D.J. drunk, that would be different, right?"

Tom's shoulders visibly sagged. "He called you, too, huh?"

"He did," Matt said. "What I'm wondering is why you didn't tell me about it?"

They were the only two people left on the field. Although the worst of the day's heat had passed, it was still sticky and uncomfortable, typical South Carolina weather, for mid-September. Matt's shirt already clung to his back.

"I made a judgment call," Tom said. "D.J. and I talked it out. He admitted he made a mistake and said he was being punished, so I figured you didn't have to know."

"You punished him?" Matt asked. If D.J. had been suspended, as acting athletic director Matt should have been told.

"Not me. His parents," Tom said. "D.J. told me he's grounded."

Matt didn't bother asking for how long. He wasn't sure he'd believe D.J.'s account, anyway.

"Not good enough," Matt said. "We need to suspend him, at least for a game, maybe two."

"What? We can't do that!"

"Why not?" Matt remembered his conversation with Jazz Saturday night, when he'd held the athletic department to a higher standard. "Because he's the starting quarterback for your winning football team?"

"I told you why. He's already been punished!"

"Not by the athletic department," Matt said. "Our rules about getting caught drinking are clear."

"We didn't catch him!"

"A father who's retired military did," Matt said. "He's a credible source."

"It's still hearsay," Tom said.

"You said D.J. admitted he made a mistake," Matt said. "How many kids have seen that photo of D.J. on Facebook? If word gets out that we knew D.J. got drunk and did nothing, what does that do to the program's credibility?"

A muscle worked in Tom's jaw. "I don't like it."

"But you see my point?" Matt prompted.

Tom nodded once.

"I can live with a one-game suspension," Matt said.

Tom finally met Matt's eyes. "We have a bye Friday. How 'bout I keep D.J. out of practice this week?"

"Not good enough," Matt said. "He needs to miss a game."

"You do realize we're playing the defending district champ next Friday?"

Matt nodded. "Do you want me to sit in when you tell D.J. about the suspension?"

Tom rubbed the back of his neck, suddenly looking older than his years. "He's my player. I'll do it," Tom said. "You can handle his mama."

Gerianne Huff was the PTA president, a loud, powerfully built woman almost as tall as her son. D.J. was her only child and her favorite subject.

"Mrs. Huff will understand why we have to suspend D.J.," Matt said.

Tom snorted. "Like hell she will."

Matt didn't waste time worrying about the football coach's prediction. He hadn't done the easy thing in insisting on D.J.'s suspension but it had been the right thing.

He left the office a full hour later than usual, rejecting the notion to ask Jazz to meet him for dinner. She seemed to be softening toward him but she was still skittish. As hard as it was, he needed to fight his nature and wait until the twins' party Sunday to see her.

After picking up a sub, he noticed the needle on his gas gauge was low. The service station where he stopped charged less for cash purchases, so he headed toward the attached convenience store. His cell phone rang, and he clicked it on. "Hello."

"You were way out of line to suspend my son."

The caller was Gerianne Huff. He wondered how

she'd gotten his cell number, then figured it didn't matter.

"I'm sorry you feel that way, Mrs. Huff," he said evenly.

"My husband and I are handling the situation." Her voice contained barely controlled fury. "You shouldn't be involved in this."

"I respectfully disagree." Matt paused outside the entrance of the convenience store. "D.J.'s my business because he's a member of a Faircrest athletic team."

"A key member," she shot back. "You need to take back that suspension right now."

The glass convenience-store door swung outward, and a couple of teenage girls left the building. Matt recognized them from school and nodded. They greeted him with huge smiles, then walked away giggling and casting backward glances at him.

"Listen," Matt said. "This is not a good time. If you like—"

"Where are you right now?" she demanded.

It wasn't any of her business but perhaps he could get across how inopportune her timing was. "At a Hess station. As I was about to say, you can make an appointment to come to my office tomorrow."

"That won't be necessary," she said and disconnected the call.

He stared at the phone for a moment, sighed and put it back in his pocket. Coaching the soccer team came with challenges but none as irritating as the ones an athletic director faced. Coaching was also a whole lot more fun.

A blonde woman wearing a shirt that was too tight

and shorts that were too short was moving away from the cash register when Matt entered the store. She smiled at him, then stopped and pointed a finger. Her nails were painted the same bright pink as her lips.

"Chicken sandwich and lemonade," she said. "You were with a boy who has a stomach the size of South Carolina."

Matt smiled back, grateful for a friendly face after the phone call. "Sadie, right? You waited on my brother and me at Pancake Palace."

"I sure did," she said. "And you're the poor guy who's trying to get a date with Jazz."

Her description of him amused Matt. Obviously Sadie didn't know him very well if she assumed he might fail. "Jazz told you about that?"

"Not willingly," she said. "That girl could be a mime, she talks so little. But I have ways of worming things out of her."

"So you know she catered my party?"

"That was you?" Sadie clapped. "Now I understand why you didn't just get some deli trays. But don't worry. I won't tell her it was a trap. I'm on your side."

He laughed. Sadie didn't look anything like his sister but her sass reminded him of Terry.

"Why *are* you on my side?" he asked.

"I'm an excellent judge of character," Sadie said. "You'd be good for Jazz."

Matt didn't try to bank his curiosity. "In what way?"

"She keeps to herself too much. You can get her to open up." Sadie rolled her eyes. "I'm trying, but Heaven knows I could use the help!"

Matt was still grinning to himself a little later as he stood by the pump, breathing in fumes and watching the automated numbers increase as gas flowed into his car.

Having Sadie as an ally was fine with him. Although Matt believed in going after what he wanted, he didn't have much practice pursuing women. The females he'd dated in the past usually made it known they were interested, often asking him out first. Jazz went to lengths to keep him at a distance even though he could swear she felt the spark between them, too.

Sadie was a few pumps away, screwing the gas cap back on her early-model Chevy. He was trying to catch the waitress's eye to wave goodbye when a dark blue minivan pulled up behind him. He didn't give the van a second look until he heard a door slam shut. The driver was Gerianne Huff.

She barreled toward him, like one of Tom Dougherty's football players intent on flattening an opponent. She stopped short, her eyes blazing and her mouth set in a stern line.

"We're not talking about this tomorrow in your office," she said. "We're talking about it now."

"You're serious?" Matt was having a hard time wrapping his mind around her sudden appearance. He regretted mentioning the name of the gas station. Either it was the only one in the area or she'd guessed right.

"Damn right I'm serious." Mrs. Huff was almost as tall as he was, with short no-nonsense hair and a scowl meant to be intimidating. "There's a big game next Friday. D.J. needs to play in it."

Matt lowered his voice. "Then D.J. shouldn't have gotten drunk Saturday night."

"You have no proof he was drunk!" Mrs. Huff spoke in a much louder voice than Matt.

"He admitted it to Coach Dougherty." Matt wasn't about to bring up the Facebook angle because she could easily claim the photo was doctored. "You know as well as I do that D.J. messed up."

"Yes! He messed up!" Mrs. Huff all but hissed. "His father and I are dealing with it. We grounded him. You don't have to do anything."

"The athletic department's policy against drinking is clear," Matt began. "Coach Dougherty should have told you—"

"Coach Dougherty said the suspension was your idea!" The volume of Mrs. Huff's voice escalated. "There could be college scouts at the game next Friday. Coach Dougherty wouldn't hurt D.J.'s chances of getting a scholarship."

"D.J.'s a junior, ma'am." Matt tried not to lose his temper. Couldn't the woman see that her leniency wouldn't help her son in the long run? "He'll have plenty of chances to prove himself."

"Not if he gets the reputation as a troublemaker!"

"Then from now on he should stay out of trouble," Matt said. The pump clicked off and he removed the nozzle, placing it back on the handle. He replaced the gas cap and took his printed receipt. "Now if you'll excuse me, I need to get going."

Mrs. Huff followed him to his car door. "This is unbelievable! You're not changing your mind?"

"That's right," Matt said.

"So you have no compassion for a kid who made a mistake?" She sounded incredulous.

"I've got plenty of compassion, Mrs. Huff. I just believe people should pay the consequences for their actions."

"I'm going to watch you like a hawk, Mr. Caminetti," she said in a soft, angry voice. "You best not make any mistakes of your own. Because you've made an enemy."

SADIE LEANED AGAINST a counter in the kitchen of Pancake Palace, grateful her number of customers had slowed and her waitress shift would end soon. Carl was wiping down the countertops while Jazz put excess pancake batter into a plastic container.

"You'll never believe who called me last night," Sadie said with all the drama the question warranted.

"Who?" Carl asked as he put elbow grease into a particularly dirty spot.

"Ace!" Sadie announced.

Both short-order cooks looked up from their work. Carl's dark eyes snapped with dislike. Carl had never met Ace, but Sadie had told him a lot about her ex-boyfriend, including the way Ace had dumped her.

"Why he call you?" Carl asked. Although his English was excellent, he tended to use the present tense and sometimes dropped words. Sadie thought his way of speaking was endearing.

"He wanted to know what we were doing this weekend," Sadie said. "He acted like he never sent that text breaking up with me!"

"What did you say?" Jazz's brows were drawn together, a worried expression mirrored on Carl's face.

Sadie straightened from the counter. "You two think he sweet-talked me into forgiving him for dumping me!"

Neither of them spoke for long moments, until Jazz asked, "Did you?"

"No!" Sadie cried. In a smaller voice, she said, "But I was tempted."

"Why you tempted?" Carl asked.

Sadie took a deep breath of air that smelled of pancakes and fried bacon. "It's not easy being a single mother."

"You great single mother." Carl was usually so quiet, this was being gabby for him.

"Thanks." Sadie didn't need props for caring for Benjy but it was nice to receive them. "But sometimes I get so damn lonely."

"It's better to be by yourself than to be with a jerk," Jazz said.

"Ace is jerk," Carl added.

Sadie had to smile. "Thanks, guys. Your support means a lot."

They both nodded, neither appearing completely comfortable with the praise. Helen Monroe barked out an order through the pass-through window, Jazz cracked two eggs onto the griddle and Carl went back to wiping up.

Sadie sighed heavily, her thoughts tumbling into words. "I just wish I could find someone as nice as Jazz's guy."

Carl's hand stilled. "Jazz, you have guy?"

"No." Jazz shook her head. "I have no guy."

"Maybe not yet, but Matt strikes me as somebody who gets what he wants," Sadie said. "It's obvious he wants you."

"Why would you say that?" Jazz asked, an edge to her voice.

Sadie couldn't figure her out. Just the other day, Jazz had commiserated with Sadie about dating the wrong kind of men. Sadie had a very good feeling about Matt.

"I ran into him at the gas station and I could just tell," Sadie said. "Oh. A weird thing happened. This tall woman driving a minivan was yelling at Matt because her son couldn't play in some football game. I'm pretty sure it had something to do with the kid drinking. Is Matt a football coach?"

"Athletic director," Jazz answered.

"That makes sense," Sadie said. "I tell you, though, the woman was not happy."

"What did Matt say?" Jazz asked.

"Something about school policy," Sadie replied. "That everybody's tough on underage drinking nowadays."

"No," Jazz said. "What did Matt say about me?"

"Oh, that." Sadie was messing with her. She knew what Jazz had meant. "He told me about you catering the party."

"He told you about this Sunday?" Jazz sounded shocked.

"This Sunday?" Sadie wrinkled her nose. "I was talking about last Saturday. Are you going out with Matt this weekend?"

"I'm not going out with him." Jazz seemed reluctant

to elaborate. "I'm doing the baking for a party his sister's throwing for her twins."

Sadie grinned. "So you are spending Sunday with Matt!"

"Not with him, with—"

"The eggs are burning," Carl announced.

Behind Jazz, tufts of black smoke rose from the griddle. Jazz whirled, grabbed a spatula and scraped the ruined mess into the trash can.

"I better go check on my tables," Sadie said quickly. She needed to pass both short-order cooks en route to the dining room. She patted Jazz gently on the back in sympathy and smiled at Carl.

He was already turning back to his work when he muttered something in a soft voice.

"What did you say, Carl?" Sadie asked.

"Nothing." Carl didn't meet her eyes.

But Sadie knew Carl had said something. She just couldn't be sure she'd heard correctly. Because it had sounded an awful lot like, "*I'm* a nice guy."

CHAPTER SIX

TERRY CAMINETTI PINCKNEY really knew how to throw a party.

The triple-chocolate fudge brownies, coconut cupcakes, peanut-butter cookies and soccer-ball-shaped cake she'd commissioned Jazz to bake for the Sunday afternoon event were only a start.

Terry had tied brightly colored helium balloons at regular intervals, covered picnic tables with blue plastic tablecloths decorated with rainbows and stretched a banner across the top of the rented pavilion.

Brooke and Robbie: The Chosen Ones, it read.

The setting was ideal, a shady gem of a park not far from the Citadel, the venerable military college on the upper peninsula of Charleston that had been turning out graduates since the mid-1800s.

The party had barely started and already it had energy. Robbie kicked a soccer ball around a grassy field with some early arrivals while Brooke and another girl played an intricate hand-clapping game. Jazz had watched the twins while arranging her baked goods on one of the shaded picnic tables, noticing little things that could mean either nothing or everything.

The widow's peak at Brooke's hairline that was shaped exactly like Jazz's.

The longish slope of Robbie's nose, a Lenox family trait.

The slim legs that accounted for most of their height, the same way Jazz was built.

Yet Jazz still hadn't attempted to find out the exact date of their birth.

"Everything looks and smells so yummy!" Terry hustled over to Jazz's side, dressed in a red T-shirt that said Me A Mamma. She snagged a peanut-butter cookie and bit into it. "Tastes yummy, too."

"Thanks," Jazz said. "Now that I've put everything out, I'm gonna go."

"Go! You can't go!" Terry didn't seem to believe in holding back emotion. "The party's barely started."

More guests began to arrive, Matt included. He wore dark sunglasses, a gold T-shirt that called attention to his tan and shorts that showed off muscular, hair-sprinkled legs.

Robbie had intercepted him before he reached the pavilion and roped him into demonstrating how to juggle a soccer ball. Matt was grace in motion, keeping the ball in the air with his feet, knees and chest.

"Wow!"

"Cool!"

"Your uncle's the bomb!"

The children's voices carried to Terry and Jazz, who managed to tear her eyes away from Matt. Terry was watching Jazz instead of her brother.

"I put everything on disposable trays." That way, Jazz wouldn't have to return for her dishes or rely on someone to bring them to her. "And you've already paid me. So there's no reason for me to stay."

"Here's a reason," Terry said. "I'd like for you to stay."

"But I'm not a guest."

"I'm the hostess and I say you are. You said yourself your work is done. And I can guarantee you the Caminettis know how to have fun," Terry said. "Isn't that right, Matt?"

Jazz had been so preoccupied with Terry, she hadn't seen Matt approach. He flipped his shades up onto his thick hair. Faint color stained his cheeks, hinting at what he'd looked like as a boy. It was only a vague hint. The boy had grown into a fine-looking man.

"You can't beat fun." Matt grinned and sampled a cookie, giving Jazz a thumbs-up as he chewed. "What are we talking about?"

"Terry, where do you want this thing?" Kevin called from where he had wheeled an oversized cooler through the grass.

"Be right there, babe," Terry said to her husband. To Matt, she added, "Convince Jazz we want her to stay, okay?"

Terry hustled away, shouting orders to her husband, leaving them as alone as they'd get at a party for children. Nobody was within twenty feet.

Jazz remembered Sadie's claim that Matt was trying to win her over and braced herself to resist him. She mentally prepared excuses about why she needed to leave. He dipped his head close to hers and she could smell his clean, warm scent.

"If you don't stick around," he said in a whispery, confidential voice, "you'll miss out on the Caminetti Shuffle."

"What's that?" she asked.

"Can't tell you," he said. "You've got to stay and see for yourself."

"But…but…" Her manufactured excuses had evaporated and she couldn't resurrect them. All she was left with was the truth. "I don't belong here."

His nose crinkled. "How do you figure that?"

"I'm not—" she tried to push the word out past the lump in her throat "—family."

"So what? Neither are most of the people who are coming," Matt said. "Terry believes in the more, the merrier."

"But I won't know anybody." Why couldn't she come up with better excuses?

"Then you can hang out with me." He winked at her. "I'll introduce you around. We'll start with my parents."

He gestured to a couple coming toward them wearing shorts, T-shirts and sneakers who looked barely old enough to have a son Matt's age. Matt resembled his father, who was tall and trim with the same golden-brown hair as Matt, but Matt had his much-shorter mother's warm smile.

"Who's this pretty young lady, Matt?" his mother asked.

"She's a friend who did the baking." Matt phrased his answer to make it sound as if Jazz were a guest first and employee second. She didn't see how she could disagree graciously. "Mom, Dad, this is Jazz Lenox. Jazz, Carol and Len Caminetti."

"It's lovely to meet you." Carol's eyes, the same light brown as Matt's, shone with curiosity.

"You, too," Jazz said.

Len pumped Jazz's hand. "So you and Matt are friends. What does that mean?"

"It means we're friends," Matt declared before Jazz could respond. "You just got back from Tallahassee, right, Dad? How was your trip?"

"The Seminoles won, so it couldn't have been better." Len extended his arm and repeatedly bent his elbow while humming an Indian war chant.

"Don't let my husband freak you out, Jazz." Carol Caminetti laid a hand on her husband's arm to still the motion. "Len played football for Florida State and that's their fight song. He used to coach the Faircrest High team, too. He's a football fanatic."

"The whole family's into football," Len nodded. "Carol was a cheerleader back when I played. Terry cheered, too. And now our son Danny is playing. He's only a sophomore but he's starting Friday night."

"We're soccer fans, too," Carol Caminetti interjected. "Did Matt tell you he was a scholarship goalie at Clemson?"

"No, he didn't." Jazz knew that Clemson had a big-time college athletic program. She was impressed but not surprised that Matt had the drive and dedication to perform at a high level. Not only hadn't Jazz played sports, but she also hadn't gone to college.

"Now Matt coaches high school and youth soccer," Carol continued. "He even does some goalie training for the Charleston Kicks. That's the local pro soccer franchise. Is the team still in season, Matt?"

"The season just ended," Matt answered. "They'll

start up again in the spring, just like my high school team."

"You can see why our grandchildren are always coming to Matt for soccer tips," Carol said.

She was a grandmother any child would be lucky to have. If Jazz had kept her twins, they wouldn't have any grandparents to fuss over them.

"Soccer's okay for Brooke but I've been talking to Robbie about peewee football," Len said. "I think Robbie may be up for it. He's excited about watching Danny play Friday night."

"We all are," Carol said. "I hope you're not too busy being the A.D. to watch him, Matt. I can remember football games where Len hardly saw a down."

Jazz was having a hard time following the conversation, something Matt must have realized.

"My dad was the Faircrest A.D. for twenty years after he quit coaching football," Matt explained.

"Loved every minute of it even though I hated giving up coaching." Len slapped his son on the back. "I can't tell you how happy I am that my son is following in my footsteps."

Carol swept a hand at the field where the twins were playing with an increasing number of other children. "I'm going to say hello to Brooke and Robbie. Are you coming, Len?"

"Sure am," Len said, moving away from them with his wife. Len gestured toward a gangly teenager who was a younger, thinner version of Matt. "Would you look at that? Danny already got the scarves out of the car for the Caminetti Shuffle."

Jazz saw Danny set a small box down on the picnic

table farthest from them. Matt raised a hand in greeting. The boy turned away and jogged to where the children were playing.

"Danny must not have seen me," Matt said. "I'll introduce you to him later."

Jazz was almost positive Danny's eyes had touched on Matt's, but it seemed unlikely that Danny would snub his brother. As for Jazz, she couldn't ignore what Len Caminetti had said about scarves.

"I'm getting more and more curious about this Caminetti Shuffle," Jazz admitted.

"That's the genius of not telling you what it is," Matt said. "You haven't left yet."

Screams of laughter sounded from the field. Danny was in mock pursuit of Robbie, taking care to stay just behind him as the little boy pumped his arms and legs with almost manic energy. Matt's parents looked on, his father clapping, his mother standing with one hand on Brooke's shoulder.

Jazz finally admitted to herself that she wasn't going to leave. At this point, she didn't think she could make herself.

MATT NAVIGATED THE logjam of children clamoring for burgers and hot dogs, intent on warding off the trouble that was brewing.

"Hey, Matt, come back here!" His brother-in-law, Kevin, stood by the grill, wisps of white smoke curling around him. "Hungry kids scare me."

Matt clapped the shoulder of the nearest adult, a divorced father who had custody of his children for the weekend. Matt had noticed earlier the guy wasn't mingling well.

"Can you fill in for me at the grill, buddy?" Matt asked.

"Love to!" The man broke speed records getting there.

Normally Matt would stay by Kevin's side until the food was gone, but Jazz needed him more. She'd been out of harm's way, sitting by herself watching the children play. Then the sneakiest of the Caminettis had joined her.

"Your coconut cupcakes are absolutely divine," his mother told Jazz as Matt approached. "It's not something I'd expect a South Carolina girl to make."

Translation: Are you from around these parts?

"The cupcakes are my own recipe," Jazz said.

"How talented you are!" Matt's mother clapped her hands. "But you must have some traditional Southern favorites. What's your specialty?"

A tactical maneuver. Evidently his mother hadn't elicited the response she was seeking with her first question.

"Chicken bog." Jazz named a stew rich in sausage, rice and chicken that was popular in the Lowcountry. His mother had her answer. Jazz was indeed a South Carolina girl.

"If the way to a man's heart really is through his stomach," his mother exclaimed, "you must have men falling in love with you right and left."

Translation: Ever been married? Engaged? In a serious relationship?

Matt slowed his steps, eager to hear the answer to that one himself.

"I'm not sure I agree with that saying," Jazz said.

"You're kidding me!" his mother exclaimed. "Who have you been cooking for that you'd say that?"

A trapped look came over Jazz's face. Matt could relate. He'd been on the receiving end of his mother's subtle probing often enough. He banked his curiosity and kept advancing.

"Sorry to interrupt," he said when he was six feet away, "but Jazz hasn't met Danny yet."

He extended a hand to help Jazz up from the picnic table bench. She reached for it so quickly Matt stifled a smile. When she was on her feet, she said, "Matt's right. I haven't met Danny."

"By all means, go meet him." His mother sounded as gracious as ever but Matt sensed her frustration. "I can always catch up with you later, Jazz."

Translation: I'm not through grilling you yet.

"Later it is." Matt guided Jazz toward a thicket of woods, near where Danny had been talking to their father a short time ago. She slipped her hand from his and folded her arms over her chest. He immediately missed the connection.

"Sorry about my mom," he said. "She's the one who should have been a cop. She'd be great in an interrogation room."

Jazz chuckled, a warm, pleasant sound. "I think she's sweet."

"She is," Matt said. "Sweetly determined to find out all she can about the woman at the party with her son."

"I'm not here with you," Jazz said.

He winked at her. "Let's not argue semantics."

"But I—"

"There's my brother." Matt was relieved to spot Danny sitting alone on a tree stump, holding half a hot dog and a Coke. It was important to Matt that everyone in his family meet Jazz. He wasn't ready to puzzle through why that was.

"Hey, Danny," Matt said in greeting.

Danny said nothing, a rarity for a kid who usually wouldn't shut up. His brother's face was an unreadable mask.

"Jazz, this is my brother, Danny." Matt watched his brother carefully to try to figure out what was going on. "Danny, this is Jazz."

"Nice to meet you, Jazz." Danny, like all the Caminetti siblings, had impeccable manners. Their mother had made sure of that.

"You, too," Jazz said. "Matt tells me you play football."

"Yeah, that's right." Danny polished off his hot dog and stood. "No offense, Jazz. But I'm outta here."

He walked away without meeting Matt's eyes, his steps eating up the ground. Matt stared after his brother, speechless.

"That was strange," Matt said to Jazz when he found his voice. "I don't know what's up with him."

Jazz touched his arm. "Maybe you should find out."

Matt glanced behind them at the parking lot, which was within easy get-away distance. "You won't leave?"

"I haven't left yet." She nodded in Danny's direction. "Go after your brother."

Matt complied, jogging to make up the distance his brother had gained on him. "Hey, Danny. Wait up!"

Danny didn't stop. He didn't even turn. Matt sped up, reaching out a hand to catch Danny's forearm. The teenager wrenched away from him without losing a step. Matt kept pace.

"Something wrong?" Matt asked.

Danny laughed dryly without looking at him. "Ya think?"

The teenager trudged into the woods, with Matt following close behind. Some of the bushes had taken on fall hues but the scenery was the furthest thing from Matt's mind. "How am I supposed to figure out what's wrong if you won't tell me?"

Danny whirled, his brown eyes blazing. "You really don't know?"

"I really don't."

"You suspended D.J.!" Danny blurted.

His brother typically dropped by the athletic office every few days, but it occurred to Matt that he hadn't seen Danny since the suspension had been announced. Although some of the other football players had been shooting Matt glares all week, it never occurred to Matt that Danny wouldn't understand.

"How could you do that after I told you I was starting?" Danny appeared hurt as well as angry, his lower lip jutting forward.

Everything clicked in place. High school teams typically went with a running attack because strong-armed quarterbacks like D. J. Huff were rare. Danny was a wide receiver.

"You think D.J.'s backup won't throw to you?" Matt asked.

"I know he won't. Thanks a lot." Danny shot him one last glare before stalking into the woods.

Matt let him go this time, frustrated he could say nothing to make things better. His gaze zeroed in on Jazz the instant he turned back to the picnic, even though dressed in a beige top and khaki shorts she seemed to be trying to blend into the background. She sat facing outward at a picnic table away from the pavilion. He joined her.

"That didn't go well," he remarked.

Jazz looked at him with gentle eyes. Because she didn't ask what was wrong, he wanted to tell her.

"Danny thinks the backup quarterback won't get the green light to throw to him," Matt said. "I suspended the starter for getting drunk."

Whatever she was about to say died on her lips. She nodded toward the man making a beeline for them. "Here comes your father."

Even from a distance, Matt could see the deep furrow in his father's brow. His stomach tightened. That look usually meant only one thing. His father was disappointed about something Matt had done. Again.

"I need to steal my son for a few minutes, Jazz," his father announced, then slanted her an assessing look. "Unless you already know about the quarterback?"

Of course, Matt thought. Danny must have filled their father in when they'd talked earlier. If his father hadn't been out of town this week, he would have cornered Matt before now.

"I know Matt suspended him," Jazz said.

"Then stick around and help me talk some sense into this boy of mine," his father said, "because suspending D. J. Huff was a bad idea."

"Why do you say that?" Matt asked. It didn't compute. Matt's father had earned high regard over his career as A.D. for being honest and fair.

"Because it could hurt your chances of making the A.D. job permanent." His father spoke in a voice low enough not to carry. "The people at Faircrest take their football seriously. They want to win."

Matt gaped at his father. "At the expense of integrity?"

"Nobody's telling you to compromise your integrity, son." His father shook his head to emphasize the point. "You just need to realize black and white make gray."

"Come again?"

"Your brother said the Huff boy wasn't arrested."

"That's right," Matt said. "D.J.'s girlfriend's father caught the kids drinking in his basement."

"See? That's a gray area right there," his father said. "This girlfriend's father, maybe he doesn't like the Huff kid. Maybe he wants to get him in trouble."

"There's also a Facebook photo of D.J. that backs up the father's story," Matt said. "D.J. was drunk, Dad. He didn't even deny it when Tom asked for his side of the story."

His father leaned closer, his voice not much louder than a whisper. "I hear there are quite a few applicants for A.D. To get the job, you need to learn when to let things slide. With a big football game coming up, this is one of those times."

"I can't believe this!" Matt exclaimed. "You're the one who always told me I couldn't cut any corners to be a winner."

"Yeah, basically," his father said. "But we're talking about school politics here. I'm trying to help you keep the job."

"I'm gonna keep the job by doing things the right way," Matt said. "That means enforcing the rules."

His father turned to Jazz, his hands upraised. "You seem like a smart girl, Jazz. Help me out here. Tell Matt he's not looking out for his best interests."

"I don't…" Jazz's voice trailed off almost before she began speaking. She was gazing down at her hands. One second went by, then two, before she raised her head and met his father's eyes. "I think Matt's doing the right thing."

"What?" his father exclaimed. "You must not realize how important football is to people around here. They want a winning team."

"They should want an athletic director who looks out for their kids," she said. "I drank in high school and got into trouble because of it. I wish someone like Matt had made me follow the rules."

Her voice was steady but Matt sensed instantly that the revelation had been difficult for her. Yet she'd opened up that window into herself to support him.

"Well, I…" his father sputtered, then tried again. "I shouldn't have asked you to—"

"Uncle Matt! Grandpa!" Robbie's excited cries broke into the conversation. He ran up to them, barely stopping in time not to crash into the picnic table. "It's time for the Caminetti Shuffle!"

His father tore his gaze from Jazz and ruffled Robbie's hair. "Then let's all go shuffle."

Robbie ran ahead of them, stopping every few feet to urge them to go faster, unaware that the Shuffle wasn't foremost on everyone's mind.

"You're making a mistake, Matt," his father said in a soft voice when they were almost to a starting line marked with a yellow ribbon.

We'll see about that, Matt thought.

JAZZ'S HEART HAMMERED, but it had nothing to do with the Caminetti Shuffle. She'd made a mistake in revealing that nugget about her past but she'd disliked the way Matt's father had been pressuring him.

The situation couldn't be more cut and dried. The athletic department had a policy against teenage drinking. The quarterback had violated it. Matt had suspended him.

End of story.

If Jazz had faced consequences for drinking when she was a teen, maybe she wouldn't have graduated to sex and drugs. Not only might she have stopped Luke from going into the convenience store on that fateful night, but it was also possible she wouldn't have been with him at all.

"Where's Uncle Danny?" Robbie was tugging on Matt's hand, a visible reminder of why Jazz should keep quiet about her past. "We need him for our team!"

Party guests all around them were breaking into trios. An older couple had snagged Matt's father. Brooke was with Terry and Kevin. Matt's mother circulated among the participants, handing out colorful scarves.

"I don't think Danny's playing, Robbie," Matt said. "We can have Jazz fill in for him."

The little boy appeared stricken. "But Uncle Danny has to play! How else are we going to win?"

The Caminetti brothers and their nephew had obviously teamed up before. Jazz tried not to take the rejection personally and released a long-held breath. "I can try to find Danny for you."

"There's no time." Matt squeezed her shoulder. "And I happen to think she's a winner, too."

Robbie slanted Jazz a dubious look, negating the warm burst of pleasure she'd gotten from Matt's comment. "Do you even know how to play?" Robbie asked.

"Not yet." Jazz tried to think of something positive to say. "But I'm a pretty good dancer."

"Uncle Matt!" Robbie wailed. "She thinks the Caminetti Shuffle is a dance!"

"That's because I haven't explained it yet," Matt said.

"It's not a dance?" Jazz indicated the two colorful scarves his mother had just handed Matt. "Then those aren't for waving to the music?"

Matt laughed. Robbie scuffed a tennis shoe on the grass, the corners of his mouth downcast.

"The scarves are for tying our ankles together," Matt said. "The Caminetti Shuffle is a four-legged race. It's the same concept as a three-legged race except we use three people instead of two and scarves instead of burlap sacks. The fastest team wins."

"Me, Uncle Matt and Uncle Danny are usually the fastest," Robbie said. Jazz didn't doubt it. Matt and his brother were proven athletes. She wondered why somebody—Brooke possibly—hadn't objected to them being on the same team.

"None of us like to lose." Matt used one of the scarves to loosely tie Jazz's ankle to Robbie's. He gazed up at her from his crouched position. "Brooke's team usually gives us a run for our money."

The little girl was a member of one of the other six teams that were lined up behind the starting line in the open field. She stood between her parents while Kevin tied their ankles together.

"We're gonna beat you, Brooke!" Robbie yelled to his sister.

Brooke stuck a tongue out at her brother. Jazz noticed that she didn't guarantee victory.

"The person in the middle gives the orders." Matt was busily tying his ankle to Robbie's ankle. "It's impossible to make good progress unless all three players are in sync."

"Listen up." Robbie explained his system, which involved assigning numbers to each of their four "legs." Nobody was supposed to move a leg until Robbie called out its corresponding number.

"I think I've got it," Jazz said when Robbie was through with the lesson.

Matt finished tying the scarf, stood up and gave Jazz a reassuring smile. "Robbie has the strategy down pat. Listen to him and you'll be fine."

Matt's mother strode to the middle of the field, additional scarves flowing behind her. She positioned herself in front of the competitors and raised her arms.

"The Caminetti Shuffle will begin when the scarves drop," she announced in a theatrical voice. "Ready! Set! Go!"

She lowered her arms with dramatic flourish, the scarves billowing behind her.

"One and three!" Robbie commanded. He waited until their team took a step with the legs corresponding to the numbers before barking more orders. "Two and four! One and three! Two and four!"

The concept was simple enough. A trio that was in sync would eat up the ground, barely noticing the constraints of the scarves. The scarf on Jazz's ankle tightened and loosened as she struggled to match the length of her strides to those of her teammates.

Shrieks of laughter rang out on both sides of them. The team of teenagers to the right was using the hop technique. The end players stepped in unison with their outside feet, then the middle player jumped when they took a step with their inside feet.

The teens mistimed a jump and went down in a heap. "We're out!" one of the kids shouted. All three broke out in hysterics.

"One and three! Two and four!" Robbie kept issuing his orders.

"Aiiee!" The team to the left couldn't get their timing down, either. A young man took too long a step, stumbled and put a hand down to break his fall. His teammates toppled after him like laughing dominoes.

"Brooke's team is getting ahead!" Robbie bemoaned, breaking his drill-sergeant-like rhythm.

His twin used an alternative strategy, walking normally and expecting her parents to match her strides. Brooke's team took over the lead. Robbie, Matt and Jazz were fourth.

"We need to speed up!" Robbie cried.

Jazz knew that meant *she* needed to go faster.

"Match your strides to Robbie's," Matt advised. "Let him set the pace."

"I'll try!" Jazz said.

"One and three! Two and four!" Robbie resumed his count.

Jazz concentrated on shortening her steps to synchronize with Robbie's tempo. Adrenaline coursed through her as they passed threesomes on the left and the right until only Brooke's team was in front of them.

The yellow tape serving as a finish line approached.

"We're gaining on them!" Jazz shouted.

Robbie counted faster. It was either speed up or fall. They sped up. Brooke, Kevin and Terry were just two steps ahead, then one, then...

"It's a tie!" cried Carol Caminetti, who'd hurried to the finish line ahead of the team. Matt's mother waved her two gaily colored scarves in celebration.

Robbie whooped and slapped palms with Jazz. The little boy's cheeks had turned almost as red as his hair. Excitement radiated from him, warming Jazz.

"Take that, Brooke!" Robbie yelled to his sister.

"I don't care if you won," Brooke called back.

"They didn't win, honey," Terry told her daughter. "It was a tie."

"Next time we *will* win!" Robbie promised. "Jazz has the hang of it now!"

"I think I just had good partners," Jazz said.

"We are the best!" Robbie grinned at Matt, who put his hand out for slapping. By the resounding contact, Robbie might have gone a little too heavy on the enthusiasm.

"Wow! You're really competitive," Jazz told the little boy.

"Mom says it's because of my ecological sign," Robbie announced.

"Astrological," Matt corrected. He bent down to untie the scarf binding him to Robbie and glanced up at Jazz. "Terry's into that kind of stuff."

"My mom says it's the reason Uncle Matt's so competitive, too. We're both Leos." Robbie put his hands out like claws and roared like a lion.

Jazz's heart rate, already elevated because of the exertion, quickened. She didn't put much stock in astrology but did know her twins had been born under the Leo sign of the Zodiac.

"What sign are you, Jazz?" Robbie asked.

"Gemini," Jazz said. Ironically, it was the sign that featured twins. "My birthday's June tenth."

Jazz took a deep breath. She'd been presented with the perfect opportunity to get the answer to the question that had kept her awake nights. Making her voice as casual as she could, she asked, "When's your birthday, Robbie?"

"July twenty-fourth!" Robbie responded the way Jazz knew he would, then added the clincher that erased any doubt. "I'm eight."

CHAPTER SEVEN

BROOKE AND ROBBIE were her children.

Jazz had known the truth in her heart from the second she'd spotted the twins at the park. Now, as she watched Robbie sprint over to his sister and adoptive parents, she understood why she hadn't sought verification.

Robbie was jumping up and down in front of his sister, no doubt celebrating because their team had snatched away a sure victory.

"Cut it out, Robbie." Terry laughed and encircled both children with her arms so that one twin was on each side of her. "You're both winners to me."

"To me, too." Kevin put his arms around his wife's neck from behind and they all laughed.

The twins weren't her children, no matter that they'd spent nine months in her womb, Jazz thought with a shudder.

They were Terry and Kevin's children.

Jazz's vision blurred, the image of the happy family turning hazy as her eyes filled with unshed tears.

"Jazz, are you all right?" Matt's voice seemed to come from a distance.

She blinked and the haze disappeared, enabling her to clearly see what she had to do.

"Jazz?" Matt gazed at her with concern. "Talk to me. You look pale."

"I don't feel so good." It was the truth.

He pressed a hand to her forehead. "You don't feel warm but maybe you should sit down."

"No." Jazz shook her head. "I need to go home."

All she'd ever wanted was for her twins—no, for Brooke and Robbie—to land in a happy home where they could enjoy an uncomplicated childhood.

A birth mother who'd spent time in prison was a complication.

She turned toward the parking lot and fled, needing to put distance between herself and all the things she couldn't have. Matt included.

"Wait a minute." Matt caught up to her before she'd taken a dozen strides. It dimly occurred to Jazz that she was always running from him but seldom getting away. "It's not safe for you to drive home when you're feeling like this."

Jazz fished in the deep pocket of her shorts for her car keys. "I'll be fine."

She'd arrived at the picnic early to deliver the baked goods so her car was in one of the first parking spaces. She hit the remote but Matt beat her to the driver's door and blocked the way.

"Let me drive you home," he said.

She shook her head. She needed to get away from the Caminettis, not spend more time with them. "That's not necessary."

"Then humor me," he said. "Because I'd never forgive myself if I let you drive off and you got in an accident."

He cocked his head, his gaze steady on hers as though she mattered. It had been a very long time since anyone had looked at her that way, longer still since someone had cared enough to want to protect her.

Jazz crossed her arms over her chest and felt her hands trembling. Considering the shock she'd received, Matt could be right. Getting behind the wheel of her car could be a bad move.

"If you drive me home," she asked slowly, "how will I get my car back?"

"I'll bring it over after the party," Matt said. "My whole family's here. I won't have any trouble getting someone to come with me when I drop it off."

It seemed to Jazz there was a simpler solution to the car shuffle but her brain wasn't functioning at full capacity.

"Okay," she said finally.

They took his car, a newer-model coupe. He'd parked in the shade, so the leather bucket seats felt cool and comfortable even before he switched on the air-conditioning. She leaned back against the headrest, but it was impossible to relax. Her mind raced, conjuring up images of Brooke and Robbie.

Matt slanted her a sideways look as he pulled out of the parking lot. "How are you feeling?"

"Better," she lied. She'd stopped shaking but it was sinking in that she might never see Brooke or Robbie again. That she *should* never see them again. "It must have been the heat."

"The heat'll do it," he said, accepting her explanation even though the high today was only supposed to reach the low eighties.

"I'm sorry you had to leave the party," she said. "Everyone's probably wondering where you are."

"Let 'em wonder." Matt turned onto U.S. 17 and followed the highway out of town, across the bridge over the Ashley River and past the circular high-rise hotel that towered above the streets below. She gave him directions to her apartment building and prayed the trip would pass quickly.

"I hope you get back before they cut the cake." Jazz started to say the names of the twins but couldn't manage it. She went with something less personal. "Your niece and nephew will be disappointed if you're not there."

"I doubt they'll notice," he said. "It's not like Terry throws them only one party a year. She's like a serial celebrator."

"What do you mean?"

"Adoption day. Birthday. Last day of school. Halloween. First day of winter." He shook his head. "She's always coming up with an excuse for a party."

Jazz tried to smother her curiosity but it was no good. Besides, at this point she couldn't see any harm in learning more about the twins. "Why do you think that is?"

"Terry knows she's lucky to have them." Matt kept his attention on the road as he drove. "She tried to get pregnant for a long time before she adopted. Her first adoption attempt, well, it didn't go so well."

"The first attempt?" Jazz prodded.

"Terry and Kevin adopted a baby girl a few years before they got Brooke and Robbie. A cute little thing they named Polly." Matt stopped at a red light and turned to face her. "The birth mother was a teenager

DARLENE GARDNER   113

who didn't have the support of the birth father. She handpicked Terry and Kevin to be the parents."

Jazz was almost afraid to hear the rest. "What happened?"

"A few days before the adoption was to become final, the birth mother changed her mind." Dark sunglasses covered Matt's eyes but his jaw was set, his lips tight. "It was an open adoption, so she'd seen Polly a bunch of times. She said she couldn't give her up."

"That must have been devastating for Terry and Kevin," Jazz said.

"They were heartbroken. The whole family was." The light turned green and Matt put the car into Drive. His profile looked chiseled, and he appeared to be gripping the steering wheel too tight. "Terry even talked about giving up the whole adoption idea."

"Except she didn't," Jazz said, stating the obvious.

"She still wanted to be a mom in the worst way." Matt's voice turned hard. "So I told her not to let the birth mother have any contact this time."

Jazz's throat seized, making it impossible for her to speak even if she'd wanted to.

"Terry eventually agreed that the open adoption was the problem. When the adoption's closed, the birth parents still have time to change their minds but the risk isn't as great." Matt flicked on the turn signal. "This is your street, right?"

Jazz hadn't noticed how near they were to her home. "Uh-huh." It was all she could manage to say.

Within moments Matt pulled the car into the parking lot in front of her apartment building, a sprawling collection of two-story brick buildings that showed their age. He put the car in Park and shut off the engine.

"Luckily the story has a happy ending." Matt's smile was back. "Now nobody can take Brooke and Robbie away from us."

Jazz whispered, "They're lucky children, to be loved so much."

"Yes, they are," he said. "And our family is lucky to have them."

Jazz drew in a deep breath but couldn't seem to fill her lungs. The temperature inside the car felt as if it had risen ten degrees.

"Thanks for the ride." She yanked opened the passenger door, got out of the car and shut the door with more force than she'd intended. Behind her, she heard the door on his side open.

"Wait!" he called. "I'll walk you to the door."

"That's not necessary," she called over her shoulder, not breaking her stride, fleeing from him yet again. "I'm feeling much better."

She didn't give him a chance to inform her that he walked women to the door regardless of how good they were feeling. She already knew that.

"When you come back with my car, you can leave my keys in the glove compartment." Jazz was backpedaling now, determined to put as much distance between them as possible. "I have an extra set."

"But—"

"Thanks again." She rounded the corner of the building where her apartment was located. When she was sure she was out of sight, she stopped and covered her face with her hands.

Matt couldn't have been more clear about his opinion of open adoption and how protective he felt toward his sister.

How would he react if he discovered Jazz was the woman his family didn't want around the twins?

Jazz hoped she'd never find out.

THE TV CHEF SWEPT her right arm in an arc to indicate the impressive array of ingredients on the granite countertop in front of her.

"Today's show is on power cooking. I'm going to demonstrate how to make multiple meals at once and freeze them for later use." The chef smiled at the camera with blinding white teeth that contrasted with her red blouse. "It's just what the busy family ordered."

Jazz pointed the remote at the nineteen-inch screen and switched off the television. She was an admitted television-cooking-show addict but this episode didn't apply to her.

Jazz had no family.

Scant hours ago she'd verified that she'd given life to Brooke and Robbie, but she'd also given them away. Now they were part of Matt Caminetti's family, and she was alone. Her situation was no different than it had been a few months ago, but after spending time with the Caminettis the silence surrounding her felt more acute.

Jazz's gaze landed on her mother's yearbook, which had been sitting on her coffee table since the day she received the box of her belongings in the mail. Before she could change her mind, she picked up her cordless phone, dialed information and asked for listings in Florence, South Carolina.

"William Smith," she told the automated voice. While she waited for the results, she could hear the rasps of her own breathing.

Long seconds passed before a live operator came on the line. "We have a number of William Smiths in Florence. Do you have a street address or middle initial for him?"

Jazz's shoulders slumped, the tension leaking from her. With a name as common as William Smith, Jazz should have anticipated the multiple listings.

"No," Jazz said.

"Can I look up another listing for you?" the operator asked.

"No, thank you." Jazz was about to hit the disconnect button when something occurred to her. "Wait! I mean yes." She took a deep breath. "Do you have a listing for a Belinda Smith in Florence?"

Jazz counted the seconds that passed by her pounding heartbeats. There were five of them.

"I do have a Belinda Smith," the operator finally said. "Would you like me to connect you to that number?"

Jazz would have refused if the operator intended to connect her to William Smith, but this was his twin. Surely Jazz could summon the nerve to pry information from his twin. She hoped. "Yes, please."

A series of mechanical beeps were followed by the ringing of a phone, then a woman's upbeat voice. "Hello."

The phone Jazz held was shaking. She realized it was because her hands were trembling. "Belinda Smith?"

"Yes, this is Belinda. Who's calling?"

Jazz hadn't thought this through but it was too late to turn back now. What could she possibly say that would sound plausible?

"I'm a friend of your brother Bill." Jazz's voice sounded shaky. She strived to gain control of herself. "I've, uh, lost track of him and was hoping you could tell me how to get in contact with him."

"Sure can." Belinda didn't seem to find anything suspicious about the call. "Bill's a postal clerk in Beaufort, works the counter at the downtown branch. You want his phone number?"

"That's okay." Jazz already had more information than she dared hope for. The man who might have fathered her lived and worked in Beaufort, a coastal town only about an hour's drive from Charleston. "That's all I need."

"You sure, honey?" Belinda asked. "What's your name, anyway? I can tell Bill that you called next time I talk to him."

"Thanks for your help," Jazz said and hung up. She leaned her head back against the top of the sofa, immediately realizing her mistake.

If Belinda Smith had caller ID, a glance at her phone's display would tell Belinda who'd called. Would the name Jazz Lenox mean anything to her? Would Belinda link Jazz to Marianne Lenox and figure out why Jazz had called?

Unlikely, considering Jazz wasn't certain herself of the reason. She was no more likely to confront Bill Smith than she was to spill the secret that she'd given birth to the twins.

She stared at the receiver, unaccountably afraid Belinda Smith would call her back demanding answers. Or maybe Matt Caminetti would phone to check on her phantom illness. And to think she'd been looking forward to the one Sunday per month she had off from her telemarketing job.

Jazz leapt to her feet, loathe to spend the rest of the night in her apartment fearing the phone might ring.

Within minutes Jazz was headed to the apartment pool, dressed in a bathing suit, flip-flops and a cover-up, and carrying a beach towel.

A middle-aged woman who'd moved in next door to Jazz a few months ago came toward her carrying canvas grocery bags. Jazz had seen her leaving for work at odd hours in a white uniform, so concluded she was a nurse of some sort.

"Nice evening for a swim," the woman—Jazz didn't know her name—remarked.

Jazz stepped to the side, making room for her neighbor to pass. "Yes. The weather's perfect."

The chlorinated water was also ideal, even though the pool area could have used updating like the rest of the apartment complex. The chain-link fence needed repair and some of the chairs were missing slats. The pool itself was large enough to swim laps in but only if no one else were present. Luckily, Jazz was alone.

She dove into the pool and cut through the water with practiced strokes, keeping her head down and taking rhythmic breaths.

Banishing Bill Smith from her mind was easy but Brooke and Robbie were tougher. The twins had occupied a corner of Jazz's heart long before she found out their names and developed a troublesome attraction to their uncle.

She concentrated on clearing her mind and enjoying the silky sensation of the water sliding over her. She swam until her arms and legs grew tired and her lungs burned, then she swam some more.

She slowed down for the last two laps until, finally, she reached out her hand to touch the edge of the pool. Lifting her head, she shook back her wet hair and saw Matt Caminetti leaning against the fence, watching her.

"Hey, Jazz," Matt said. "I thought that was you."

"What are you doing here?" Jazz blurted out.

He held up a set of keys. "I brought your car back."

"I thought you were going to leave the keys in the glove compartment." She was slightly out of breath, she wasn't sure whether from the exercise or his surprise appearance.

"I wanted to see how you're feeling," he said. "But it looks like you're good."

Shame coursed through Jazz. Matt had done nothing to deserve to be treated so rudely. On the contrary, he'd been an absolute gentleman.

"Thanks. I'm fine now." She was in the shallow end of the pool but kept submerged up to her neck. "And thank you for bringing back the car."

"Think nothing of it." Matt unlatched the door and stepped into the pool area. "I'll put the keys with your stuff."

He set them down near her beach towel but seemed in no hurry to leave.

"Isn't someone waiting for you?" she asked.

"Nope," he said. "We came in three cars. I drove yours. My cousin drove mine. And his wife drove theirs. They're already gone."

"I hate that you went through so much trouble," Jazz said. Especially because she could have driven her own car home.

"I was glad to help," he said.

She shouldn't prolong their encounter. It seemed rude, however, not to ask him about the party. "How did everything go after I left?"

"Great," he said. "The caterer who baked the cake did a terrific job. It was a big hit. She's really quite talented."

Jazz felt heat tinge her skin even though she was still in the water. "Thanks for saying that."

"Hey, next time you want a compliment, just feed me. I'll be happy to oblige."

She ignored that comment. There wouldn't be any next time.

"How did things go with your dad and brother?" Jazz hadn't meant to ask that question. Once she had, she realized how much she wanted to know the answer.

"About the same." Matt sat down on the end of one of the lounge chairs, leaned forward and rested his forearms on his knees. "Danny didn't talk to me. My dad talked too much."

"Your father should trust your judgment," Jazz said.

Matt laughed without humor. "My dad only trusts his own judgment. You know, it's funny. I thought he'd be happy about me and this A.D. job, but he always finds something to criticize."

"I could say a few critical words about him," Jazz retorted, then covered her mouth. "Sorry. I shouldn't have said that."

"That settles it," Matt said. "You have to go out with me."

She didn't understand. "Because I was about to bad-mouth your father?"

"Because we'd be good for each other." His gaze was unwavering. "And because I can't stop thinking about you."

With the pool lights shining down on him, Matt looked as golden as when she'd first seen him bathed in sunlight at the park. Now that she'd gotten to know and like him, he was even more handsome.

Her heart hammered. "I wish you wouldn't."

"Don't you think about me?"

"No," she said instantly.

"Now, why do I think you're not telling the truth?" he asked softly.

If she were on dry land, she could put a quick stop to the conversation by returning to her apartment. In the pool, she was a captive audience.

She straightened and instantly realized it was a mistake. The water came to just below her chest. Although she was wearing a modest one-piece bathing suit designed for swimming, Matt's eyes caressed her body. She felt her nipples harden.

"You think I'm lying because you're a man and have a hard time believing a woman isn't interested," she said, striving for flippancy.

She waded through the water, annoyed at her body's response. Matt stood up and approached the ladder with her beach towel. She hesitated, then climbed out of the pool and reached for the towel.

He circled behind her and wrapped her in the towel, bringing his mouth close to her ear.

"I don't find it difficult to believe a woman isn't interested," he whispered, sending a shiver cascading down her neck. "I just have a hard time believing *this* woman isn't."

Clutching the towel so it covered her, Jazz turned to face him. Another mistake. This close to Matt she could smell the warmth of his skin and see the faint beginnings of his beard and the tawny color of his eyes.

"Why is that?" She tried to make her voice haughty but it came out breathless.

"Because you want to kiss me as badly as I want to kiss you." His voice was as soft and sensuous as the water had been against her skin.

Anger roiled inside her, at him for being right and at herself for being weak.

"So what if I do?" she retorted.

He laughed and pulled her into his arms, pressing his mouth to hers before it registered what she'd admitted.

Matt kissed like a man who knew what he wanted. His mouth slanted over hers, the taste of him heady and exciting. The towel dropped away, hitting the cement with a soft thud so only the bathing suit covered her. His body felt warm against her pool-chilled skin. He coaxed her into opening her mouth and he deepened the kiss, his tongue sliding against hers.

Her mind grew hazy, the reasons she shouldn't be kissing him beyond reach. She tried to summon them, knowing they were important, yet she was helpless to fight the feelings that swamped her.

Jazz could try to fool herself into believing the reason Matt had gotten past her defenses was because it had been a long time since she'd let anyone kiss her. That wasn't it. She hadn't been tempted by other men, only by this man.

One of his hands was at the small of her back while the other caressed the nape of her neck. The kiss drove all thoughts from Jazz's mind except the need to be closer to him. She felt him grow hard, and excitement raced through her that she'd had that effect on him.

Without warning he pulled back, disengaging his mouth from hers and placing his hands on her shoulders to keep distance between them. She almost cried out in protest.

"We'd better stop." Matt's hair was mussed from where she'd stabbed her fingers through it. He sounded out of breath. "Anybody could see us."

Jazz blinked and clarity slowly returned. Matt was right. They were in clear view of a half-dozen apartments. She'd forgotten herself so totally that being discreet hadn't occurred to her.

Neither had it sunk in that she was kissing the uncle of her twins, a man she'd decided earlier tonight was off-limits. Like the rest of his family.

She yanked away from his touch, picked up the towel and secured it around herself. She couldn't let him know that she still felt vulnerable. "I'm not inviting you inside my apartment."

"Okay." He shoved his hands into his pockets. She

got the impression it was so he wouldn't reach for her again. "We can take things slow."

Jazz closed her eyes, wondering how she'd gotten herself into this predicament. She accepted her fair share of the blame but he was at fault, too. He was far too forceful, too used to getting what he wanted. She snapped her eyes open. "Why can't you take no for an answer?"

"That kiss didn't seem like a no," Matt said, sounding far more reasonable than she did.

She shook her head, desperate to get him to understand. "Listen. I can't go out with you. I can't see you anymore, period."

"Why not?" He looked confused. Why wouldn't he be after the way she'd reacted to his kiss? She needed to accept that he wasn't going away without a good explanation. She could tell him part of the truth, she realized. That might be enough.

"There are things you don't know about me," Jazz began.

"I know you're a good person," he countered.

"That's just it. I'm not." She sucked in a breath to fortify herself for the rest of the confession. "I spent five years in prison for armed robbery."

Matt threw back his head and laughed. "Yeah, right. And I'm a mass murderer."

"That's the reason I work at Pancake Palace," she continued and watched the humorous light in his eyes fade. "Not many other places will hire ex-cons."

Matt's brows drew together. "You're serious?"

"Yes," she said.

His mouth hung open, his shock evident.

"Now you understand." Jazz needed to get out the rest of it before she lost her nerve. "I'm not somebody you should have introduced to your mother."

She grabbed for her cover-up and car keys before heading quickly from the pool area, not waiting to hear his response.

Jazz blinked back tears. The stunned look on his face had said it all: Matt wouldn't be pursuing her anymore.

A tear slid down her face. She didn't bother to wipe it away. More were coming.

SADIE PLOPPED DOWN next to Carl Rodriguez on the wooden bench a few doors down from Pancake Palace on Monday, in the spot where Carl liked to take his late-morning break.

"So what do you think is up with Jazz?" She asked the question that had been on her mind all morning, the reason she'd taken a break at all. Sadie usually worked straight through, not because she got off any earlier when she did but because she needed to maximize her tips.

Carl screwed the cap back on his bottled water. Sadie had noticed he did everything with forethought, whether it was answering a question or filling an order.

For the hundredth time, she wondered how such a deliberate man had wound up in prison. She'd never ask, though. She liked Carl. She didn't want to risk feeling differently about him if she found out his crime.

He looked her straight in the eyes, a big point in his favor. Most men's gazes dipped to her D cups. Although

Sadie was pleased that nature had endowed her with such bounty, after a while the leering got old.

"I think Jazz is okay," he said.

"C'mon!" Sadie cried. "She's been quieter than a mime in church!"

One corner of his mouth lifted, an expression typical of Carl. She wondered what he'd look like if he let his smile break completely free. With his dramatic dark coloring, he'd probably be hot.

Sadie blinked back her surprise at the direction her mind had gone. She'd never once thought of Carl in those terms before.

"Jazz, she not as noisy as you." Carl delivered the line with a charm that made it impossible to take offense. She pretended to, anyway.

"Hey! I'm not noisy," Sadie teased. "I'm effervescent."

His eyes crinkled at the corners. "That a big word. Who tell you that?"

"A conceited jerk who said he was trying to improve my vocabulary." Sadie rolled her eyes. "I can't believe he dumped me first."

Carl's brown eyes turned serious. They reminded her of melted dark chocolate, the kind that dripped over hot-fudge sundaes. "You need more confidence," he said.

"I have tons of confidence," she shot back.

"Then why you date these…what do you call them? Jerks."

"Well, it's not like I know they're jerks when I agree to go out with them!" Sadie said. "They don't go around with Jerk Alert signs on their foreheads."

"But you still date them after you find out they jerks."

She couldn't deny that, not when she'd spent the better part of the last month complaining to Carl and Jazz about Ace. Except, how had the subject turned to her? She'd sought out Carl to discuss Jazz.

"I think something happened this weekend with Matt." She kept talking before Carl could object to the change of subject. "Something bad. Or else Jazz would have told us about the party."

"She didn't want to tell us," he said. "When you ask what happen, she say nothing."

"Exactly!" Sadie pointed at him. "That's why I think something's wrong. She really likes this guy, I can tell."

"How you can tell?" Carl asked.

Sadie thought of how Jazz's entire body seemed to go on alert whenever Matt's name was mentioned. But that wasn't something a guy would understand. "I just can. And I really want things to work out for Jazz with Matt."

"Why?"

She blew out a breath. "Really, Carl? You have to ask that?"

"Sí," he said, the Spanish affirmative somehow making him seem more intriguing. What? Carl? Intriguing?

"I like Jazz. Can't you tell there's something missing in her life? I think it's a man."

Carl started to say something, but Sadie preempted him. "You're going to ask why I think that, aren't you?"

He nodded.

"She keeps to herself way too much. It's like she doesn't know what it is to be happy. I think Matt could make her happy."

Carl didn't respond for several seconds, as was his habit. "How about you?" he asked finally. "Do you look for a man to make you happy?"

She met those melted-chocolate eyes for long seconds and felt something stir inside her. Something she didn't exactly know how to handle.

Damn Carl for making that comment a few days ago about being a nice guy. If that was what he'd said. She still wasn't sure of it.

"I'm happy already." Sadie stood up, extended her arms above her head and executed a twirl. "Sometimes I even spontaneously break out in dance."

Carl threw back his head and laughed, showing even white teeth and that unrestrained smile she'd been wondering about.

And now Sadie knew she was right.

When he smiled, Carl Rodriguez was smokin' hot.

"Are you busy Friday?" he asked.

Her heart nearly slammed to a stop. Carl was going to ask her out!

"My nephew, he play football," Carl continued before she could respond. "I go always. Benjy might like to go. Maybe you and Benjy meet me there."

Not a date. At least, she didn't think so. But what if it was? Sadie needed to have more than a six-year-old on hand for emotional support.

"I'll get Jazz to come, too," she said airily.

Carl raised a dark eyebrow. Sadie chose to believe

it was because he didn't think she could convince the other short-order cook to do anything.

"I'll talk her into it," she assured him. "A woman who can dance like this can do anything."

Sadie shimmied all the way back to the restaurant, with Carl's laugh trailing her. Sadie herself wasn't laughing. In her attempt to help Jazz, she'd complicated her own life.

She knew hardly anything about Carl except he'd been in prison—and that her newfound attraction to him wasn't going away anytime soon.

CHAPTER EIGHT

THE DRIZZLE FALLING on the soccer field Tuesday night had turned into a steady rain, which hadn't prevented Matt from giving in to his players' pleas to continue the end-of-practice scrimmage.

"C'mon, Coach," one of the thirteen-year-olds had begged. "We've barely been practicing an hour."

That was because Matt had been late. Again. This time he'd been dealing with a scheduling mix-up with the girls' volleyball team. Since Matt had taken over the A.D. job from Carter, there was always something. He'd already had to line up the father of one of his players to help him coach the soccer team, starting with the next practice.

"A few more minutes and we'll call it quits!" Matt shouted to be heard above the drum of the rain. He wasn't scrimmaging with his players because the teams had even numbers.

"But we're having fun, Coach!" one of his hardest-working players countered.

Matt was usually the one who didn't want to leave the field. Not so tonight. He had a burning need to discover the details of the incident that had landed Jazz in prison.

He'd surfed the internet both Sunday and Monday nights searching for answers but had come up blank.

Tonight he planned to call his brother-in-law for guidance about how to access public records, leaving Jazz's name out of it.

"Get off me!" The angry shout came from Alex Price, the team's top goal scorer, who everyone called Lex.

A tall, lanky defender named Dylan had been shadowing the speedy forward as Lex raced down the sideline with the ball. Dylan had probably thrown one too many elbows.

"You get off me!" Dylan shouted back, following up his comment with a shoulder shove.

Lex lost control of the ball and it skittered down the field through the wet grass. Instead of chasing it, Lex extended both arms and pushed Dylan back. The taller boy's feet went out from under him and he fell hard on his rear end, water splashing up from the ground.

Dylan sprang to his feet and charged Lex, tackling him in a move better suited for football than soccer. The two boys went down in a tangle of arms and legs, grunting as they hit the ground.

"Hey, break it up!" Matt sped toward the battling duo, his athletic shoes making squishing noises.

The rest of the team stopped running, with a few of the players joining Matt at the fight scene. Lex and Dylan wrestled with each other, throwing wild punches.

"I said break it up!" Matt hauled Dylan off Lex, positioning his body between the teammates before Lex scrambled to his feet. Matt grabbed some wet material from the jerseys of both boys and held the two of them apart with his arms extended. They struggled to get at each other.

"Stop it!" He gave both boys a hard shake. "What's gotten into you two?"

Matt's tactics finally paid off. Both Lex and Dylan stopped straining against his hold, although he could feel the tension in their bodies.

The rain came down harder. Water spilled from the bill of Matt's ball cap, but he could still see the rest of the players gaping at them.

"The next practice is Thursday at six. I'll see you all then," Matt called. Nobody moved. "Go on. Get out of here."

After another moment's hesitation, the boys ran toward the parking lot around the corner of the school building, where parents congregated to pick them up. A few of them made tents with their hands to keep the rain off their faces.

Matt released his hold on the two boys. Lex gazed after his teammates, even taking a step in their direction.

"Don't even think about it," Matt warned. "The three of us are staying right here until we get this thing figured out."

Lex and Dylan glared at each other through faces that were thankfully unmarked. They'd been wrestling when the punches started flying, preventing either boy from landing an effective blow.

"Start talking," Matt said. "You're teammates. You're supposed to have each other's backs."

"It's his fault!" Dylan bellowed.

"That's not true," Lex countered. "He started shoving me first. I didn't do nothin'."

"You were with Becky last night!" Dylan shouted.

Matt almost groaned. Oh, great. His players were barely into their teens and they were fighting over a girl.

"Who's Becky?" Matt asked.

"My girlfriend." Dylan peered around Matt to level his teammate with another glare. "Lex was making out with her last night."

"Who told you that?" Lex demanded.

"Doesn't matter who told me." Dylan practically spit out the words. "You shouldn't have touched her."

"I didn't touch her!" Lex said.

"You're lying!"

"Ask her," Lex said. "And then ask her what I told her to get you for your birthday, you dumb-ass."

"What?" Dylan said.

Lex turned away, his face an angry mask.

Matt figured he better answer for Lex or they'd be out in the rain all night. They were already soaked to the skin.

"I think Lex is trying to say he was with Becky because she wanted advice about what to get for your birthday," Matt told Dylan. He turned to his other player. "Right, Lex?"

"Yeah." Lex stared at the ground. "That's right."

"But...but..." Dylan sputtered. "Why didn't you tell me why you were with her?"

"I would have," Dylan said, "but you never asked."

Out of the mouths of babes, Matt thought. His players could have avoided the entire misunderstanding if

Dylan had come straight out and asked Lex for the full story.

The way Matt should have the other night with Jazz.

"Are you two good now?" Matt asked the boys, his mind already leaping ahead to what he had to do later tonight.

Lex and Dylan nodded, sneaking sheepish looks at each other.

"Then shake on it," Matt ordered, waiting until they did as he instructed. "Now listen up because I'm only saying this once. I'm letting you off with a warning this time. But if you two disrupt another of my practices, you're off the team. Understood?"

Lex nodded.

"Yes, Coach," Dylan said.

"And next time don't be so quick to believe the worst of each other," he added. "Now go on and get out of here."

The boys didn't need to be told twice, running side by side through the raindrops in the direction of the parking lot. Matt followed at a slower pace.

Not only couldn't he get any wetter than he already was, but he also needed to figure out how to approach Jazz. Because the best way to find out about the armed robbery that had landed her in prison was to ask her about it.

THE DETERGENT-SCENTED AIR in the apartment complex laundry room was heavy with humidity on Tuesday night as Jazz folded the extra-large men's polka-dot boxer shorts. She placed them on top of a neat pile that already included boxers decorated with superheroes.

All three of the washing machines were going through their cycles, unlike the dryers. They were quiet, yet filled with dry clothes. You'd think a guy with odd taste in undergarments would whisk his clothes away as soon as they were dry.

Jazz reached into a dryer and fished out another pair of boxers, this one with a Bugs Bunny theme. She shook her head.

Matt Caminetti wouldn't have to be embarrassed by his underwear. He'd look good in something sleek and black. And if he did go for boxers with cartoon characters or superheroes, he could pull that off, too.

Not that Jazz would ever find out what Matt wore under his clothes. She'd scared him off for good with her revelation that she was an ex-con.

Who would have guessed her strategy would work so well?

She carefully transferred her wet clothes to the now empty dryer. At least she didn't have to worry about Matt approaching her at the football game Friday night. After some coaxing, she'd let Sadie talk her into going with Sadie, Carl and Benjy, figuring with hundreds in attendance, it would be easy to avoid Matt and his family.

She shoved the Caminettis from her mind, switched on the dryer and glanced at the clock ticking on the wall. Jazz's clothes should be dry at just past ten o'clock, the time she usually got off from her telemarketing job. Tonight the boss had sent half the workers home early, bad news since Jazz got paid by the hour.

She'd probably have to look for a different second job soon, even if every application contained the dreaded question: Have you ever been convicted of a felony?

Jazz's apartment complex consisted of a series of simple two-story brick structures arranged in a rectangular shape around courtyards with grass. The laundry room for her set of buildings was located at an angle from her apartment. Jazz exited onto the lighted sidewalk that connected the buildings and stopped dead.

Matt was ringing her doorbell.

Her feet felt frozen while she wondered what she should do. Matt turned away from her door, forcing Jazz's decision. She ducked into the laundry room through the open door, backing up until she was next to the whirring dryer.

What was Matt doing here?

More importantly, could she afford to find out?

A droplet of perspiration formed on her forehead and dripped down her face while she listened to the seconds tick by. Was it thirty seconds? Forty? A minute? She'd lost track. She crept to the door and peeked around the corner.

"Jazz? I thought that was you." Matt was only a few feet away. Even his bright orange Clemson T-shirt couldn't detract from the cut of his shoulders and appeal of his features. One corner of his mouth kicked up in a charming smile. She hardened herself against it.

"I went back to check on my clothes." Jazz wouldn't let herself be rattled by him. She emerged the rest of the way from the laundry room and met his eyes. "What are you doing here?"

"I came to see you," he said.

"Why?" she retorted. "I'm still an ex-con."

His smile disappeared, and she could have kicked herself. So what if he'd gaped at her like she belonged in a *Silence of the Lambs*–type movie when she told him about being in prison? Her goal had been to scare him off. And now she was getting in his face for it.

"I'm sorry. I shouldn't have said that." She rubbed her temple. "If you don't want to associate with an ex-con, that's totally your right."

His mouth dropped open. Oh, great. She was compounding a bad situation.

"Sorry again," she said before he could respond. "I understand your position. Really, I do."

She didn't sound as though she understood even to her own ears. She sounded hurt and more than a little angry.

"Forget it," she said and moved to pass him.

"Wait!" His hand gently caught her upper arm. She hated that her nerve endings tingled at his touch. "I haven't told you why I'm here."

Jazz had felt down for days, only now admitting Matt's rejection was the reason. She stood perfectly still, careful not to look at him so he wouldn't see further proof that he'd hurt her.

"I'm the one who's sorry," Matt said. "I acted like a jerk."

"There's no need to—"

"Let me finish so you understand," he interrupted. "I admit I was shocked. But I should have followed you back to your apartment and asked for the real story."

"I told you the real story," she said, still without

looking at him. "I was involved in an armed robbery. I was convicted. I went to jail."

"There's more to it," Matt said. "You wouldn't just rob somebody."

Jazz finally lifted her gaze. "How do you know?" she demanded.

His eyes were steady on hers, the hand on her arm solid and firm. "I just do."

She caught her lower lip with her front teeth so he wouldn't notice her mouth was trembling. Since her release, nobody had shown this kind of belief in her.

"I've never made any excuses for what I did," she said.

"I'm not asking for excuses. I'm asking for your story."

His manner was nonjudgmental, his gaze unwavering. A thousand times, Jazz had examined the circumstances that had led her to prison. A hundred more, she'd wondered if she should talk to someone about what had happened. Matt wasn't a shrink, but wasn't it healthy to get the things that ate at you out in the open? What would it hurt to tell him?

"You won't like what you hear," she warned.

"Why don't you let me be the judge of that?" Matt's voice was soft, his manner inviting.

Jazz nodded.

THE INTERIOR OF Jazz's place smelled delicious, like chicken, pasta and fresh bread. Since she excelled at cooking, that wasn't a surprise. The look of the apartment was the real stunner.

The wall in the main room was lemon-yellow, the

sofa and love seat were cherry-red and throw pillows added vibrant splashes of even more color. Jazz had painted her tables a startling lime-green, and eclectic art covered the walls. Nothing looked expensive but everything seemed bright and different, a marked contrast to the muted colors in Jazz's wardrobe.

Matt gestured to his orange T-shirt. "Looks like I wore the right shirt. I fit right in."

Jazz didn't seem amused. Since he'd shown up at her apartment without notice, she'd been edgy and out of sorts, not like the sort of woman who decorated her home in the colors of the rainbow. Matt couldn't blame her. He'd acted like the worst kind of moron when she'd told him about the armed robbery, asking not a single question and then staying away from her for days.

He sat on the love seat but she kept standing, not pacing exactly but not keeping still, either. With her hair down and dressed in a sleeveless beige shirt, jean shorts and flip-flops, she looked young and innocent.

Matt didn't prompt her, but waited for Jazz to tell the story at her own pace. Finally, she took a deep breath and began.

"When I was a teenager, I was seeing this guy named Luke," she said. "He was a few years older than me. I knew he'd been in juvie but I didn't care. I thought he was cool. Anyway, I was turning eighteen and he offered to take me to an expensive restaurant."

She hesitated, long enough that Matt interjected with a question. "Your foster parents were okay with you going out with a guy like that?"

Jazz's eyes widened. "You know I was in foster care?"

"Terry mentioned it," Matt said. "She probably thought I already knew."

"I was only in the system for a few years," she said. "I lived with my grandmother until she died when I was sixteen."

Matt wanted to ask why her parents hadn't been able to care for her, but Jazz already seemed thrown off track by his interruption. He couldn't take a chance that she'd clam up. He waited for her to continue.

"My foster parents, they were too busy to notice the crowd I hung with," she said. "They had two other foster kids living with them, both younger than me. I wasn't going to be there much longer, anyway."

Jazz had mentioned her eighteenth birthday. Matt assumed foster care ended at age eighteen or after high school graduation. He imagined it had been a scary time for her.

She inhaled deeply and moved from one spot in the room to another.

"My birthday was on a Saturday night. I put on my best dress, a little black number I'd found in a secondhand store. I even wore makeup." She rubbed her forehead. "Luke had gotten fired from some fast-food joint—I don't remember which one—like a week before. I was so stupid. I never even asked how he had the money for dinner at a nice restaurant."

Matt refrained from pointing out it made sense to assume Luke wouldn't have invited her out if he couldn't afford to pay.

"Luke asked where I wanted to go. This was in Florence." She named a city more than two hours northwest of Charleston. "I picked this new downtown place that was supposed to have amazing food. I thought I might be able to figure out how to duplicate some of the recipes."

She paused long enough for Matt to conclude she'd never gotten to sample the restaurant's offerings.

"Luke took a back road and stopped at this deserted convenience store along the way." Jazz quit pacing and leaned back against one of the yellow walls. "I started to get out of the car, but he told me not to come into the store. He said I should take the wheel and wait."

Jazz's chest rose and fell, although Matt didn't hear her sigh.

"I should have figured it out right then," Jazz said. "Maybe I did. I don't remember anymore. But the next thing I knew, I heard a gunshot and Luke came running out of the store. He hopped in the car and yelled at me to drive. He was holding a gun in one hand and some money in the other. I didn't know what else to do, so I drove."

She shook her head, as if to rid herself of the memory. Except she hadn't finished the story.

"The cops picked us up, of course. We didn't get five miles down the road. Thank God Luke was a lousy shot. He only winged the guy behind the counter. He said the gun went off accidentally, but our lawyer said nobody would believe that if we went to trial."

"You had the same lawyer?" Matt couldn't keep his silence any longer.

"The court appointed both of us a lawyer. It turned out to be the same one." Jazz spoke matter-of-factly, as though that was common practice. "The lawyer said if either of us went to trial, our sentences could be as much as thirty years because a firearm was used during the robbery."

"You should have had a lawyer who looked out for your interests alone," Matt said. "You didn't even know there was going to be a robbery!"

Jazz's mouth tightened before she spoke. "The hand of one is the hand of all. That's what the lawyer said. And when it comes to the law, that's the truth."

"It's not that clear-cut," Matt insisted.

"It was for us. Luke pleaded guilty and got ten years without the possibility of parole." This time Matt did hear her sucked-in breath. "I took a plea bargain and served five years."

"Five years in prison for not knowing your boyfriend was going to rob a convenience store?" Matt was incredulous.

"You make it sound like I was blameless," Jazz said.

"You were!"

"That's not true. I knew how wild Luke was and I was still with him."

"You weren't responsible for his actions," he argued.

"I was responsible for getting myself into a bad situation," she maintained. "I was no angel back then. Just the opposite. I left out that we smoked marijuana in the car before we got to the convenience store."

"Nobody was looking out for you," Matt said.

"I was eighteen, old enough to look out for myself." She was shaking her head back and forth, refusing to listen to his very valid points.

He stood up and crossed the room to where Jazz

stood with her back to the wall. He took her gently by the shoulders and waited until she looked at him. She appeared to be in pain.

"For argument's sake, let's say you deserved to be punished." Matt spoke urgently so he'd get through to her. "You did your penance. Don't you think it's time you stopped punishing yourself?"

"I'm not—"

He didn't let her finish. "Yes, you are. You even assumed I didn't want to be around you because you'd been in prison."

"That was true!"

Matt shook his head. "Not true. I didn't believe the worst of you. Well, not after I had time to think about it. That's why I came over here tonight. And I was right."

Jazz was still shaking her head. He put a hand against one of her cheeks to still the movement. She opened her mouth to say something else, and he moved his fingers so they covered her lips.

"You might not believe in yourself," Matt said softly, "but I believe in you."

JAZZ YEARNED TO BE the woman Matt thought she was.

Gazing into his eyes, she could almost see herself the way he did. As a woman who'd been victimized by circumstances and not one who had a criminal legacy.

Almost.

"You don't know everything about me." She spoke through the fingers still covering her lips.

"I don't need to." Matt slid his fingers to the back of her neck and cupped her head with a gentle hand.

The anticipation that he was about to kiss her buzzed through her veins. He had a beautiful mouth, his lower lip rich and full, his upper lip slightly bowed in the center.

She'd let him kiss her, Jazz decided. She even wanted him to, just to see if she'd blown the first kiss out of proportion. She'd told herself again and again over the last few days that no kiss could be as electrifying as she remembered.

Jazz moved forward, closer and closer to finding out. And then her mouth was on his, her fingers threading through the golden-brown strands of his thick hair.

Her lips molded to his while she breathed in the clean, warm scent that was uniquely his. Her nerve endings came alive, heightening her senses. He tasted wonderful and ever so slightly of a rich, luscious coffee.

Yes, that was it. He tasted luscious.

She pressed against the solid length of him, yearning to be closer. She felt his erection against her lower abdomen at the same time he coaxed her mouth open. It didn't take much persuading.

Matt's tongue slid against hers, arousing all sorts of sensations she hadn't felt in years before he'd kissed her by the pool. Maybe she'd never felt anything like it. Heat built inside her, flickering like the sparks before a fire broke out. She rubbed against him, feeling the heat pool at her very center.

One of his hands slid slowly down her back, settling on her rear end, bringing her closer against his arousal. Their kiss got deeper, more furious.

Jazz had never felt passion like this. It rose inside of her like a living thing until her world spiraled out of control. That could be because Matt had swept his arms under her knees and her feet were off the ground. His lips were on the side of her mouth, then at her throat. Her flip-flops slipped off her feet and landed on the carpet with a soft thump.

"Bedroom?" Matt rasped.

She couldn't tell if he was asking for directions or permission. It didn't matter. She couldn't think.

"Down the...hall," she said.

Matt took off in that direction, striding the length of the hall and nudging open the partially cracked door to her bedroom with his foot. He flipped a switch on the wall that turned on the ceiling fan and her bedside lamp.

The room was her favorite, decorated in a kaleidoscope of colors with a psychedelic bedspread set off by sky-blue walls she'd stenciled with azaleas, her favorite flower. Jazz had never allowed anyone into her sanctuary. Until now.

Matt deposited her on the bed, kicked off his shoes and quickly joined her. His mouth sought hers and the spiral inside Jazz grew tighter, wilder. She wasn't sure whether the colors she saw were in her room or in her mind.

The slats of the ceiling fan whirred overhead, stirring the air but doing little to cool the heat between them. Matt fumbled with the buttons of her shirt, and Jazz let him, glad when he had the garment unbuttoned and she could be free of it.

Then Matt's hands were on her skin, gliding across

her abdomen, moving upward. Her breasts swelled and her nipples puckered, straining against the silky material of her bra. He fumbled with the clasp.

Soon Jazz would be completely naked, with no barrier to making love with him. Was she ready for this?

Her heart pounded, her blood raced through her veins and her lungs felt as if they were in the grip of a vise.

The answer was a resounding no. She wasn't ready.

Jazz jerked backward, breaking off the kiss and pushing against his chest until their bodies were no longer touching. She scooted away, putting at least a foot between them on her queen-sized bed.

"Jazz, are you okay?" Matt asked.

She wasn't looking at him but he sounded stunned. Why wouldn't he be? She'd practically thrown herself at him and then acted as if he were sexually assaulting her.

Jazz nodded.

Matt anchored himself on one elbow and gazed down at her. His hair was ruffled, his eyes heavy lidded, his lips moist. "Are you sure? Because you don't look okay."

She inched farther from him on the bed, picked up her shirt and put it back on. Matt didn't change his position while she rebuttoned it, watching her warily. She strived to get control of herself.

"I'm sorry." Jazz took a deep breath and released it slowly. "You probably think I'm nuts."

"No," he said, "I don't."

"I wouldn't blame you. I know I'm giving off mixed signals. It's just that…" She took a deep breath and tried again. He deserved an explanation. "It's been a while and things were suddenly going too fast."

A moment passed, then another. "How long is a while?"

Jazz hadn't consciously counted up the years. She swallowed. "Since before I went to prison."

"How long ago was that?" he asked. "Six years? Seven?"

"Almost nine," she said. "I turn twenty-seven this year."

Matt smiled at her, long and slow. "You won't get any complaint from me. I kind of like that you haven't been with anyone else in a long time."

Jazz might as well tell him the rest of it. "I didn't only mean I haven't made love in almost nine years." She could only manage a whisper. "I haven't kissed anyone in that long, either."

His mouth dropped open and he shook his head. "That can't be true. Not of someone who looks like you."

Jazz stared at him, not sure where he was going with this.

"I mean, look at you." Matt gestured to her with a nod of his head. "You're gorgeous. Men must hit on you all the time."

She blinked, trying to square his words with her self-image. She'd always thought of her looks as average.

"When you're in prison," Jazz said, "you learn pretty quickly to give off signals that you want to be left alone."

"Haven't you wanted to date since you've been out?"

Jazz shook her head. She'd been too busy holding down two jobs so she could pay the rent. Not only hadn't she sought male attention, but she'd also avoided it.

"After Luke, I don't trust my judgment," she explained.

"So these signals you give off, do they work with everyone?"

She was surprised to feel herself smile. "You mean, everyone besides you?"

"Yeah, I guess that's what I mean."

Jazz shrugged. It was becoming easier to talk with every minute that passed. "Every now and then, there's a guy who doesn't get the message. But I can handle it."

"How do you handle it?"

"Different ways," she said. "Mostly I say I'm not interested. That usually works, but not always."

"I'd apologize," he said, "except when you kissed me, it didn't feel like you were signaling me to leave you alone."

Jazz wiped a hand over her face. "I wanted to kiss you. But then before I knew it we were in my bedroom and I panicked."

Matt brushed a strand of hair from her face and a little tingle spread through her.

"I'd never push you to do anything you didn't want to do," he said. "You know that, don't you?"

She nodded. She trusted him in a way she hadn't trusted anyone in a very long time. She wasn't ready to make love to him, but she didn't want him to go, either. With Matt in her bed, the world was a far less lonely place.

"Maybe you could just hold me for a while," she whispered.

Matt wrapped her into his arms. She took comfort in the even rhythm of his breathing and a peace settled over her.

Neither of them spoke a word. After a while Jazz's eyes grew heavy. Her last thought before she drifted off to sleep was that she hoped nobody else needed the dryer tonight.

Because there was no way she was leaving the warmth of his arms to fold her clothes.

CHAPTER NINE

JAZZ OPENED HER EYES to darkness.

She felt incomplete, as though something were missing. A rustling near the foot of the bed brought home what it was. Matt was no longer lying next to her.

"Matt?" Her voice sounded groggy from sleep. "What time is it?"

"Almost two." He straightened. Something was in his hands. It appeared to be a pair of shoes. "I'm heading out. I've got work in the morning."

She did, too. She needed to be at Pancake Palace for prep work in less than four hours.

Jazz pushed herself up into a sitting position. She was still in the clothes she'd worn the night before. Her eyes adjusted to the darkness and she could see that Matt was, too. His T-shirt had come loose from his shorts and he looked charmingly rumpled.

"We fell asleep," she stated the obvious.

"I didn't mean to." Matt sat down on the edge of the bed closest to her and brushed the hair back from her face. Jazz leaned into his touch. "But after I was sure you were asleep, I switched off the light. I only meant to stay a little longer. The next thing I knew, it was 2:00 a.m."

"Really?" she asked. "You fell asleep that easily?"

"Only after you did," he said. "Before then, I was too revved up."

Jazz laughed, remembering the passion that had flared between them. Yet, lying in his arms last night, she'd felt safe.

"You weren't the only one," she said. "My engine was racing, too."

"You have a beautiful engine." Matt's sensuous mouth curved into a smile she could just make out in the darkened bedroom. "All the more reason for me to get going."

"Yes." Jazz reached out to trace the outline of his lips. What was it about his mouth she found so fascinating? "You should get going."

He caught her hand and placed a kiss in the center of her palm. A shivery sensation traveled down her arm.

Jazz met his eyes. "You can do better than that."

"Ah, a challenge," he said. "You should know I can't resist one."

Without letting go of her hand, he leaned forward and claimed her lips with a gentle, undemanding kiss. She breathed in the clean, intoxicating scent of him, already sure that blindfolded she could pick him out of a dozen men. His lips graced her mouth with a series of soft, tender kisses that demanded nothing. He still held her hand, which was nestled against his heart.

Matt kissed the side of her mouth, whispering against her skin, "I should go."

Jazz turned her mouth, greedy for more of his kisses. His whiskers had grown since last night, the feel of his face against hers scratchier and somehow more exciting. Kissing him was intoxicating, spreading a sensuous languor through her body.

She lost track of time, not aware of anything except pleasure. She felt bereft when he raised his head. He inhaled, then exhaled.

"We've got...to stop." Matt seemed to be struggling to get his breathing under control. "Already I won't... be...walking straight."

She was amazed that she could giggle, even more surprised by what she was about to say. "What if I don't want you to stop?"

He became very still. Jazz could make out just enough of his expression in the darkness to pick up on his surprise. "Are you sure?"

Last night the panic had been present from the start, lurking beneath the surface, warring with the passion. The panic was completely gone now.

"Very sure," Jazz said.

Keeping her eyes fastened on his, she undid her shirt button by button, then shrugged out of it. Next she unhooked the front clasp of her bra, letting her breasts spill free.

She saw his Adam's apple move as he swallowed.

"I sure am glad you're sure," Matt said, "because you sure are beautiful."

His tone was so reverent that she laughed again, then slipped her bra completely off. He kept staring. She felt her nipples pucker.

"By the way," Jazz said in a breathy voice, "this is definitely not a case of 'look but don't touch.'"

It was Matt's turn to laugh. He reached for her, one of his warm hands cupping her shoulder, the other gliding over her back and across her stomach until moving north. His mouth closed over hers as he cupped her breast.

She gasped into his mouth. A tight spiral of need unfurled inside her. While still kissing him, she reached for the hem of his T-shirt. She helped him pull it over his head, breaking off the kiss only as long as necessary. His chest was muscular yet not overly developed, with a light sprinkling of hair.

"I sure hope you have a condom," she said.

He reached into the pocket of his shorts, withdrew his wallet and produced one.

Her eyes dipped to the waistband of his shorts. She tucked her thumbs into her own waistband.

"Race you," she said.

Matt was sliding his shorts down his lean hips before she finished unzipping. She didn't even get a glimpse of his underwear, which meant she still didn't know if he wore boxers or briefs, cartoon characters or superheroes. She giggled.

"Why are you laughing?" His voice was playful. "I won."

Jazz shimmied out of her shorts and bikini panties, then took a long look at the hard length of him. She felt a surge of feminine power.

"No," she said. "We both did."

She moved forward, meeting both his mouth and body halfway, so that they were skin to skin. Jazz slanted her mouth, granting him better access, giving herself even more gratification.

She ran her hands over the solid planes of his body and strained to be even closer to him. He reached between them. Even before he stroked her, she was slick and ready. She helped him sheath himself with the condom, then guided him so that the tip of his shaft was at her entrance.

"Now," Jazz said and thrust her hips to take all of him.

She moved with him. It had been more than eight years since she'd had sex but she was positive she'd never felt this intensity before. Matt was in no hurry, setting a tempo that led to a slow buildup of sensation, until Jazz thought she'd die from too much pleasure.

The pressure built inside her, hot and needy, so that she was the one who started to move faster. He matched her rhythm until something hot, sweet and unfamiliar burst inside her, transporting her to a different plane. He thrust inside her one more time and groaned, reaching his own climax.

They stayed that way for long moments until Matt rolled over, still keeping her in his arms so they were side to side. Jazz turned her head to smile at him.

"That was my first time," she told him.

"What?" Matt looked adorably shocked.

"Not my first time making love," Jazz clarified. "My first orgasm."

His grin was so cocky it warmed Jazz to her toes. "Sweetheart, you've been hanging out with the wrong guys."

"Is that right?"

"Absolutely." Matt kissed the side of her neck, sending shivers spiraling down her body. "In fact, I think you should go to dinner with the guy who gave you your first orgasm."

"I thought you were going to stop asking me out," Jazz said.

"This won't be a date." Matt nuzzled her neck again. "It'll be my reward for gratifying you."

She couldn't help it. She giggled again.

"How does Wednesday night sound?" he asked. "Let's say eight-thirty?"

Jazz could hardly think with his clever lips on her body. Now they were near her ear. But wasn't it already Wednesday? "I'm working tonight."

"Thursday night?"

"Also working." Jazz was busy four nights a week with the telemarketing job.

"I've got the football game Friday night," Matt said. "I need to be on the sidelines making sure things run smoothly, but you could come and sit with my family."

Reality crashed down on Jazz, heavier than a boulder. Barely forty-eight hours ago she'd made the decision to stay away from all of the Caminettis. If she made an exception for Matt, how could she avoid the rest of them?

"I can't," she said.

This close to him she could see the frown lines that appeared between his eyebrows. "Are you brushing me off?"

Jazz bit her lower lip. "Maybe a little. I'm already going to the game with some of my coworkers. Carl— he's another of the short-order cooks—has a nephew who plays for the team."

"I'm cool with that," Matt said slowly. "But let's get back to you brushing me off."

"I'm not in the market for anything serious, Matt."

"Okay," he said. "I can live with that."

Jazz needed to make things clear. "Even if it means I don't want to be around your family?"

"You don't like my family?"

"I like your family fine." An understatement. "I just don't want them getting the wrong idea about us."

"Fine. No family," Matt said. "So will you go out with me Saturday night?"

Jazz hesitated instead of blurting out her agreement. She needed to be smart and consider the situation from every angle. But hadn't she already done that? She'd told Matt of her desire to keep things casual and to stay away from his family.

"Say something." Matt grinned at her. "As long as it's yes."

She gave up trying to resist the irresistible.

"Yes," Jazz said.

"Good answer! You won't be sorry. I'll take you somewhere nice for dinner. If you behave yourself, maybe you'll even get lucky."

She laughed and moved closer to him, surprised that he was already primed and ready for her again.

"I have a feeling I'm about to get lucky right now," she whispered.

Jazz proceeded to lose herself in him, not even caring that she'd be well short of the requisite eight hours. If anything was worth losing sleep over, it was Matt.

WHAT A DIFFERENCE twenty-two minutes of high school football made.

The spotlights still shone, the band still played the

Faircrest fight song and the stands were still packed, but with two minutes until halftime Matt could no longer spot a single Free D.J. sign.

Nobody had mentioned the suspended quarterback's name since a few of the boosters had cornered Matt before opening kickoff to complain that the punishment had been excessive.

That could have something to do with the surprising play of the backup quarterback—and the score. Faircrest led defending champion Valley Field by a touchdown.

"You're a tough man to find." Matt's father appeared at the fence where Matt was watching the Faircrest drive. After a couple of long runs, the ball was near midfield.

"Can't stand still for long," Matt said. "A lot of fires to put out."

So far Matt had stopped a pregame shouting match between opposing fans, explained to people streaming into the game that only standing room was left and ordered the Faircrest students to stop chanting obscenities.

He hadn't gotten a chance to say hello to Jazz, who was sitting at about the thirty-yard line with Sadie, a young boy and a handsome, dark-haired guy who must be the short-order cook she'd mentioned. The guy sat between Jazz and Sadie.

"That's an A.D.'s life," his father said with a laugh. He nodded toward the field. "Rodriguez must have sixty or seventy yards rushing."

Arthur Rodriguez, the backup quarterback who'd spent the first part of the season on the bench, added an exciting dimension to the Faircrest attack. While

D. J. Huff was strictly a drop-back passer, Rodriguez had the speed to cut to the outside and run downfield.

"Look at this!" his father suddenly cried.

Rodriguez was rolling to the right after faking a handoff to the fullback. The young quarterback looked downfield to where Danny had a step on the defensive back and heaved a throw in Danny's direction. Matt's father clutched Matt's arm as Danny gazed back over his shoulder without breaking stride. The ball dropped into his arms.

Matt shouted along with the crowd.

"That's my boy!" his father yelled.

The defender shoved Danny out of bounds but the damage was done. The ball was at the ten-yard line and Danny had his first high school catch.

"That was some catch!" His father's smile was brighter than the lights shining on the field.

"Some throw, too," Matt said.

"That it was!" His father slapped Matt on the back. "You are one lucky son of a gun."

"Come again?"

"The Rodriguez kid is the real deal," his father said. "If you hadn't suspended D.J., he wouldn't be playing."

"That's not why I…" Matt's denial was snuffed out by the excited crowd. Faircrest had run another play and Rodriguez was streaking down the left sideline for the end zone. He was at the five-yard line, the three, the one…

"Touchdown!" Matt's father shouted.

The Faircrest players mobbed the backup quarterback. Band members lined the end zone, waiting to get on the field for their halftime performance. A half-dozen majorettes and color guards sprinted toward the football players and joined in the celebration.

"There's another fire," Matt told his father. "Got to go."

The band director was already rounding up the overly exuberant girls when Matt arrived in the end zone. Matt hung around the end line in case another celebration broke out in the minute or so that remained in the first half.

He didn't head toward Jazz until the half ended, the football players retreated to the locker room and the band struck up its opening number in the halftime show.

Matt hadn't seen Jazz in almost three days, since he'd left her bed a few hours before dawn on Wednesday morning. The few times he'd called, he got voice mail. He'd considered sending flowers until remembering her insistence that they keep things casual.

"Hey, Mr. Caminetti. Wrong direction," called a tall kid on the basketball team who'd been giving Matt dirty looks all week. "Snack bar's this way."

"No thanks." Matt patted his flat stomach. "Gotta preserve the six-pack."

The kid laughed and Matt kept moving against the tide of people intent on hot dogs, burgers and soft drinks. The stands were no longer as crowded, thanks to all the people en route to the concession stand. Sadie waved wildly as soon as Matt started up the center aisle of their section.

"Over here, Matt!" Sadie called.

Matt grinned and waved back. Sadie must not realize

he'd memorized Jazz's exact location before the game even began. Now that Matt was closer, he noticed that Jazz had once again dressed in muted colors, a brown shirt and what looked to be khaki pants. With her friends between her and the aisle, she should have blended into the crowd. She didn't.

Jazz smiled at him the way she had after revealing he'd given her her first orgasm. The smile made worthwhile every last step he'd had to fight through the crowd to get to her.

"That's Jazz's Matt." Sadie turned to the guy seated between herself and Jazz, speaking loudly enough that Matt heard from a few rows away. "Isn't he a looker?"

The guy grinned at Sadie, although not at Matt. Good. He normally enjoyed competition, but not when it came to Jazz. Of the two women, Sadie was definitely the one who'd captured the guy's interest.

"Sit down, Matt." Sadie patted the empty seat on the end of the aisle where the little boy had been sitting. "Benjy—that's my son—went to get popcorn with the boys sitting in front of us. He makes friends real easy."

"Hey, Sadie." Matt greeted the waitress, then looked around her to Jazz, meeting her eyes and smiling even wider. "Jazz, great to see you."

"You, too." Jazz's smile grew, too, and all the annoyances Matt had dealt with over the past few hours faded away except one. Jazz was too far away to kiss.

He extended a hand to the man sitting between the women. He wore a polo shirt with a Pancake Palace logo. "I'm Matt Caminetti."

"Carl Rodriguez."

Carl had a good handshake, dry and firm. He was maybe thirty-five, with thick black hair and a certain wariness about him. Matt wondered about that.

"Carl's nephew Arthur is playing quarterback for Faircrest!" Sadie sounded nervous, but Matt immediately discounted the observation. What would the waitress have to be nervous about? "Isn't he doing terrific?"

"He had a great first half," Matt agreed. "He's quite an athlete."

"I come always because Arthur's mom work nights," Carl said. "This first time Arthur play."

"He's only a sophomore, right?" Matt asked.

"*Sí*," Carl said.

"Then you'll get to see Arthur play many more times," Matt predicted.

"Matt's brother is a wide receiver for Faircrest," Jazz added. "It's his first start, too."

"Danny's got his personal cheering section over there on the fifty-yard line," Matt said. "My entire family's here."

Matt indicated where the Caminetti clan sat in a section mostly populated by the parents of the football players. Terry was looking his way and pointed him out to Brooke and Robbie. The twins jumped up and down, waving their arms. He waved back.

Matt was about to suggest that he and Jazz go over to say hello when he remembered she wanted nothing to do with his family. He could live with that. For now.

"Danny had a nice catch," Jazz said. "I'm glad he got the chance."

"The way Carl's nephew can throw, Danny should have more chances in the second half," Matt said. "It's rare for a high school quarterback to run and throw well."

D. J. Huff, the suspended quarterback, was one-dimensional. Although D.J. had a fantastic arm, he was as immobile as the statue of the falcon at the entrance to the stadium. The bird of prey was Faircrest High's mascot.

"Ooo, then maybe Arthur will get to play quarterback next week, too." Sadie voiced the thought that would surely gain momentum if Faircrest held on to win the game.

"Let's see what happen in second half," Carl said.

The answer was more of the same. Arthur Rodriguez led the team to two additional touchdowns, Danny caught a couple of passes for long gains and Faircrest won 28-14.

Matt kept busy helping troubleshoot a glitch in the PA system, supplying the visiting team with more water and dealing with a dozen other small problems. After the game ended, he stood near the exit to help ensure the thick crowd filed out of the stadium without incident, watching for Jazz.

He finally spotted Jazz and her friends among a knot of Faircrest students with index fingers raised in the air. "We're number one! We're number one!" the students chanted as they passed by.

"Bye, Matt," Jazz shouted. Sadie waved. Stopping wasn't an option unless the women were willing to risk being trampled by the happy students.

There went Matt's chance to mention to Jazz that

he could drop by later tonight if she wasn't too tired. Phoning her and begging her to let him come over didn't qualify as casual. He resigned himself to waiting until their date tomorrow to see her.

There was a slight break in the crowd after the raucous students left the stadium. Matt's parents, Terry, Kevin and the children came into view. Robbie ran up to Matt, his young face animated. "Did you see Danny catch those passes? Wasn't that super cool?"

Matt rustled his nephew's dark red hair. "It sure was."

Terry appeared behind her son, protecting him with her body from another knot of fans intent on the exit. She winked at Matt. "I'll tell you what I saw. You with Jazz."

Matt didn't get a chance to respond before Terry and Robbie were forced to move along, joining the rest of his family in the mass exodus. He wasn't sure what he could have said, anyway.

Nearly every fan wearing the maroon and black of the Faircrest Falcons wore a smile as they left the stadium. The exception was Gerianne Huff. The suspended quarterback's mother passed within a foot of Matt, her face a cold mask. Matt nodded to her. "Hey, Mrs. Huff."

She looked right through him and kept walking.

There, he thought, goes trouble.

Except, that was ridiculous. Matt could handle the Gerianne Huffs of the world. It was Jazz's insistence on keeping things casual that was bound to cause him trouble.

CHAPTER TEN

IF MATT WERE TRYING to impress Jazz with his choice of restaurants for their Saturday night date, he succeeded. Dolce Vita occupied prime waterfront real estate on the Charleston peninsula with a stunning view of the bridges that spanned the Cooper River.

The interior was equally impressive. Wooden beams, brick walls and photos of Italian landscapes gave the place an old-country feel. Italian music drifted through the air, soft enough not to interfere with table conversation. The tangy scent of tomato sauce mingled with the rich aroma of cheese and the warm scent of freshly baked bread.

"You're going to love the food here." Matt sat catty-corner from Jazz at a table for four with a view of the water that was fading as dusk deepened. A candle glowed on the table, softening his features and making him appear dreamy. Jazz almost groaned at the thought. Dreamy? She absolutely could not think of Matt that way.

"You predicted that already," Jazz told him. "Three times, I think."

A corner of his mouth lifted in a charming half smile. Charming, not dreamy. "Sorry. I don't usually repeat myself."

Matt was nervous, she realized. They'd already slept

together, yet he was pulling out all the stops to make their first date memorable.

He wore a collarless cream-colored long-sleeved shirt that opened at the throat and dark slacks that hugged his muscular thighs. He was clean shaven and his thick hair sprang back from his forehead, tempting her to run her fingers through it. He looked gorgeous.

Gorgeous? That was almost as bad as *dreamy*.

Jazz needed to get her head on straight, and that included squashing the fluttery feeling she got in her stomach every time he touched her. And sometimes even when he didn't.

"That's okay. I love it so far." She opened the leather-bound menu to a virtual feast of choices. Lobster fra diavolo. Spaghetti bolognese. Frutti di mare. "Wow. I'd give anything to work at a place like this."

"Then why don't you?" Matt asked.

She peered at him over the top of the menu. "Is that a serious question?"

"Yes."

"Places like this don't hire people like me," she said and went back to perusing the menu.

"Why? Don't you have the right kind of training?"

"I have culinary arts training," she said shortly. She'd studied in prison, preparing for work in the outside world. She also regularly checked cookbooks out of the library to keep up on the latest trends, watched TV cooking shows and experimented with her own recipes.

"Then why do you think you wouldn't get hired?" Matt wouldn't let the subject drop.

Jazz put down the menu, annoyed that she had to explain something so obvious. "Because I've been in—"

"Matt! Jazz!" Matt's sister, Terry, appeared like an apparition a few feet from their table, quickly closing the distance. Her husband trailed her. "I told Kevin that was you."

Jazz stared at the couple openmouthed, then swung her gaze to Matt. He looked as surprised to see his sister and brother-in-law as she was.

"Terry spotted you from the hostess station," Kevin confirmed, extending a hand to shake Matt's. To Jazz, he said, "Good to see you again, Jazz."

"You, too," she lied.

"You don't mind if we join you, do you?" Matt's sister kept talking before either Jazz or Matt could answer. "After all, I did turn Matt on to this place. And with this view, your table is to die for."

Kevin slung an arm around his wife's shoulders. "Hon, maybe they'd rather not have their table invaded."

"Is that true? Am I inflicting myself on you?" Terry covered her mouth with her right hand.

"No, of course not," Jazz replied at the same time Matt answered, "Well, yeah."

Matt raised an eyebrow at Jazz. She was surprised by her response, too. Simply put, she couldn't bear to hurt Terry's feelings, especially because she liked the other woman.

"You are such a stinker, Matt." Terry wrinkled her nose at him, acting just like a big sister. "Jazz doesn't mind, so you shouldn't, either. You love me."

"I'll say this about my wife. She doesn't have self-esteem issues." Kevin pulled out one of the vacant chairs for Terry, then sat down next to her when she was settled.

Jazz's heart pounded. She hadn't thought through her answer and considered how difficult it would be to have dinner with the couple who'd adopted her twins.

She inhaled slowly, assuring herself she could handle the situation. After tonight, she didn't need to see Terry and Kevin again. And it wasn't as though their dinner conversation had to revolve around the twins. They could talk about dozens of other things.

"With a good-looking husband and two great kids, what do I have to feel insecure about?" Terry asked with a laugh.

"Your lack of modesty?" Matt asked.

"Ha, ha. Very funny," Terry said.

"Where are Brooke and Robbie tonight?" Jazz blurted out the question to her own dismay.

Terry took the change of subject in stride. "My mom babysits two or three times a month so we can have date nights." Terry squeezed her husband's arm. "I love my kids like crazy but it's nice to get a break."

"They're still coming to the park with me tomorrow morning after church to work on their soccer games, right?" Matt asked.

"Robbie is. I'm not so sure about Brooke," Terry said. "She said something about going to a friend's house."

"Brooke will come to the park first," Matt predicted. "Her coach played her in the field last game. After those two goals she scored, he won't move her back to goalie. If she works at it, she could be a prolific scorer."

A pretty waitress in a tuxedo dress bustled over with

additional menus and place settings, and conversation stalled until after they ordered. Jazz chose the chef's special, a parmesan-crusted, pan-seared flounder with a side of pasta.

"Sounds divine," Terry said, "but then everything is good. Have you been here before?"

Jazz shook her head. "First time."

"With your catering business, you'll really appreciate it," Terry said.

Terry thought Jazz had her own catering business? Jazz took a deep breath. Her real job was far less impressive. "I'm not a caterer. I'm a short-order cook."

"Really?" Terry paused with her glass of ice water halfway to her mouth. "Then you're wasting your talents."

"That's what I've been trying to tell her," Matt said. "Lots of restaurants in Charleston would be lucky to have her."

Jazz clenched her teeth. Was Matt trying to provoke her into admitting she was an ex-con or was he really that clueless?

"It's an idea," Jazz said. There wasn't much else she could say. Nobody would believe she'd rather work at Pancake Palace than one of Charleston's excellent dining establishments.

"A very good idea," Terry said.

Kevin soon changed the subject to last night's high school football game, a topic still going strong when the waiter brought their entrées.

"So those people you were sitting with last night, Jazz, that was the new quarterback's uncle and his girl-friend?" Terry asked.

"Carl is Arthur's uncle, but he and Sadie are only friends," Jazz answered, but what if that wasn't so? Had she unwittingly horned in on what Carl had intended to be a date? Except, then why had Benjy been along? Unless it was because Carl had listened to Sadie complain that the men she dated didn't take an interest in her son.

"The Rodriguez kid is good," Kevin summed up. "Too good to be second string."

"We'll see what happens next game," Matt said.

"I already know." Kevin paused. "I went to your parents' house this afternoon to borrow some tools, and your dad was on the phone with Tom."

Jazz chewed her food slowly, savoring the flavor of the flounder dish, wondering who they were talking about.

"Tom Dougherty's the high school football coach." Matt directed the explanation to Jazz. "He and Dad have been friends since Dad was the A.D. at Faircrest."

"Tom's planning to use both quarterbacks next Friday," Kevin said. "He's thinking about alternating them by series."

Terry winced. "Mama Bear will not be happy about that."

"D. J. Huff's mother," Matt explained to Jazz. "D.J. is the quarterback I suspended for a game."

"D.J.'s mother is in the junior league with me and all she talks about is D.J. and football," Terry said. "She was mad as a hatter at Matt for suspending him."

Jazz wondered if Mrs. Huff was the woman Sadie had seen yelling at Matt at the service station. It seemed like a good bet.

"But enough about football," Terry interrupted. "Tell us how long you two have been dating."

Jazz exchanged a look with Matt. She interpreted his nod as encouragement to answer the question any way she wanted.

"Actually," she drew out the word, "this is our first date."

"Get outta here!" Terry exclaimed. "It is not!"

"Yeah," Matt said. "It is."

"But I thought...you just seem to fit together so...you never said..." Terry sputtered, then started over. "Why didn't you just tell us to get our own table?"

"I tried," Matt said.

"Try harder next time," Terry admonished. "And take Jazz for a romantic walk along the Battery, why don't you? I promise Kevin and I won't come along."

MATT WALKED ALONGSIDE Jazz through White Point Gardens, the park at the southernmost point of the city of Charleston peninsula. A salty breeze rustled through the leaves of the park's massive oak trees as Matt and Jazz passed Civil War cannons pointed toward the harbor and a latticed gazebo commonly used for outdoor weddings.

During the day horse-drawn carriages laden with tourists passed by the park but at night the area was relatively quiet. Matt led Jazz across Murray Boulevard to the sidewalk that rimmed the seawall. The moon was three-quarters full, shedding light on the rippling water of the harbor. It splashed gently against the low wall, bringing with it the scent of the sea.

"I don't always listen to my sister," Matt said, "but in this case, a walk was a good idea."

"Terry's nice." Jazz didn't elaborate. She'd said little at dinner, too. Matt was afraid he knew the reason.

"Hey, I'm sorry about Terry...I swear I didn't know she and Kevin would be at the restaurant."

Jazz cut her eyes at him. "I know you didn't."

"Good." Matt breathed a little easier. "Although I guess I shouldn't have been surprised. Terry and Kevin can walk to the restaurant from home. They live south of Broad."

Broad was Broad Street, a well-maintained thoroughfare that divided Charleston's priciest real estate from the rest of the city. Lavish house museums, hundred-year-old homes with beautiful gardens and charming bed-and-breakfasts lined the narrow streets, creating a living-history experience.

"Their house must be terrific," Jazz said.

"It's been in Kevin's family for generations. He's just the lucky dog who has it now. I tell him that all the time."

"Where do the twins go to school?" Jazz asked.

"A private school a few blocks north of Broad Street. They can walk there."

"Sounds nice."

"They've got a nice life," Matt said. "But then they're good folks. I've got to say, though, I was surprised you invited them to eat with us."

"Me, too." Jazz shook her head. "I didn't want Terry to feel like I thought she was too pushy."

Matt put an arm around her, touched by this softer

side of her. "Terry would have gotten over it. She knows she's pushy."

Jazz let his arm stay where it was. It felt like a triumph to Matt.

"She's not *that* pushy," Jazz said. "I was glad she didn't ask more questions about me."

They'd talked a little about Jazz's job, her love of cooking and her running, but that was the extent of it. Matt's curiosity wasn't close to being satisfied. "Would you mind if I do?" he asked.

"Depends on the questions."

Not the answer he was looking for, but he'd roll with it. "Do you have any brothers or sisters?"

"It's only me," she replied.

"How did you end up being raised by your grandmother?"

This part of Murray Boulevard was even quieter than the stretch of road beside the park. Lights shone from the windows of the grand houses across the street from the sidewalk along the harbor. The lapping of the water and the whoosh of the breeze filled the silence.

"I thought we were keeping things casual," Jazz said.

Not if Matt could help it. He held back the thought, surprised at its ferocity.

"You know all about my family," he said. "It's only fair I know something about yours."

"I don't know that much about you. You never told me where you grew up."

"James Island." He named a community about five miles from where he lived now. "In the same two-story, three-bedroom house on the river where my parents still live. There's a dock and a pool out back. When I was growing up, kids my age were everywhere. We used to stay outside playing until it was too dark to see. Your turn."

He felt her shoulders tense under his arm. Jazz didn't say anything for some time.

"I lived in a mobile home with my grandma about five miles outside of Florence. My mom didn't live with us but she was around." Jazz spoke so quietly he had to strain to hear her. "One of them was always in trouble for something. Shoplifting. Petty theft. Public drunkenness."

Her shoulders moved up and down, as though she were taking a deep breath. "My mom was convicted of possession of marijuana with intent to distribute, although I never believed that. She liked her drugs too much to sell them."

"What happened to her?"

"She died of AIDS when I was nine."

"And your grandmother?"

"Lung cancer when I was sixteen. She was a tough old broad, but she smoked like a train." Jazz's smile held no joy.

"I'm sorry," Matt said.

"Ironic the woman who lived next door was constantly bugging her to quit. She had granddaughters who visited, so I spent a lot of time over there."

"Why didn't your neighbor take you in?" he asked.

"She moved into a nursing home before Grandma died." Jazz's voice was wooden.

"How about your dad?"

"I've never met him," Jazz said after a moment. "My mom always claimed she didn't know who he was."

"But you don't believe that," Matt stated.

She gave him a sharp, guarded look. "Why would you say that?"

"I can hear it in your voice." Matt rubbed her shoulder, aching for the girl she'd been, better understanding the woman she'd become. He wished she realized how much strength of character it took to get from where she'd been to where she was now. "Any leads on who he might be?"

He felt her body stiffen under his hand.

"Why do you assume I'm looking for him?" she asked.

"Aren't you?"

"I wasn't." She seemed to notice how telling her reply was because she didn't even take a breath before continuing. "I'm not looking for him now, either. Not really. It's just that..."

"What?" he prodded when her voice trailed off.

Just when he feared she'd clam up, she started talking again, slowly at first, then more rapidly. She didn't stop until she'd told him about finding the snapshot inside her mother's yearbook and her theory that a postal clerk in Beaufort could be her father.

"If you like, I'll come with you when you go talk to him," Matt offered.

"That's not necessary," Jazz said. "I decided not to follow up on it."

"What?" Matt stopped walking and turned to face her. "Why wouldn't you? The guy could be your father."

"You're the one who's against open adoptions," Jazz reminded him.

"You're not adopted." He didn't understand why she'd brought up adoption. Her situation had nothing to do with it. "You owe it to yourself to find out if this postal clerk is your father. If he is, he owes you a hell of an explanation."

"Not if I don't ask for one. Besides, I can make a pretty good guess what he'd say, anyway. Why should I listen to how he didn't want to be part of my life?"

"You don't know that," Matt said. "Maybe your mother never told him she was pregnant. You've got to go to Beaufort, confront this guy and find out."

Jazz narrowed her eyes at him. "Do you always do that?"

Matt angled his head. "Do what?"

"Push," she said. "You were the same way at the restaurant when you suggested I should start applying for chef jobs."

"You should." Matt tried to sound like the voice of reason. "You can't succeed if you don't try."

"Oh, yeah?" Jazz retorted. "So you think it doesn't matter that I'm an ex-con? You think everybody would overlook that tiny little fact?"

So that was what this was all about, Matt thought. Jazz was as afraid of how her father would perceive her as she was of finding him.

"Not everybody," he said. "But you'll never succeed if you're afraid of failure."

"I've heard you say stuff like that before. That's jock lingo, isn't it?"

She was on the mark. Matt used to memorize inspirational sports quotes to motivate himself. The quotes weren't the sole reason he'd gotten a soccer scholarship to a Division One school but they'd helped him reach his potential.

"There are parallels between success in sports and in life," he said. "I'm trying to get you to see you don't need to let your past hold you back."

"Well, don't," she snapped. "I'm doing fine the way I am."

Matt didn't believe that. Jazz was existing instead of living because of this fatalistic notion that she couldn't outrun her past. She worked two jobs, neither of which seemed to fulfill her, and she seemed to spend a lot of time alone.

"You could be doing better," Matt said.

Jazz gave him a smoldering look, then pivoted and headed back in the direction they'd come, moving so quickly Matt had to jog a few steps to catch up.

"Hey, wait a minute!" he called. "Where are you going?"

"I want you to take me home." Jazz ate up the ground with her quick strides.

Matt jogged to catch up to her. "Whatever I said to make you mad, I'm sorry."

"Just like a man," she muttered.

"What?"

"How can you be so clueless? You made it a point to tell me I don't measure up!"

"That's not—"

"So how about I make things easy on you?" She sounded angry but her voice shook. "Don't call me again."

Aw, hell. How had Jazz gotten such a wrong impression?

She increased the length of her strides. They were between streetlights, where the visibility wasn't as good. He started to tell her to be careful of her footing when she stumbled and lost her balance.

He caught her before she went down and helped her stand upright, keeping his hands wrapped around her upper arms. She glared at him. "Let go of me, Matt."

"I will," he said. "After you listen to what I have to say."

"I've heard enough."

"You haven't heard this." An urgency to make her understand filled him. "I should have made it clear that I think you're amazing."

"But you—"

"I can't stop thinking about you, Jazz. It's been this way since the first time I saw you."

Matt thought he saw moisture on her cheek. He brought his thumb to her face and wiped away a tear.

"If you only take one thing I say to heart, let it be this," he said. "I like you just the way you are."

Matt replaced his thumb with his lips, kissing her tearstained cheek before moving to her mouth. He kissed her once, twice, three times, demanding nothing and getting no response. Just when he feared she'd pull back, she melted into him, her mouth pressing to his.

He'd spoken nothing but the truth. He only wished Jazz agreed.

PORTABLE FOLDING CHAIRS lined the soccer field where a game was in full swing on Saturday a week later.

Young teenage boys in blue jerseys squared off against boys wearing green, racing up and down the field after a ball while parents cheered.

Matt paced the sideline on the far side of the field, shouting instructions and encouragement. He was the only Caminetti in sight. Jazz had made very sure of that before she approached the field.

In the week since she and Matt had dinner with Terry and Kevin at Dolce Vita, Jazz hadn't encountered a single one of Matt's family members. She'd seen plenty of Matt despite their busy work schedules. Just last night, he'd stopped by after the Faircrest football team won another game with Arthur Rodriguez as quarterback. This morning, Matt had persuaded her to come to the soccer game. Considering he'd been in her bed at the time, Jazz hadn't stood a chance of refusing.

"Are you with the Berzerkers?" A thirtyish woman wearing a ball cap over frizzy brown hair leaned back in her chair, addressing her question to Jazz.

"I don't know what a Berzerker is," Jazz admitted.

The woman laughed. "Join the club. It's the name of the blue team."

"That's not the team Matt Caminetti coaches, is it?" Jazz asked. Surely Matt would have mentioned such an unusual name.

"The Berzerkers aren't that lucky," the woman said. "Matt's coaching the Pythons. They're up 2-1."

"How much longer in the game?" Jazz had delayed her arrival by design because coming to the game had seemed too much like what a girlfriend might do.

"The second half just started," the woman said. "The Python fans are on the other side of the field."

"Thanks," Jazz said.

She opted to sit at midfield on the metal bleachers occupied by only a few other people, presumably the ones who didn't own portable chairs.

The two women nearest the bleachers, both wearing the green of the Pythons, turned to look at Jazz when she sat down. One of them said something to the other. Jazz only hoped they weren't speculating about who she was.

Yes, she and Matt were carving out time for each other and sleeping together. Things were going great, partly because he hadn't mentioned either the chef job or the postal clerk who might be her father all week. But Jazz wasn't Matt's girlfriend. She'd let herself be persuaded to come to the game because...Matt talked about his team a lot and she was curious? Hmm.

The play on the field couldn't keep her attention, not when the Pythons' coach was so much more interesting. In black shorts and a green T-shirt, he looked vibrant and muscular.

Matt had a hand on the back of one of his players, a compact boy a full head shorter than he was. Matt said something to the boy while gesturing at the play on the field. There must have been a break in the action because Matt clapped his player on the shoulder and the boy ran onto the field to replace a teammate.

"Let's go, baby!" A woman on the Pythons' side of the field jumped from her chair and waved a green towel like a lasso.

The boy who'd substituted into the game received the ball off a throw-in. He controlled the ball with his feet, cut to the middle of the field and split two Berzerker defenders. Kicking the ball in stride, he sent it past the goalie's outstretched arms into the top corner of the goal.

"Yee-haw!" the woman waving her towel yelled. "Way to strike, Pythons!"

The goal scorer leaped into the air, pumping a fist. He raced to the sidelines, straight for Matt. Player and coach slapped palms. Matt's grin was so wide, Jazz could see the white of his teeth from across the field.

Jazz was on her feet, too, although she didn't remember leaping to them.

She sat down, still watching Matt. He gestured to his players with both hands palms down. The celebration was over and he was signaling that they should keep their heads in the game. Matt would make a wonderful father. He was already a fantastic uncle—to Jazz's biological children.

A weight settled over her heart. Additional evidence about what a great guy Matt was would make it harder when the inevitable time came to part ways.

"You look familiar."

It took Jazz a few seconds to realize the tall, thin woman sitting a few feet away on the bleachers was addressing her. The woman had a pixie cut and was probably in her forties. Jazz had never seen her before in her life.

"Sorry," Jazz said. "I don't think we know each other."

The woman's nose wrinkled as she stared at Jazz. She had sharp features, made to appear more prominent by her short hair. "Weren't you at the football game when Faircrest played Valley Field?"

"Why, yes." That had been eight days ago. Jazz hadn't attended last night's game even though Sadie had invited her. The risk of running into Matt's family was too great. So was the possibility she'd be in Carl's way if his intention was time alone with Sadie and her son, Benjy.

"I thought that's where I'd seen you before," the woman said. "You were with a man, another woman and a little boy, right?"

"Right," Jazz said.

"The man had on a shirt with a restaurant name." The woman tapped her chin. "Now, what was the name?"

"Pancake Palace," Jazz answered. This was getting weird. "I'm surprised you remember all that."

The woman shrugged her thin shoulders. "I'm good with faces, and I wasn't sitting far from you. I've heard about that restaurant before, though I can't remember why."

Jazz thought it was time she switched things up and asked some questions of her own. "Is your son a Python?"

"Oh, no." The woman pointed out a tall, somewhat awkward boy who played for the Berzerkers. "That's my Ryan. Number seventeen on defense."

Ryan was substantially taller and heavier than the other boys.

"He plays youth football, too. We like him to do soccer for his cardio." The woman tilted her head. "You're too young to have a son on the team, aren't you?"

Brooke and Robbie were ten, only a few years younger than the players.

"Maybe a little," Jazz said, volunteering nothing more.

The woman went back to watching the game and Jazz resumed her study of Matt. He clapped his hands, exuding an air of composure. She couldn't hear everything he yelled to his players but what she did hear was positive.

"Good job!"

"Way to defend!"

"What a save!"

"He's quite the looker, isn't he?" the woman remarked.

Jazz tore her gaze from Matt. The woman was studying her with a knowing smile. So much for denying she'd been looking at him. "Matt's a handsome man."

"You're his girlfriend, aren't you?" the woman asked.

"No!" Jazz's response was instantaneous. "No, I'm not."

"I'm sorry," the woman said before Jazz could ask why she wanted to know. "I didn't mean to pry. It's just that the way you were looking at him was so…oh, never mind. Forgive me?"

Jazz nodded. She stood, eager to get away from the woman.

"You're going?" The woman's eyes widened. "There's only a little time left in the game."

"Yes." Jazz didn't owe the nosy woman an explanation.

She climbed down the bleachers and got a few feet

before three short whistles signaled the end of the game. Matt's players shouted triumphantly and congregated around him on the sideline. Joy wreathed Matt's face. When, Jazz wondered, had she last felt that kind of elation?

The answer struck her with startling speed: When she was in bed with Matt.

Matt cut the celebration short, lining his players up for the postgame handshake. He trailed the field.

Somebody bumped Jazz with a chair they were carrying over their shoulder.

"Sorry," a man said.

"That's okay." Jazz should thank the man for knocking her out of her Matt-induced stupor. Her half-formed plan had been to leave before Matt saw her. Too late.

"Jazz!" Matt called. He separated from his players and sprinted across the field, his legs long and toned. Admiring him was becoming a pastime of hers. Sometimes, after they made love, she found herself running her eyes over the quiet strength of his body.

She had to stop this; she needed to be cool and collected when she greeted him. She couldn't let him guess what she was thinking.

Matt ran directly to her, put his hands under her arms and swung her around three hundred and sixty degrees. Her head was spinning and she was laughing when he set her down.

Before Jazz could say a word, Matt kissed her right on the mouth. Her world went topsy-turvy again but this time it could have been from the kiss. He grinned at her.

"What was that for?" She sounded breathless, probably because she was.

"I'm glad you made it, that's all."

"I didn't think you knew I was here," Jazz said.

"Are you kidding? I noticed you as soon as you got here. A couple minutes after halftime, right?"

"Right." Jazz could breathe again. "Congratulations. That was a good win."

"That was a blast!" Matt said.

"Coach has a girlfriend!" the boy who'd scored the second-half goal chanted in a singsong voice. He was flanked by snickering teammates.

Matt slung an arm around Jazz. "Yes, I do," he told the boys with good cheer.

Out of the corner of her eye, Jazz noticed the woman from the bleachers watching them. Jazz should set everyone, especially Matt, straight about the temporary nature of their relationship.

Not now, though.

Not when Matt's arm felt so good exactly where it was.

CHAPTER ELEVEN

THE NEXT DAY Matt placed the last of the dirty plates into the dishwasher in his parents' kitchen, which still smelled of roast beef, mashed potatoes and gravy. He walked toward the butcher-block table his mother had just wiped down, bent and kissed her on the cheek.

"I'm out of here," Matt said. "I'll see you at the football game on Friday, right?"

"What do you mean you're out of here?" His mother was so short she had to tilt her head back to gaze up at him. "You heard your father. It's a beautiful afternoon to take the boat out."

His mother spoke loudly enough to be heard over the hum of conversation, childish giggles and barks coming from the adjacent room. It sounded like Brooke, Robbie and probably Danny were playing with the family's cocker spaniel while the adults talked.

"I can't go out on the water today," Matt said.

His mother carried a dish towel in one hand. She balanced her empty hand on her rounded hip. "Why not? I thought you reserved Sundays for family."

All of the Caminettis did. For as many Sundays as Matt could remember, his mother had cooked a big meal after the family attended early-morning church services. They usually sat down to eat around noon, then spent the rest of the afternoon together. Matt had expanded on the tradition, taking Brooke and Robbie to the park in the late mornings to work on their soccer games while his mom prepared the food.

"I'm meeting Jazz at Folly Beach," Matt said, naming a laid-back beach community that was about a ten-minute drive from his parents' house on James Island. "Jazz works Sunday nights, so it's our only chance today to spend some time together."

"I knew that girl was more than a friend!" His mother clapped her hands together. "Why didn't you invite Jazz over for Sunday dinner?"

Matt had almost issued the invitation a half-dozen times. Family was important to him. As much as he loved spending time alone with Jazz, his preference on Sundays would be to share her with his family.

"Jazz wants to take things slow," Matt said.

"But she's already met the lot of us," his mother said. "You tell that girl that if she can master the Caminetti Shuffle, she can come to Sunday dinner!"

Matt wished it were that simple. He wasn't exactly sure why it wasn't. "I just might do that."

"And if Jazz asks if she can bring dessert, say yes," his mother said. "I haven't had cake as delicious as the one she made for the twins' party since Emma McDowell was in my Junior Women's club."

Now, there was a name Matt hadn't heard in a while, although for one summer he'd seen Mrs. McDowell a few times a week. She'd hired him to do yard work for her after he finished eighth grade, rewarding Matt with cookies and lemonade as well as cash.

"Do Mrs. McDowell and her husband still own that restaurant in North Charleston?" Matt asked.

"They sold it about a year ago but now their daughter Kathy is going into the restaurant business," his mother said. "I hear she's opening a new place in downtown Charleston in a few weeks."

At his mother's comment, an idea took form. Matt rolled with it, the way he always did when opportunity presented itself. "Do the McDowells still live in the area?"

"They sure do," his mother said. "Emma and Steve are in that corner house on Orange Grove Road, the same as always."

That was the nugget of information Matt needed before he dialed information and asked for a number for the McDowells. By the time he met Jazz at Folly Beach, he'd already spoken to Mrs. McDowell and discovered what he needed to know.

"This was a good idea," Jazz said as she walked beside him along the edge of the surf, sandals in hand. She looked young and carefree in oversized sunglasses, shorts that bared her long legs and a fitted T-shirt. Her sandy-brown hair blew about her face, tousled by the breeze.

"It would have been a better idea if you didn't have to go into work early," Matt said.

When Matt had met Jazz in the parking lot beside the Folly Beach pier, she'd greeted him with the news that she needed to be at the telemarketing call center two hours earlier than usual. That gave them exactly one hour at the beach, enough time for a walk, not enough time to stop for a drink at the restaurant at the end of the pier.

"We're switching over to fall hours," Jazz explained.

"My boss says people are more likely to be home earlier on Sundays now that summer's over. It'll give us more chances to make sales."

The flip side was that Matt would have even fewer opportunities to be with Jazz.

"Are you okay with working longer hours?" he asked.

Jazz kicked at the water and it sprayed in front of them in an arc. "Yes and no. I could sure use the money. But between your job and my two, we don't have a whole lot of time to spend together."

Matt could think of two solutions, but bringing up either of them, especially his mother's Sunday dinner invitation, was fraught with land mines. He breathed in the scent of the sea. Better to encourage Jazz to reach those conclusions on her own.

"So what are we going to do about that?" Matt asked.

"What can we do about it?" Jazz slanted him a warning look. "And don't you dare say I should get a better-paying job! Because I can't."

Matt dug in the pocket of his shorts and pulled out a folded piece of paper. It fluttered in the breeze. "What if you had a lead on a job?"

"Matt Caminetti," Jazz said, drawing out the syllables of his name, "what have you done?"

He dodged a teenage boy running toward the water with a boogie board. October had begun but it was still nearly eighty degrees. A smattering of people were enjoying the beach, although very few of them were in the water.

"I can only tell you if you promise not to get mad," he replied.

Jazz threw up her hands, startling into flight a nearby egret. "Now, how can I make a promise like that?"

Matt started to put the slip of paper back in his pocket. "Then you'll never know what the job was."

"Okay, I won't get mad," Jazz blurted before the paper made it all the way out of sight. "Even if I think I should."

"Curiosity is your Achilles' heel," Matt teased. "You were the same way with the Caminetti Shuffle."

Jazz didn't laugh. "What's on the slip, Matt?"

"A contact." Matt pointed out a jellyfish in their path, waiting until they'd walked safely past it to continue. "I used to do yard work for a couple who owned a restaurant in North Charleston. Turns out their daughter's opening a new place downtown and isn't through hiring yet. The mother gave me her daughter's phone number."

"Did you mention my felony conviction?" Jazz asked over the sound of the ocean waves.

"Why would I? It's not the mother's restaurant."

"So her daughter won't know about it, either," Jazz stated.

"Well, no," Matt said. "But the McDowells are good people. I'm sure their daughter won't hold your past against you."

"You don't know what she'll do." Jazz seemed to be making a concerted effort to hold on to her temper.

"Neither will you if you don't call her," Matt pointed out. He held out the piece of paper to her with a raised eyebrow. Water from the crashing waves cascaded over his bare feet.

"I won't call her," she said.

"Take the number anyway. It won't hurt to have it handy in case you change your mind."

Just when Matt was certain Jazz was about to repeat her refusal, she snatched the paper out of his hand and shoved it in the pocket of her shorts.

"If you're not careful," Jazz said, "I'm going to change my mind about dating you."

"Won't happen," Matt said. "You're too taken with me."

"Really? And what do you base that on?"

"This." He swept his arms under her legs and picked her up out of the surf. She squealed.

"What are you doing?" Jazz cried.

"What do you think?" he asked with a grin. "I'm sweeping you off your feet."

Matt kissed her and felt his own equilibrium go topsy-turvy. He hoped she phoned Mrs. McDowell's daughter, not only for her sake, but also for his, because spending only a few hours a week with her wasn't nearly enough.

"That was nice," she said after he set her back down. "But I'm still not going to call about that job."

On a Saturday six days later, Jazz waited on a padded bench inside the reception area of what was already an eye-catching restaurant. The dining room décor was done in lime greens and navy blues, conveying a fun tone.

Jazz wiped her damp palms on the skirt of the pretty

salmon-colored dress she'd bought on sale. Kneading her forehead did nothing to ease her pounding headache.

She was way out of her league. She should have stuck to her vow not to call the number Matt had given her for Kathy McDowell, except something he'd told her kept running through her mind.

You can't succeed if you don't try.

The seconds ticked by, lengthening into minutes. Had she been forgotten? It must have been at least fifteen minutes since the teenage boy had unlocked the door to let her into Charles Towne Flair and said he'd get Kathy.

Footsteps finally clicked on the tile floor. Jazz dropped her hand from her forehead. A rail-thin woman appeared from the back of the restaurant, her dark hair piled atop her head in a messy bun. She wore jeans and a T-shirt, and green paint streaked her nose.

Jazz got to her feet so quickly she saw stars. Oh, great, she thought. If she fainted, she really wouldn't have a shot at this.

"Sorry to keep you waiting. I forgot to ask the painters to do the trim on the windows." The woman stopped at the deserted hostess stand and rubbed at the smudge on her nose, succeeding only in spreading it. "I'm starting to think I shouldn't be doing the painting myself.

"By the way, I'm Kathy McDowell. And you must be here about the assistant chef job."

Fighting to regain her equilibrium, Jazz nodded. "My name's Jazz Lenox."

"Oh, yes!" Kathy beamed at her. "You're Matt Caminetti's friend. My mother just loved him when he was a kid. Did Matt tell you she used to buy Oreos just for him after she found out they were his favorite cookie?"

"No, he didn't." Jazz had seen Matt as many times over the past week as their busy schedules allowed, but they hadn't talked any further about the McDowells. Jazz hadn't even mentioned that she'd set up an interview.

"Matt was something even back then. Such a looker that I used to sneak peeks at him from the living room window." Kathy laughed. "I'm pretty sure he knew it but he never let on. Is he still a great guy?"

"He's a great guy," Jazz agreed. Her palms felt damp. Considering she wouldn't be putting herself through this if not for Matt, she might revise her opinion if this interview went poorly.

"I can get you an application, but why don't we talk first?" Kathy sat down on the bench Jazz had vacated, inviting Jazz to join her with a sweep of her hand.

Jazz lowered herself next to Kathy, trying not to think about how much she wanted the job. She craved a look at the kitchen.

"I don't know how much you know about the restaurant, so I'll give you the entire spiel," Kathy said. "We're trying to appeal to a wide crowd by keeping our food moderately priced and specializing in American staples like steaks, pasta, seafood. The difference will be in unexpected twists in the recipes that give the food new flair. Sound good so far?"

"Sounds great," Jazz said. Like her dream job.

"The opening's in two weeks, so I need to finalize my hiring soon. I only have a couple openings left and the competition's pretty fierce."

Jazz frowned. Competition was Matt's forte, not hers.

"Ideally I'd like an assistant chef to be able to take orders but also to have the capacity to work independently." Kathy gave off the impression of an astute businesswoman despite her green nose. "Do you have a résumé?"

Jazz had hoped to get by without having to provide one. "Not with me."

"You can send it along later," Kathy said. "For now, just tell me about your experience."

If Jazz had been superstitious, she would have crossed her fingers behind her back. She'd learned the hard way that life was about absolutes. Either Kathy would consider her job experience adequate or she wouldn't.

"I'm a short-order cook at Pancake Palace." It nearly felt as if her tongue had tripped over the words. "We serve breakfast food, pancakes mostly, for breakfast and lunch."

One of Kathy's eyebrows rose. It, too, was speckled with green paint. "And before that?"

"Before that I studied culinary arts," Jazz told her, deliberately vague.

Kathy brightened and leaned toward her. "Where was that? The Culinary Institute of Charleston?"

Jazz's stomach dipped and rolled. Here was the moment of truth. "Camille Griffin Graham. It's a corrections institute in Columbia."

"I see," Kathy said slowly. To her credit, she didn't flinch. "What kind of training did you have?"

"The program was run by the woman who supervises food services at the prison." Jazz bit her lip, wondering how to make herself sound more impressive. "But I've been cooking pretty much my whole life, since I was ten or eleven, at least. I watch cooking shows and read cookbooks and invent my own recipes."

Kathy didn't look impressed. "How long have you worked at Pancake Palace?"

"Three years," replied Jazz.

"That long?" Kathy gave her a measured look. "Then it's been a while since you've cooked anything besides breakfast food?"

Jazz was about to tell her about the catering jobs but what was the use? Kathy McDowell had made up her mind not to hire Jazz the moment she'd heard the words *corrections institute*.

"You don't have quite the right background for this job," Kathy said. "I'd suggest enrolling in some additional training to make yourself a more attractive candidate."

"Thank you for your time." Jazz stood up, irritated at herself for believing that she even had a chance at a restaurant of this caliber.

"You're welcome," Kathy said. "I'm sorry it didn't work out."

"I'm sorry to have bothered you." Jazz managed to keep her poise until she was on the sidewalk outside the restaurant. She gasped for air and her hands trembled, which was ridiculous. The job interview had held no surprises.

She got into her car, intending to drive straight home but finding herself turning down the street where Matt's town house was located. She had an almost overwhelming need to tell him what had happened, if only to get him to understand he shouldn't make her want things that were out of reach.

By the time she remembered why they weren't getting together until tonight—Matt had afternoon plans—Matt's town house was in view. His silver coupe was in the driveway.

Unaccountably glad Matt was home, Jazz parked behind his car and hurried up the stairs to his town house. She jammed her finger against the doorbell, not sure if she were more eager for his support or his admission that she was right. The only certainty was that she longed to see him.

The door opened but it wasn't Matt who greeted her. It was Brooke. The little girl twirled a long red strand of hair around her index finger, smiling shyly and humming.

"Hey, Brooke." Jazz could barely speak; the twins being here hadn't occurred to her at all. In the nearly three weeks since the party where she'd found out the truth, Jazz had tried not to think about the twins. Now the yearning was back, immediately, and even stronger than before. "I didn't expect to see you here."

"Uncle Matt's watching us," she said.

"You're not supposed to answer the door to strangers, Brooke!" Robbie's voice didn't quite drown out the thuds of his running footsteps. He joined his sister, doubling Jazz's longing for what might have been.

"Oh, hey, Jazz." Robbie turned around and shouted, "Uncle Matt, Jazz is here!"

Brooke covered her ears.

"Ask her in," Matt called back.

"Come on in." Robbie stepped aside to allow her

entrance, then dashed for the kitchen. With another silent glance at Jazz, Brooke followed her brother.

Jazz hesitated, her mind warring with her heart. The battle was lost almost before it began. She stepped inside the town house and closed the door.

Matt was sitting on a kitchen chair, bent over to tie the laces on one of his sneakers. He smiled at her, his eyes crinkling at the corners. His white Charleston Kicks soccer T-shirt brought out his tan, making him look vibrant and healthy.

"Hey, Jazz. I didn't think I'd see you until tonight. Not that I'm complaining." Matt winked at her. "What are you doing here?"

She shelved the urge to tell him about the failed job interview. This wasn't the right time for I-told-you-sos. The twins flanked him, with Brooke humming a nonsensical tune and Robbie practically vibrating with energy.

"I was in the neighborhood," Jazz answered.

"We're going to the fair!" Robbie exclaimed. "We were just leaving."

"I take them every year." Matt moved on to the laces of his other shoe. "We're getting a late start because all three of us had soccer games this morning."

"We all won but Brooke!" Robbie glanced at his sister. She kept humming and didn't rise to the bait. "And now we're going to pick out which cows should win the blue ribbons!"

"There are 4-H competitions at the fair," Matt explained. "Robbie likes to guess the winners."

Brooke stopped humming. "I don't like cows."

"But you like the bumper cars, right, Brooke?" Matt asked. "You and Robbie always have fun on those."

"Let's go, Uncle Matt!" Robbie exclaimed. "We've got to get there quick!"

Matt finished tying his second shoe and got to his feet. "We usually go for the entire day but I told them we needed to leave by six today."

Jazz appreciated Matt not saying that was because of their dinner date. She couldn't bear it if the children blamed her for cutting short their good time.

"Do you want to come?"

The softly voiced question came from Brooke. She gazed up at Jazz with green eyes that were shaped the same as Jazz's own eyes. The breath caught in Jazz's throat and something loosened in her chest.

Jazz's gaze flew to Matt. He shrugged and cocked his head, conveying that it was up to her. What else could he do after her insistence that she avoid his family?

"C'mon, Jazz," Robbie cried. He dashed for the door, calling over his shoulder. "Let's go!"

Brooke merely gazed at her, waiting for her answer.

In the weeks Jazz and Matt had been dating, Jazz had convinced herself she could keep her distance from the twins. Now she understood she'd been fooling herself.

"Yes," Jazz said. "Let's go."

THE COASTAL CAROLINA FAIR pulsed with life. Crowds roamed the midway, music blared from the carnival rides and the scent of cotton candy drifted through the air.

Jazz drank in the atmosphere, taking a mental snapshot of Matt walking between the twins, Robbie skipping along next to him, Brooke's hand in his. The four of them had arrived at the fair barely an hour ago and already she had a storehouse of memories, some involving 4-H cows. They'd have to be enough to last her through the years to come.

"Let's ride the roller coaster next!" Robbie cried. "I think there's one with two coasters that race each other!"

"Sounds good to me," Matt said. Jazz was starting to see why the children loved being at the fair with him. So far, every one of their suggestions had sounded good to him. "We can do girls versus boys."

Brooke said nothing. She was gazing at the small crowd that had gathered at one of the smaller of the pavilions scattered throughout the fairgrounds. By listening closely, Jazz could hear the strains of music over the noises of the midway.

"Why don't we check out the pavilion first?" Jazz squinted to make out the printing on the sign in front of the structure. "A dance company's performing."

"Let's go!" Brooke said.

"A dance company." Robbie sounded like the words pained him. "Who wants to see people dance?"

"It's better than going on some dumb old roller coaster," Brooke said.

"Since when do you think roller coasters are dumb, Brooke?" Matt asked, frowning.

The little girl didn't answer.

Robbie put his hands together in prayer. "Please, Uncle Matt. Don't make me watch people dance!"

"Don't make me go on a roller coaster!" Brooke countered.

Matt looked helplessly from one child to the other. It was the first time Jazz had ever seen him at a loss around the children. She stepped forward.

"How about if Brooke and I watch the dancers, and Matt and Robbie go on the roller coaster?" Jazz checked the time on her watch. "We can meet back here in front of the lemonade stand at two o'clock."

"Thank you!" Robbie barreled toward her and hugged her waist, the contact over almost before it began. A sweet ache started near Jazz's heart.

"You are a genius." Matt leaned down and gave her a swift kiss on the lips. He winked at her before leading Robbie away.

Jazz watched the pair of them retreat, then felt a small hand tug at her sleeve. Brooke gazed up at her with complete trust on her pretty freckled face. The ache intensified, growing even sweeter.

"Are you and Uncle Matt going to get married?" Brooke asked.

"Married?" Jazz had never permitted herself to think of a future with Matt. She wouldn't now, either. "Of course not. Where'd you get that idea?"

"I heard Mommy tell Daddy that Uncle Matt should marry you," Brooke said. "Mommy said you're nice."

What could Jazz say to that?

"Your uncle and I are just friends."

Brooke's red head swung back and forth. "Nuh-uh. Friends don't kiss."

They were within sight of the pavilion stage. A mix of young men and women performed a choreographed, high-energy dance to a pop tune Jazz had heard before but couldn't identify.

"Look, Brooke! It's already started." Jazz wasn't above using distraction to get out of a sticky situation. "Let's find a good seat."

Brooke skipped ahead, finding space on an aluminum bleacher two rows from the stage. She sat down, her attention riveted on the dancers. With her foot tapping in time to the music, Brooke's smile was brighter than those worn by the performers.

"This is so cool!" the little girl whispered to Jazz between numbers. She kept her eyes straight ahead, as though afraid of missing something.

The dance company's production might indeed have been cool. The dancers were probably putting on a terrific show. Jazz couldn't say for sure because she was watching Brooke.

The girl clapped in time to the music, her huge smile not fading even once. When the performance ended twenty minutes later, Brooke's young face glowed with pleasure.

"I loved that!" Brooke stayed in her seat while others filed out of the pavilion. Jazz knew instinctively that Brooke was savoring what she'd seen. Jazz often did the same thing after watching something she enjoyed.

"Do you dance, Brooke?" Jazz asked.

Brooke shook her head, her smile finally fading. "I play soccer."

"Can't you do both?" Jazz asked.

"Mommy and Daddy only allow us to do one activity," Brooke said. "They want us to make good grades."

Jazz couldn't fault Terry and Kevin for ensuring the children's schedules weren't overloaded, but surely there must be a way to get Brooke involved in dance.

"I'll tell you a secret if you promise not to tell Uncle Matt," Brooke said in a quiet voice.

Jazz wasn't keen on keeping secrets. Something about Brooke's serious expression convinced her to make an exception.

"I promise," Jazz said.

Brooke cupped a hand to her mouth, leaned close to Jazz and whispered in her ear. "I don't like sports."

The child drew back and Jazz examined her small face, where unhappiness had replaced the joy.

"I don't understand," Jazz said. "Why can't you tell Matt that?"

"Because *he* likes sports," Brooke said.

JAZZ WAS STILL THINKING about Brooke's secret a few hours later. She and Matt stood outside the bumper car arena, watching the small vehicles bash into each other. Robbie's car was behind Brooke's and gaining. A collision appeared inevitable.

Matt slung his arm around Jazz's shoulders. "I'm glad you came with us. Are you having fun?"

"I am." Jazz was grateful Matt hadn't brought up her aversion to spending time with his family. It would be tough to explain why she'd made an exception, ever harder to justify why she couldn't do so again. "Where else could I get a hug for not forcing someone to watch dancing?"

"That hug was more for the roller coaster." Matt

scrunched up his face. "I've got to admit something here. I wasn't keen on the dancing, either."

"So Brooke wouldn't have seen the dancers if I hadn't been along?" Jazz couldn't quite believe that.

"Oh, I would have taken her to see them." Matt gave her a lopsided grin. "I just wouldn't have liked it."

Jazz's mind whirred, because here was her opportunity to talk to him about Brooke and soccer. But how could Jazz broach the subject without breaking her promise?

"I've never seen anyone enjoy dancing so much, but it's not surprising," Jazz said. "Have you noticed that Brooke is always humming? She's quite musical."

"She's good at a lot of things," Matt said. "You should see her on the soccer field."

Robbie's bumper car bashed into Brooke's for what must have been the third or fourth time. Brooke giggled, the same way she had the other times he'd caught up to her. She didn't seem interested in retaliating.

"I don't think Brooke is very competitive," Jazz said.

"I've noticed." Matt didn't sound pleased. "We're working on that."

"Why?" Jazz asked. "Why are you working on it?"

He seemed puzzled by the question. "Brooke is a good athlete. Once I can get her to have a hunger for winning, she can be a great athlete."

"Maybe she's fine the way she is," Jazz said. "Maybe she doesn't need to be pushed into things."

Matt dropped his arm from her shoulders and turned to face her. "Are we still talking about Brooke?"

"Not entirely," Jazz admitted.

"I don't get it."

That was because she hadn't explained why she'd showed up unannounced at his town house. One look at Brooke and Robbie, and her brain had turned the consistency of oatmeal.

"I went to Charles Towne Flair this morning to apply for that assistant chef job," Jazz stated.

"Terrific!"

"No. Not terrific. Kathy McDowell turned me down flat."

"I'm sorry." Matt rubbed her shoulder. He actually looked surprised. "Did she say why?"

"Why do you think?" Jazz's voice was sharper than she'd intended. "She mentioned something about me needing more training but I'm sure it was because I've been in prison."

"Maybe it *was* because of the training thing," Matt said. "Maybe you should—"

"You shouldn't have pushed me to apply, Matt," Jazz interrupted. "You set me up to fail."

"I disagree," he said. "The only way to get ahead in the world is to take chances."

"And what? Fall flat on my face?"

"If that's what it takes," he said. "As long as you get up, dust yourself off and try again."

Jazz wasn't convinced but couldn't think of a comeback. She couldn't stay angry at him, either, not when his intent was to help her out.

"Is that what you tell Brooke?" Jazz asked.

The little redhead was getting out of her bumper car,

appearing not the least bit upset that her brother had repeatedly gotten the better of her.

"As a matter of fact, it is," he said. "If Brooke is going to be a top soccer player, that's a lesson she has to learn."

Jazz bit her lower lip, thinking about how to phrase her words so she wouldn't break her promise to Brooke. "Maybe you should ask Brooke sometimes how she feels about the game."

"She loves soccer," Matt proclaimed. "Both kids do."

"Just ask her," Jazz said.

Robbie burst through the exit and maneuvered around the people waiting in line for the next rotation, with Brooke following at a less breakneck clip.

"That was so much fun!" exclaimed Robbie.

"Yeah, that was fun!" Brooke said.

Matt grabbed Robbie under the arms and lifted him.

"Put me down, Uncle Matt. I'm too big to pick up!" Robbie shouted, but the boy was laughing through his protests.

Matt tossed his nephew a foot or so in the air and caught him. Brooke giggled along with her brother.

"So you think that's funny?" Matt asked his niece. He set Robbie down and picked Brooke up, giving her the same treatment until all three of them were in hysterics.

A tide of emotion hit Jazz like a tsunami. She couldn't fool herself any longer.

Since the moment she'd spotted the twins in the

park—no, since they were born—she'd loved them with all her heart.

And now she loved their uncle, too.

CHAPTER TWELVE

SADIE BURST INTO the kitchen at Pancake Palace the following Wednesday, such a frequent occurrence that Jazz didn't turn from the griddle.

"Oh, my gosh!" Sadie cried. "I am so excited I could faint!"

Carl was standing next to Jazz, cracking eggs into a fresh batch of pancake mix. He chuckled. "You not kind of girl who faints."

"Okay, then," Sadie said. "I'm so excited I could run screaming around the parking lot, waving my arms and throwing in a couple of leaps."

Carl's chuckle turned into a full-fledged laugh. Jazz joined in.

"What's so exciting?" Jazz asked.

"Lady Gaga is coming to Charleston!" Sadie all but shouted.

"Lady who?" Carl asked.

"Lady Gaga!" Sadie repeated. "She's a singer with terrific style. Her outfits are amazing! How can you not know who she is?"

"I don't—how you say it?—get much around," Carl said.

"Get around much," Jazz corrected with a smile. "Don't feel bad, Carl. I barely know who Lady Gaga is, either."

"Well, you're both missing out," Sadie said. "One of my customers—two eggs over easy with hash browns— told me she just heard on the radio that Lady Gaga will be at Gaillard Auditorium in two weeks! She's adding a spot to her tour."

"You are going?" Carl asked.

Sadie's sigh was audible above the eggs frying on the griddle. "Probably not. I'm sure the tickets will be too expensive." She brightened. "But it's still exciting that Lady Gaga will be in the same city as me!"

"How about I buy the tickets and take you?" Carl made the offer in an offhand manner, but Jazz noticed his hand tighten on the spoon he was using to stir the pancake mix.

"But you...I thought..." Sadie sputtered, a rarity for a woman who always had a lot to say. "Why would you want to go if you've never heard of her?"

Carl didn't turn around from his work. "You like her," he said, his voice rough.

"I know," Sadie said, "but—"

Carl didn't let her finish her sentence. "Think about it. If you want me to get tickets, I get them."

He poured some of the pancake base onto the griddle and dropped in some fresh blueberries. Clearly he was through discussing Lady Gaga.

Jazz glanced over her shoulder. Sadie met her eyes, panic clearly visible on her face. "Help," she mouthed silently.

But what kind of advice could Jazz give Sadie? Jazz had romantic problems of her own, if you could call being in love with a gorgeous man who thought he was her boyfriend a problem.

It wasn't as though Jazz could dispense advice even if she had any. Jazz, Sadie and Carl worked the same shift. At no time would Jazz be alone with Sadie. Or so she thought.

Sadie was waiting for her a short time later when Jazz emerged from one of the two stalls in the ladies' room. The waitress's back was to the sink, her panic visible.

"You've got to help me figure out what to do!" insisted Sadie.

"Did you follow me in here?" Jazz asked.

"How else could I talk to you about Carl?" Sadie moved aside to make room for Jazz at the sink. "Because I'm pretty sure he asked me out. You did think Carl was asking me out, right?"

"Yes, I did," Jazz said.

"That's what I thought." Sadie put both hands on her own head and grabbed at her blond hair. "Oh, what am I going to tell him?"

"I don't understand what the big deal is." Jazz turned on the faucet and washed her hands. "You already go to football games with Carl. You're going again this Friday night, aren't you?"

"Yes, but I meet Carl in the stands! I have Benjy with me! Those aren't dates!"

Jazz switched off the faucet and tore a paper towel from the dispenser. "You like Carl, right?"

"Sure I do," Sadie said.

"And you want to go to the concert?"

"I'm dying to go to the concert."

"So go with Carl." Jazz balled up the paper towel and tossed it in the wastebasket.

"Would you and Matt come with us?" Sadie asked in a hopeful voice.

"Matt isn't a Lady Gaga fan," Jazz said. It was a guess but probably a good one.

"So what? I've seen the way Matt looks at you. You could ask him to do just about anything and he'd say yes."

Jazz prayed Sadie's impression was wrong. Falling in love with Matt hadn't changed the fact that Jazz would eventually have to break things off. When she did, she hoped Matt wouldn't hurt as much as she would.

In any event, asking Matt for favors at this point would complicate an already messy situation.

"Sorry, Sadie. I don't feel comfortable with that," Jazz said. "You need to figure out whether you want to date Carl, anyway."

"That's the problem," Sadie wailed. "I don't know if I want to date him. Carl's different from anybody I've ever gone out with."

"Isn't that a good thing?" Jazz asked.

"I suppose," Sadie said, but she didn't sound convinced.

Jazz needed to be getting back to the kitchen but resigned herself to hearing Sadie out. Work could wait. It wasn't as though she was heading back to her dream job. She immediately shoved the thought from her head. After her experience at Charles Towne Flair, she'd best stop dreaming.

"Then what is it?" Jazz asked.

At Sadie's helpless shrug, Jazz suddenly feared she understood the waitress's reservations. "It's not because Carl killed a man, is it?"

Sadie's eyes bugged out and her mouth gaped open. She couldn't have looked more shocked. "Carl killed somebody?"

Jazz nearly groaned. "You didn't know." It was a statement, not a question.

"How could I know?" Sadie asked.

"It was in self-defense," Jazz clarified. "And why didn't you know? It's not a secret. Carl told me the first week we worked together."

"I never asked him. I guess because I didn't want to take a chance I'd feel differently about him," Sadie said.

"Would you feel differently about me if you knew my crime?" Jazz asked.

Sadie's eyes narrowed. "You didn't kill somebody, too, did you?"

"No," Jazz said stoically, "I didn't kill anybody."

"It's different with you, anyway, because you're not a man."

The door banged open. Helen Monroe stuck her graying head inside. "I thought I'd find you two in here. Could you hurry it up? Some of us don't have the time to take bathroom breaks."

Helen didn't wait for an answer.

Sadie stuck out her tongue at the closed door.

"I really don't like that woman," Sadie said as she and Jazz left the restroom together. "And I still don't know what to do about Carl."

Even though it went against Jazz's longstanding determination not to get involved in someone else's problems, she couldn't hold back the words.

"You could take a chance," she said.

TAKE A CHANCE. Take a chance. Take a chance.

Jazz could hardly believe she'd dispensed the advice, let alone that she was following it herself.

"You can let go of that steering wheel." Matt sat next to her in the passenger seat of her car, which she'd parked facing the bland, one-story building that housed Beaufort's downtown post office. "We're not going anywhere with the ignition turned off."

"I was thinking of turning the car back on," Jazz said.

"After I left work early and you called in sick to your telemarketing job?" Matt shook his head. "You don't want to do that."

Oh, but she did.

"What if I drive back to your town house and cook you dinner?" The idea appealed to Jazz but could she get Matt to go along with it? "After we eat, I'll let you have your way with me. Just to be clear, I'm talking about sex."

"I like the sound of that." Matt reached over, removed the keys from the ignition and handed them to her. "Let's do it after you talk to Bill Smith."

Jazz's stomach cramped when she envisioned entering the Beaufort post office and confronting Bill Smith.

"Maybe I should have warned him I was coming," Jazz said.

"I thought you said it wasn't the kind of thing to tell someone over the phone," Matt said.

Jazz had called the downtown post office earlier in the day to make sure Bill Smith was at work but had declined when a coworker offered to put him on the line. Now she understood that she'd been putting off the moment of truth.

"I can't just walk up to him while he's working and tell him I could be his daughter, either." Jazz swiped a hand over her forehead, which felt clammy. "We should have come up with a plan during the drive down here."

She'd picked him up at Faircrest High School after calling to tell him of her impulsive decision. But during the hour drive to Beaufort they'd talked of inconsequential things, mostly because Jazz changed the subject whenever Matt brought up their mission.

"We can make a plan now," Matt said. "It's nearly five o'clock. How about you tell Bill Smith you have something to discuss with him and ask him to meet us for a cup of coffee?"

Matt's plan sounded logical while they were in the car. Once they were inside the post office waiting in a line that was moving surprisingly quickly, it was a different matter.

Four clerks were on duty, only one of them male. The male clerk looked like an older version of the good-looking teenage boy in Jazz's mother's snapshot. His hair wasn't quite as thick and his waist not as trim, but the clerk was recognizable as the Bill Smith who had meant something to Jazz's mother.

Jazz watched Smith hand an elderly gentleman his change. "Come on back and see me again, ya hear."

His next customer, an older woman with salt-and-pepper hair, shuffled up to the counter as though her feet hurt. "What can I do for you?" Smith asked in a loud, cheerful voice.

Jazz couldn't see anything of herself in Bill Smith but that didn't necessarily rule him out.

"Do you realize you're squeezing my hand really hard?" Matt whispered in Jazz's ear.

Jazz immediately loosened her grip. She'd been so busy wondering whether Smith's friendly smile would disappear when it was Jazz's turn at the counter that she hadn't even realized she was holding Matt's hand.

There were only two people waiting in line in front of them. One of the female clerks yelled "Next!" and then there was one. The temperature inside the post office seemed to rise twenty degrees.

"I can't do this," she told Matt.

"Sure you can," Matt said.

Jazz shook her head and dropped his hand, walking quickly toward the exit and feeling like the worst sort of coward. The air outside was sweet and cool. A soft breeze washed over her, almost as if it were propelling her forward. She stepped down from the sidewalk into the parking lot, not stopping until she'd reached her car. Only then did she notice Matt wasn't with her.

Oh, no!

She hurried back the way she came, desperate to get to Matt before he put in motion something that couldn't be stopped. He was exiting the building when she reached the entrance. She gaped at him, waiting for him to tell her what she already knew.

"Bill Smith said he'd meet us at a coffee shop in about a half hour," Matt said. "It's near the waterfront about four blocks south of here."

"But...but I changed my mind!" Jazz cried.

"If you didn't want to talk to him," Matt said, "you wouldn't have driven down here."

"But I..." Jazz could barely process her thoughts over the panic clawing at her. "I'm afraid, Matt."

He took her hand, his brown eyes softening as they gazed at her. "There's nothing to be afraid of. I'll be right there with you every step of the way."

The next thirty minutes passed in a blur. Jazz was barely aware of Matt driving the four blocks and parking alongside a street dotted with shops and businesses. At another time, she would have treasured the view of the blue water dotted with boats but she barely paid attention to the view. She refused Matt's offer to buy her a drink when they entered the coffee shop and sat down at a table facing the front door.

Eventually the door swung open and in walked Bill Smith, wearing the same blue short-sleeved collared shirt and gray pants he'd been wearing at the post office. He looked around, located their table and headed straight for them.

Jazz told herself to calm down, to think rationally. At this point, Bill Smith was just a man, nothing more.

"What's this about?" Bill stopped beside the table. He was smiling but not as broadly as he'd been in the post office.

"Sit down and join us," Matt invited. He gestured to his half-empty cup of coffee. "Unless you'd like to get some coffee first."

"No, I'm good." Bill pulled back a chair, lowered himself into it and looked straight at Jazz. "Do I know you from somewhere? You look familiar?"

Jazz gulped. He'd given her an opening. She needed

to summon the courage to take it. "I'm Jazz Lenox. You knew my mother."

"Oh, yeah?" His eyes narrowed but they looked more assessing than suspicious. They were almost exactly the same shade of gray as Jazz's eyes. "What's your mother's name?"

"Marianne Lenox," Jazz said.

"Marianne? Yeah, I remember her." He nodded. "We went to high school together. How's Marianne doing?"

"She died when I was nine," Jazz said.

"Oh, jeez. I didn't know. I'm sorry to hear that," Bill said. "But I'm kind of stumped. I don't understand why you want to talk to me."

The scent of coffee, which Jazz normally enjoyed, was nearly overwhelming. She looked at Matt for help. He nodded, encouraging her to continue.

"I was looking through my mother's yearbook and found a snapshot of you," Jazz said. "There was also a newspaper clipping about you starring in a high school play."

Bill tilted his head. "And?"

Jazz blew out a breath. "And I thought you might have been important to her."

Bill didn't say anything for a long while. A muscle worked in his jaw. "How old are you?"

"I was twenty-six this past June," Jazz said.

Bill started shaking his head before she finished her response. When he spoke, it was in a whisper. "Are you here to tell me you think I might be your father?"

Jazz nodded. Under the table, Matt squeezed her hand.

"This is unreal." Bill ran a hand through his hair. His smile was definitely gone. "Never in a million years would I have expected this."

"Are you saying it's not possible?" Matt asked the question foremost in Jazz's mind.

"Oh, it's possible," Bill said. "It's just a shock. Everyone knew Marianne dropped out of high school because she was pregnant but she never told me the baby could be mine."

"You didn't think to ask?" Matt's voice held an edge.

"Hell, no. Marianne was a good-time girl. I could think of a half-dozen other guys who—" Bill abruptly stopped talking, gazing across the table at Jazz. His eyes were kind. "What I mean to say is Marianne wasn't a one-guy girl."

The information came as no surprise. Jazz's grandmother had repeatedly referred to her own daughter in a lot worse ways. The old woman had told the teenage Jazz that promiscuity was the reason Jazz would never know the identity of her father. But that was before Jazz had looked through her mother's yearbook and discovered Bill Smith had a twin and had played in a jazz band.

"There's only one photo in my mother's yearbook," Jazz pointed out. As evidence, it was flimsy, but with Matt at the table Jazz couldn't reveal she'd given birth to twins. "I thought that meant you were...special. Then there's my name. According to the yearbook, you played in a jazz band in high school."

"I liked Marianne. I did," Bill said. "But none of that proves anything."

"A DNA test would," Matt said.

Jazz held her breath waiting for Bill's response. If Matt hadn't brought up the DNA test, Jazz would have. Now that she'd come this far in her quest to find out if Bill Smith was her father, she longed for a definitive answer.

"No way." Bill shook his head vehemently. At his raised voice, the few other patrons in the coffee shop looked their way. Bill leaned across the table, lowering his volume. "I'm not taking any DNA test."

"It's the only way to find out for sure if Jazz is your daughter," Matt pointed out.

"Look, nothing against you, Jazz. But my life is great just the way it is," Bill said. "I've got a wife and three kids who aren't even out of high school yet."

"You might have four kids," Matt said.

"And I might not." Bill looked Jazz straight in the eyes. "Listen, I'm sorry about this. I am. But I'm not one for stirring the pot. I'm going to leave well enough alone."

Tears stung the back of Jazz's eyes but she didn't protest. Dimly she noted that Bill had rejected her even before finding out she had a criminal record. If he knew, he'd probably be more adamant about refusing to take the DNA test.

"I understand," Jazz said softly.

"You understand?" Matt blurted out. "How can you understand this guy, Jazz?"

It was Jazz's turn to place her hand over Matt's. "I do."

Bill got to his feet. He paused, appearing as though he wasn't sure what to say. "I'm sorry."

Then he was gone and along with him what was perhaps Jazz's only chance to find her father.

"Damn that guy." Matt pushed back his chair and half rose. "I'm going to talk some sense into him."

"No, don't." Jazz's voice was stronger than it had been all afternoon. "I meant what I said, Matt."

How could Jazz not sympathize with the postal clerk's position when she'd taken a similar stance with Brooke and Robbie? The situations weren't exactly the same but they had strong parallels.

Just as Jazz would never know if the man who'd just walked out of the coffee shop was her father, the twins would be in the dark about the identity of their birth mother.

Bill Smith wasn't the only one who intended to leave well enough alone.

SOMETHING WAS OFF.

The certainty hit Matt the instant he entered The Watering Hole the next night and spotted his father at a back table away from both the pool tables and dartboard.

Because of its prime location on King Street in downtown Charleston, the bar was always at least half-full, even on a Thursday night like tonight. The few times Matt had met his father for a drink, Len Caminetti had been front and center. That his father was sequestered away from the action didn't come as the only surprise.

Tom Dougherty, the Faircrest High football coach, was at his father's table.

"Hey, Matt!" His father half stood and called to him. "Back here!"

The old friends had obviously been at the bar for a while. The pitcher in the middle of the table was almost empty, the same as their beer mugs. Tom's hand was wrapped around his. The football coach nodded at Matt when he reached the table.

Matt swung his gaze from his father to Tom. "What's going on?"

"What do you mean?" His father's raised voice didn't fool Matt. Len Caminetti believed the best defense was a good offense. "Me and T.D. are having a drink."

Matt pulled back a chair, the legs scraping against the wooden floor, and sat down. He needed to make this quick. He'd slept at Jazz's place last night after the fiasco with Bill Smith. She'd put on a brave face, claiming she couldn't miss what she'd never had, but it was obvious the rejection had stung. Whether Jazz admitted to needing the support or not, Matt intended to be waiting when Jazz got off from her telemarketing job tonight.

"You hardly ever ask me to meet you for a drink, Dad," Matt said. "And you didn't tell me Tom would be here."

"What? You got something against T.D.?" His father gestured at the football coach.

"Of course not," Matt said. "I work at Faircrest. Tom's so popular right now he's like an icon."

Tom laughed. "Ain't that the truth? Win a couple football games and everybody loves you."

"Everybody except Gerianne Huff," his father clarified.

There was an empty mug on the table. Matt reached for the pitcher and filled it with beer. "Has Mrs. Huff been making trouble for you, Tom?"

The football coach had given up on the notion to rotate his two quarterbacks after a single game, awarding the job outright to Arthur Rodriguez. The sophomore had come through, leading the team to a decisive victory last Friday. The next game was tomorrow night.

"Trouble for *me?* No." Tom shook his head. "Mrs. Huff can't say much when the team's winning, so she's going after another target."

Matt took a swig of beer. "Who?"

"You," Tom said.

"I don't understand," Matt said.

"That's why T.D.'s here," his father said. "I asked him to come after he told me what Gerianne did."

It was as if the other two men were speaking a foreign language Matt didn't understand. "What did Mrs. Huff do?"

"She's telling everyone you shouldn't be A.D. because you're dating an ex-con," Tom said.

Matt's breath caught. He'd spotted Gerianne Huff talking to Jazz in the stands at his youth team's soccer game the weekend before last but dismissed the encounter as unimportant. He wondered how Mrs. Huff knew Jazz had been in prison. Surely Jazz hadn't told her.

"Yeah, I know. It's ridiculous, Matt. But you can't just let Gerianne go around lying about you." Matt's father's face had turned red with indignation. "Tell Matt what happened after school today, T.D."

"I saw Mrs. Huff go into Ray's office. So I asked

him what was going on, her being the mother of one of my players," Tom said. Ray was Ray Middleton, the school's longtime principal and one of Tom's closest friends. "I probably shouldn't be telling you this, but I figure somebody's gotta warn you. Mrs. Huff didn't only complain about you dating an ex-con. She bitched about your support of Carter Prioleau, too."

Matt hadn't talked to the former A.D. since he'd thrown Carter the goodbye party and realized Carter's true nature. That didn't mean Matt was going to apologize for being wrong about the man.

"She should mind her own business!" Matt snapped.

"But she didn't," his father said. "And now you've got to defend yourself or you might find yourself out as A.D."

"Not going to happen." Matt had never in his life gone after something as hard as he had the athletic director position and failed to achieve his goal. "I'm getting that A.D. job."

"Not until you clear this up. But that should be easy enough." His father frowned. "Unless you *are* going out with someone besides that pretty caterer."

"Jazz is the only woman I'm dating." Matt hadn't been remotely interested in anybody else since he'd met Jazz.

"That's what I told T.D. here." His father jerked a thumb at his friend. "What I don't get is why Mrs. Huff would lie about Jazz."

Matt had hoped to safeguard Jazz's privacy but didn't see a way out of telling his father the truth. "Mrs. Huff isn't lying. Jazz served five years in prison."

Matt went on to explain the circumstances, emphasizing the raw deal Jazz had gotten. The two men listened in silence, with Matt's father tapping his chin thoughtfully. When he was through explaining, Matt reached for his beer mug.

"It's a good thing you haven't been dating Jazz long," his father said.

Matt's arm froze, his mug suspended in midair. "Why's that?"

"You have to ask?" his father said. "If you keep going out with her, it'll hurt your chances of becoming A.D."

Matt set down his mug. "Those were the same words you used about me suspending D. J. Huff."

"I was wrong about that," his father admitted. "But who could have known there was a better quarterback than D.J. waiting in the wings?"

"I would have suspended D.J. even if he was the only quarterback on the roster," Matt said.

"I already told you I was wrong about that one," his father said. "But I'm right about this."

"I don't agree." Matt felt his jaw tighten. "Nobody has the right to tell me who I can and can't date."

"Wake up, son," his father whispered harshly. "You work at a school. You're around teenagers every day. Mrs. Huff is out to get you, but she has a point. Parents want to know they can trust your judgment."

"I've proven they can trust me," Matt said.

"Then find a nice girl who hasn't been in prison." His father turned to his friend. "Right, T.D.?"

"I already heard some of my football players talking

about it," Tom said. "The news is spreading fast. Don't forget Mrs. Huff is the president of the PTA."

"You think she'll bring it up at a PTA meeting?" Matt was incredulous.

"I think she blames you for D.J. losing his starting job," Tom stated.

"This is serious, son," his father said. "There's no telling how far Gerianne will go."

"Your father's right," agreed Tom. "From what I understand, you hardly know this Jazz. It would be different if you were in love with her."

Matt stood up, leaving most of his beer behind. "I've heard enough."

"Think long and hard on it, son," his father called after him. "This is your future we're talking about."

Matt couldn't think of anything else for the next hour. He was still dwelling on the situation at a few minutes past ten o'clock while he waited in the courtyard of the office building where Jazz worked as a telemarketer.

He was angry at his father but the older man had only spoken the truth. If Matt continued to date Jazz, he could face repercussions.

She emerged from the building with an older woman, laughing about something. A streetlight caught her in its glow. Her hair was long and loose and she wore a red shirt with a blue-jeaned miniskirt. She looked beautiful and vibrant and alive.

"Jazz!" Matt called her name.

Jazz turned in his direction, smiled and hurried toward him. Matt caught her in his arms and kissed her as though it had been years instead of hours since he saw her.

That was when Matt knew that it would take something far more powerful than gossip to keep him away from her. Because this tender feeling wrapping around his heart felt an awful lot like love.

CHAPTER THIRTEEN

JAZZ BIT INTO HER grilled bratwurst sandwich two days later, chewing slowly to enjoy the rich flavor as long as possible.

"Do you realize you're making an *mmm* noise?" Matt asked, amusement in his voice.

Jazz swallowed, temporarily closing her eyes in bliss.

"I can't help it," Jazz said. "It's so good!"

They were eating lunch on Saturday while walking around the farmer's market in Charleston's Marion Square. More accurately, Jazz was eating lunch. Matt had already finished. He'd met her at the downtown Charleston location after his youth soccer team had won another game to stay undefeated.

The atmosphere in Marion Square was more reminiscent of a carnival than a farmer's market. White tents shaded the vendors, crowds roamed the grassy aisles and belly dancers in colorful costumes performed on a makeshift stage.

Jazz was the happiest she'd been since Bill Smith had refused to take the DNA test.

"You shouldn't have met me here, you know," Jazz said. "Now tonight's menu won't be a surprise."

She'd volunteered to cook for him, only partly because she was dying to spend more time in his fabulous kitchen. She was eager to show off her skill, too, which was why only the freshest ingredients would do. She was thinking of serving macadamia-crusted brie along with a rich, flavorful she-crab soup. For the main course, she'd go with grilled salmon accompanied by seasoned rice from recipes she'd invented. She'd finish on a flourish with cherries jubilee.

Matt put his arm around her and kissed the side of her head. "You're glad I'm here, though."

She laughed. "Cocky, aren't we?"

"Hey, I tell it like it is," he said. "I can't help if I'm irresistible."

He didn't know how right he was. Jazz *was* glad of his company and irresistible wasn't far off in describing her reaction to him. Sometimes—okay, most of the time—she couldn't get enough of him.

Jazz took the last bite of her bratwurst sandwich before she was tempted to do something stupid, like admit her need for him was insatiable. Her affliction was getting worse every day, due in no small part to his thoughtfulness. He'd spent every moment he could with her since their trip to Beaufort, wisely refraining from discussing what had happened.

"I'll tell you what will be irresistible," she said. "Tonight's meal."

"Confidence. I like it." He winked at her. "So where to?" Matt looked to the left and to the right. "We seem to be in the wrong section."

While they were eating their bratwurst, they'd wandered near the stage. The belly dancers were gone, replaced by six teenage girls performing an energetic tap dance. Smiles wreathed their young faces.

"Thataway." Jazz pointed to the opposite end of the grassy square in response to Matt's question. She'd scouted a fish market with a large selection and reasonable prices before he'd arrived. "Follow me."

She threaded her way through dozens of people who'd stopped to watch the tap dancers, Matt following in her path. Many of the onlookers were smiling and clapping. Jazz paused to take a look. The practice the girls must have put into the routine was paying off. They were in perfect synch.

"They're very good," Jazz said.

"Surprisingly good." Matt had a better view than she did because his height enabled him to see over the heads of the people in front of them. "I didn't know girls that young tapped."

"Oh, yeah," Jazz said. "A typical curriculum at a dance school is a blend of tap, jazz and ballet."

Matt put his hand on the small of her back. She wasn't about to analyze why she found even that slight touch thrilling.

"You didn't take dance growing up, did you?" Matt asked.

"Not hardly," she retorted. Did he really think the difficult childhood she'd described to him could have included dance lessons? "Why do you ask?"

"You sound like an expert," he said.

That was because Jazz had phoned a dance school earlier in the week and peppered the receptionist with questions, aiming to be prepared in case the knowledge could help Brooke.

"I must have heard it somewhere, is all," Jazz said. On stage, the six girls formed a chorus line. Leaning with their bodies slightly forward, they performed an intricate tap routine while swinging their arms in unison.

"Brooke would love this!" Jazz couldn't hold back what was on her mind. "Terry should bring her here on Saturdays."

"Terry's busy on Saturdays with soccer," Matt said. "She's been lucky that Brooke and Robbie's games are usually at different times so she and Kevin can watch both."

Jazz was about to question again whether soccer was the right choice for Brooke but didn't get the words out.

"I go to their games when they don't conflict with my team's," Matt said. "I'm pretty sure that's the case next Saturday. Maybe you can come with me."

He made the offer with nonchalance, as though she'd never objected to spending time with his family. She couldn't blame him after they'd spent last Saturday at the fair with the twins. So she needed to set him straight. Again.

"Excuse me. Coming through," the female half of a young couple called from behind them. It was easier for Jazz to resume walking than to step aside.

To the side of the stage was a sizable area where artisans sold handwrought crafts. One booth featured leafy green houseplants. Another offered baked goods sold by teenage girls wearing maroon-and-black cheerleader uniforms. A sign above the booth announced proceeds from the sale would help the cheerleaders travel to a regional competition.

"Aren't those cheerleaders from Faircrest High?"

Jazz squinted to make out the logo on their uniforms. "Yes. They are from Faircrest."

"I didn't know anyone from school would be here," Matt muttered under his breath.

"They should be in a good mood after that win last night," Jazz said. The football team had notched another victory, although Jazz hadn't been there to see it. She might have gone with Carl and Sadie if the waitress hadn't canceled at the last minute.

Three cheerleaders were working the booth, which didn't have any customers at the moment. Two of the girls, both petite brunettes, gazed in their direction. One of the brunettes said something to the third girl, a taller blonde. The blonde scanned the area before her gaze seemed to settle on Jazz and Matt. All three of the cheerleaders giggled.

Jazz peered over her shoulder but didn't see anything behind them that could have elicited laughs.

"Where's that fish market again?" Matt asked.

It took Jazz a second to process his question. She pointed in the general direction they'd been headed. "Over there. But don't you want to buy something to support the Faircrest cheerleaders first?"

"No," Matt said.

The giggles from the booth had grown louder. Jazz noticed a fourth girl she hadn't seen before, probably because she wasn't wearing a cheerleader's uniform. She was younger than the others and resembled the blonde, which led Jazz to believe she was a younger sister.

"I'll do it!" Jazz heard her say.

The youngest girl detached herself from the others

and walked toward them. Matt put a hand on Jazz's back, gently urging her to move.

"Excuse me, ma'am," the girl called, barely able to speak through her giggles.

Jazz stopped and pointed to herself. "Are you talking to me?"

The girl nodded, finally getting her laughter under control. "We were just wondering, uh, what you did."

"I don't understand," Jazz said.

"You've got a lot of nerve coming over here and bothering us," Matt said at the same time. His lips were tight, his jaw set. "What's your name?"

The girl gaped at them, then turned and dashed back to the booth. The older girls were watching, hands over their mouths, twittering more than laughing.

Matt's hand once again exerted pressure on Jazz's back. "C'mon, let's get out of here."

Jazz resumed walking, frowning as she tried to make sense of the girl's question. "What did that girl mean?"

"It's not important," Matt said, his tone clipped.

Except the opposite must be true or Matt's manner wouldn't be so brusque. He was practically shuddering with anger, though not at Jazz, at the young girl. *We were wondering what you did,* the girl had said. What could that mean other than...

"Was she asking what I did to get sent to prison?" Jazz shook her head, almost immediately discounting the notion. "No. That doesn't make sense. How would that girl know I'd been in prison?"

Matt didn't reply, which was like waving a red flag in front of her face. He was hurrying her even though the booth with the Faircrest cheerleaders was no longer in sight. A muscle flickered in his jaw.

"Matt?" Jazz stopped walking steps from a stand offering a variety of hot and cold soups. People were milling about nearby, still, Jazz and Matt were relatively alone. "Did that girl know I'd been in prison?"

Matt's gaze flickered away before his eyes came to rest on her. They looked pained. "Probably."

Jazz's hand flew to her throat. "How?"

He exhaled, shaking his head. Obviously he'd rather not explain. "Do you remember talking to a woman a few weeks ago at my team's soccer game? Tall, short hair, in her forties?"

"Yes." Jazz recalled the woman instantly because the encounter had made her uncomfortable. "She asked if I was your girlfriend. She said she'd seen me at the football game with Carl and Sadie."

"That was Gerianne Huff," Matt said. "She's the mother of the quarterback I suspended. He's since lost his starting job."

"And?" Jazz asked.

"And somehow she found out you have a record," he said.

Jazz remembered Mrs. Huff asking about the name of the restaurant on Carl's T-shirt. The owner of Pancake Palace didn't broadcast that he hired ex-cons but neither did he hide the fact. Years ago the *Post and Courier,* Charleston's daily newspaper, had even done a feature story about a short-order cook who'd been involved in a high-profile crime. The cook no longer worked at the restaurant but a surprising number of people remembered the story.

"That doesn't explain how the girl knew." Jazz gasped and covered her mouth. "Oh, no. It's all over school that you're dating an ex-con, isn't it?"

Matt crossed his arms over his chest. "It doesn't matter."

"Of course it matters! You work at a high school." Jazz couldn't believe she hadn't considered the ramifications being involved with her could have on Matt before this minute. "If the students know, so do their parents."

"My private life is nobody's business but mine."

"That's not true. Didn't you tell me you could be fired for bringing embarrassment to the school? Isn't that what was going to happen to your friend Carter?"

"Apples and oranges," Matt said. "Besides, you're not an embarrassment. Even if you had been guilty, you've paid your debt to society."

"Really? So the principal hasn't spoken to you about me?" Jazz could tell from the mutinous cast of his face that she'd hit the mark. "He has, hasn't he?"

"It's not worth worrying about," he said. "Principal Middleton won't fire me."

That might be true but Matt was glossing over the fact that Jazz could cost him the chance to run the athletic department. She couldn't let that happen, not when there was no future for her and Matt.

People passed them on both sides, crowding in on them, making Jazz feel as though her heart were being squeezed tighter.

"Let's go somewhere else and finish talking about this," she said.

"There's nothing more to say." Matt sounded

authoritative but he must have known there was plenty more to discuss.

"Please." Jazz put a hand on his arm. "I really want to leave."

He frowned. "Without stopping at the fish market?"

"Yes," she said.

Matt's shoulders dropped along with the corners of his mouth. "Should I follow you to your place or do you want to follow me to mine?"

They'd driven to the farmer's market separately, so his question made perfect sense. Except Jazz could envision what would happen if they went somewhere Matt was free to touch her: She wouldn't be able to think clearly and they'd end up in bed.

"Waterfront Park is nearby," she said. "I'd rather go there."

Matt nodded once but she felt no relief that he'd agreed to her suggestion. Giving up her newborn twins had been the hardest thing she'd ever done in her life. What she was about to do would rank a close second.

AT ANY OTHER TIME, Matt would have enjoyed a visit to Charleston's Waterfront Park.

A thick canopy of oak trees afforded plenty of shaded benches. A large fountain at the main park entrance led to a wide wooden pier with stunning vistas of the Cooper River and the towering bridges that connected Charleston to Mount Pleasant.

Today Matt barely glanced at the view. He was preoccupied coming up with the words to convince Jazz to ignore the gossip.

"Let me start, because I know what you're going to

say." Matt was beside Jazz on a shaded bench under the wooden canopy, no doubt a seat she'd chosen over the more romantic swings. "You're blowing this thing at school way out of proportion. It's nothing to worry about."

"Oh, really?" Jazz didn't look convinced. "Is that what the principal told you?"

Matt hesitated. Principal Middleton had called Matt into his office the day before, exactly as Tom Dougherty had warned.

"Just tell me the truth, Matt," Jazz said. "Please."

"Okay, he did want to know about you," Matt confessed. "I told him how you'd ended up in prison but only so he'd understand you weren't some hardened criminal."

"Did he mention the employment contract you signed?" Jazz asked.

In retrospect, it hadn't been a wise move.

"You're not an embarrassment, Jazz." Matt had delivered the missive in more heated terms to the principal. "The only thing that should matter anyway is job performance."

"Matt, I—" she began.

"No, let me finish. I don't care what other people think. I care about you." Matt hadn't intended to tell her this soon how deep his feelings ran, but the time seemed right. He filled his lungs with air and said, "I'm in l—"

"I think we should stop seeing each other," she interrupted. Her eyes flickered to his, then away.

He felt like a wrecking ball had hit him in the

gut. "What? Because some small-minded people are gossiping about us?"

"That's part of it," Jazz said. "I can't let you lose your job because of me, especially since we both know what we have is temporary."

She'd told him as much upfront, yes, but everything had changed. Hadn't it?

"You don't think things have been going well?" Matt could have pointed out that the sex had been fantastic but he was referring to so much more. He'd spend time with her even if he couldn't touch her.

"Well enough," Jazz said. "But it can't last."

"Why not?" Matt demanded.

"It's exhausting to be with you, Matt," she said. "I never would have applied for that chef job or confronted Bill Smith if not for you."

"You were the one who tracked Bill down," he pointed out.

"Yes, but you didn't even let me change my mind when we got to Beaufort," she said. "You were the one who arranged for me to talk to him."

"I was trying to help."

"I know you were. That's my point. You go full speed ahead, no matter the obstacles." She stared down at her hands, then raised her gaze to the water. "It's enough for me to be out of prison with an apartment and a job."

They were back to her job situation again. Matt hadn't brought up the subject in a week but couldn't hold back his opinion now.

"I don't believe you," he said. "You work sixty hours a week at two jobs to afford your apartment. You can't tell me you don't want something better for yourself."

"See what I mean?" Jazz's voice held a sharp edge. "You won't accept that everybody isn't as hard-charging as you are. You're the same way with Brooke."

"What does Brooke have to do with this?" Matt asked.

"Quite a lot, actually." Jazz bit her lip. "Not Brooke, specifically. Your family. You're so close to them that dating you is like dating your family."

Her change of subject took him aback. One minute she was claiming they should break up because of a personality conflict and now she was bringing his family into the equation.

"You like my family." It was a fact, not an opinion. She'd even told him so on a number of occasions. "You had a great time at the fair with Brooke and Robbie."

Jazz gazed off into the water. In the distance, a dolphin jumped, its sleek gray body appearing, then disappearing under the ripples. She didn't seem to notice.

"When Brooke and I were watching the dancers at the fair, she asked if you and I were getting married." Jazz spoke so softly he had to strain to hear her over the whistle of the sea breeze. "She got the idea from Terry."

"So what? You know what Terry's like. She never has a thought she keeps to herself."

"So your family already thinks we're serious," Jazz said. "I don't blame them. Things between us have been moving way too fast."

"Then we'll slow them down," he said. "Yeah, maybe we have things to work on in our relationship but we *can* make it work. You haven't given me one reason to believe otherwise."

"How about this?" Something hard and determined flashed in her face. "You don't know the real me, Matt. There's something about me that's so big I can never tell you."

Now they were getting somewhere. Her other reasons hadn't made sense but this one had the ring of truth.

"You can tell me anything," Matt insisted.

"Not this. It's something you'd never be able to forgive."

"Try me," he said.

She shook her head back and forth. "You're not listening to me. I can't tell you. Ever."

He couldn't buy that. He wouldn't. "If this secret is the real reason you're breaking up with me, you have to tell me," he implored.

"Stop pushing me!" she cried. "Can't you see it's not only what you want that's important?"

"Of course I can."

"Then you have to accept that it's over."

Everything inside him rebelled at her words. He could tell she cared about him. He could see it in her eyes every time she looked at him, except she hadn't met his eyes once since they'd arrived at the park.

"Look at me and tell me that's what you really want," he challenged. Until she did, he wouldn't be convinced.

For a couple beats of his heart, she kept staring out at the water. Then she turned and met his eyes. Hers were clear and unblinking.

"I want us to be over, Matt." She had a toughness about her he'd never seen before.

His impulse was to try to get her to change her mind,

to tell her he loved her and nothing on earth would change that, not even the terrible secret she wouldn't tell him. But now that she'd met his challenge, he couldn't.

Matt needed to accept her at her word even though his heart felt like it was being trampled by an elephant.

It really was over.

THE REMNANT OF the old bridge was deserted except for the lone fisherman halfway across the broken span, his pole leaning against the railing, the fishing line dangling perhaps fifteen feet to the water below.

Sadie hadn't seen another car since she'd gotten out of her little red Kia on Monday afternoon and started walking across the bridge. Even though she wasn't even ten miles from work, Sadie wouldn't have known this place existed if she hadn't followed Carl's pickup here.

She wouldn't have pegged Carl as a fisherman, either, but then she knew very little about him.

He didn't let on that he was aware of her approach but she'd seen his head turn at the slam of her car door. She pulled back her shoulders and thrust out her chest anyway, strutting like she was wearing spike heels and a little red dress instead of her waitress uniform and soft-soled shoes.

Her mama always said nobody could tell you were faking it if you were flaunting it.

"Hey, Carl," she drawled when she was twenty feet away. Might as well pretend meeting on this John's Island bridge wasn't unusual. "Are the fish biting?"

His dark gaze flickered to her, then returned to the

water. An egret flew overhead. She could smell salt water and the earthy scent of plough mud.

"I get here right before you," he said. "You almost lose me back at Highway 17."

She'd followed him on a whim as they were both leaving the parking lot after work. She hadn't switched over to the left lane quickly enough when he'd turned onto a side road. But luckily, after she'd made a U-turn, the road had led straight to this old bridge.

The sun beat down on them, making it feel warmer than the seventy degrees she'd heard it was on the radio. Sadie needed her deodorant to do yeoman's duty, but that was more because of her nerves than the temperature.

"It's a beautiful day, isn't it?" Sadie raised her face to the sun.

Carl didn't respond, which was the way things had gone at work, too. She'd make a comment about something that happened this past weekend and hear only silence. Usually either Jazz or Carl said at least a few words in response. Today Jazz had been preoccupied with something she didn't want to talk about. And Carl, who wasn't a chatterbox at the best of times, didn't even smile and chuckle like he usually did when Sadie blathered on.

She had an awful feeling it was because she still hadn't given him her decision about the Lady Gaga concert. She hadn't even mentioned it since last Wednesday, and that was five days ago.

"How was the football game on Friday?" Sadie had been meaning to ask him that question all day. She'd know herself if she hadn't phoned Carl to cancel at the eleventh hour. "Did your nephew get to play quarterback?"

"Faircrest win," Carl said. "Arthur, he play whole game."

"That's fantastic!" Sadie said. Carl had to be pleased even though he didn't sound like it. From everything she'd heard, Carl was like a second father to Arthur. "Isn't that fantastic, Carl?"

"Yes," Carl said in a voice devoid of emotion. "Is fantastic."

Sadie couldn't ignore his dismissive tone any longer.

"Are you mad at me about something, Carl?" she ventured.

He yanked back his fishing pole but she hadn't seen anything tug at the line. After a moment, he rested the pole in its previous position against the railing. "Why I be mad?"

Enough, Sadie thought, was enough. She balanced her fists on her hips and closed the distance between them so they were almost touching.

"Why, I don't know, Carl," she huffed. "Maybe because you ignored me all day until I felt like I had to follow you all the way out here to this bridge in the middle of nowhere and now you won't say two words to me."

He continued gazing out at the water.

A car, at long last, passed on the road adjacent to the old bridge. It needed a new muffler and more horsepower. Carl probably couldn't have made himself heard over the noise, but Sadie wasn't in the mood to give him the benefit of the doubt.

"Well? Say something!" she demanded.

Carl finally met her eyes. His were dark and unfathomable.

Sadie braced herself to be verbally slammed for wavering about the Lady Gaga concert.

"If you don't want to go to football game, you say so," Carl said. "You don't make up story that Benjy is sick."

"That's what all this is about?" Sadie's voice was loud enough it would have drowned out the bad muffler if the car wasn't already gone. "You didn't believe me when I said Benjy was sick?"

Carl nodded. *"Sí."*

She thumped him once on the chest. "Benjy threw up twice on Friday. It turned out he'd eaten a whole bag of candy and about a gazillion potato chips but I didn't know that at the time."

"You really think he sick?" Carl still sounded doubtful, damn him.

"I really thought he was sick." Sadie had to wait for her temper to cool. "So now can we go back to being friends again?"

"You and me," Carl said, "we not friends."

"Of course we're friends! Why would you say something like that?"

"You and Jazz talk about why I went to prison," he said. "But you say nothing to me."

"Jazz told you that?"

"Jazz say I should explain to you," he said. "Is explanation what you want?"

Sadie was never less sure of anything in her life. She nodded anyway. "Sure."

"I go to bar," Carl said. "I have drink. I get in fight. I kill a man."

He returned his attention to the fish that weren't biting. His chin was raised, and his profile looked strong and noble.

Had Carl killed a man in self-defense, as Jazz had claimed? Or had he gotten drunk and violent, as he'd just suggested? Sadie would have to make up her own mind because it was clear that was as much of an explanation as she was getting.

She needed some space and distance to sort out everything in her mind but she couldn't leave yet. Carl hadn't mentioned the concert but it lay between them, unseen but in the way. Sadie couldn't keep him waiting on her answer any longer.

"About the concert invitation…" She paused, not sure what she was going to say. Jazz had advised her to take a chance.

Could she?

"There is no invitation," Carl said. "I take it back."

"You can't take it back!"

"I just do." If Carl had crossed his arms over his chest and thrust out his lower lip, he couldn't have sounded any more stubborn. "I already buy tickets, so you can have them. You go with someone else."

"But I don't want to go with someone else." The certainty that coursed through Sadie was so absolute, she couldn't believe it had been so long in coming. "I want to go with you."

"Too late," Carl said.

"It most certainly is not too late." Sadie grabbed him by the front of his shirt and turned him away from his fishing pole. Carl still smelled like the pancakes they served at work but Sadie happened to really like pancakes. "This thing between us, it's just starting."

His expression didn't soften one bit. "What thing?"

"Carl Rodriguez, do I really have to explain it?" Sadie was getting that tingly feeling she'd started experiencing when she was around Carl. The difference was this time she wouldn't fight it.

He nodded once.

She pulled down his head and claimed his mouth. As sensation flooded her and she melted into a kiss as rich as fine wine, she discovered kissing Carl was something she should have done a long time ago.

CHAPTER FOURTEEN

JAZZ PUMPED HER ARMS and lengthened her stride later that Monday afternoon, ignoring the stitch in her side and the ache in her legs.

She usually stopped running about a block before she reached the parking lot of her apartment building and walked the rest of the way home to cool down.

Not today. Today she considered blowing on by. Except the stitch was getting worse and her breathing was louder than the music at some rock concerts.

She reached the outer edge of the parking lot and slowed. Exercising until she collapsed wouldn't serve any good purpose. She'd still have dumped the man she loved—and she'd still be an ex-con who had no right to be around her children, no matter how much she loved them, too.

A heaviness came over her limbs, weighing them down, making it feel as if she were moving through quicksand.

A woman passed by in her PT Cruiser, beeping the horn and waving from the car's open window. It was Jazz's next-door neighbor Gabriela de la Cruz, dressed in her nurse's uniform, heading for work on the hospital pediatric floor. Jazz had finally introduced herself and learned her neighbor's name and precisely what Gabriela did for a living.

"Jazz! Over here!"

The shout came not from Gabriela's car, but from the apartment complex parking lot. Sadie was slipping through the parked cars, rushing toward Jazz. "I'm so lucky to have caught you."

Jazz didn't reciprocate the feeling. Initially she'd been eager to get to Pancake Palace after her emotional weekend, to take her mind off the breakup, but work this morning had been another sort of ordeal.

Sadie had kept chattering at Carl even though the other short-order cook had said nothing in return. Jazz nearly yelled at the waitress to open her eyes and see what she was doing to the poor guy.

"I was driving home when I got to the turn for your place." Sadie talked as she approached the sidewalk. "Before I knew it, here I was."

Jazz bent at the waist and braced her hands on her thighs above her knees while she tried to catch her breath from her hard run. Sadie didn't seem to notice that Jazz hadn't greeted her.

"I need to ask a favor." Sadie had finally reached her. She sounded almost as winded as Jazz.

Jazz raised her head without changing her position. "Is this about Carl?"

"Why, yes," Sadie said.

Jazz straightened, closing a few steps until she was directly in front of Sadie. "I held back last time when you asked for advice. This time I won't. Stop jerking him around!"

"What? But I'm not!"

"Carl is a really good guy." Jazz had to stop herself from shoving her forefinger into Sadie's breastbone.

"He needs a woman who doesn't make him feel like a criminal."

Sadie, for once, didn't have a response.

"Carl picked a fight at a bar. Do you know with who?" Jazz didn't wait for Sadie to answer. "His brother-in-law. And do you know why? Because the bastard beat up his sister and broke her jaw and one of her arms."

Sadie gasped. "Carl killed his sister's husband?"

"He didn't mean to." Jazz no longer cared that it wasn't her story to tell. "But during the fight his brother-in-law fell against the corner of a table and cracked his skull."

"Oh, my gosh," Sadie said. "I didn't know that."

"I'll tell you something else you don't know." Jazz spoke in a raised voice. "The guy's family didn't shed any tears for him. You know that quarterback you watch on Fridays?"

"Arthur?" Sadie named the sophomore boy who had taken over as starter for the Faircrest football team.

"He's the dead guy's son," Jazz said. "Arthur doesn't even use his father's last name. The boy doesn't hold a thing against Carl. He's proud to be a Rodriguez."

"Because Carl was defending his mother," Sadie finished.

"That's right. I'm not saying what Carl did was right or that he shouldn't have gone to prison. But I am saying he's a good guy who's paid his dues."

Emotions chased across Sadie's face but Jazz couldn't identify them.

"So either go to the concert with Carl or tell him

you're not interested," Jazz said. "But if you reject him, don't do it because you're afraid of him."

"I'm not afraid of Carl," Sadie said, this time with her characteristic spunk. "And I already told him I'd go to the concert with him."

Jazz felt her mouth gape open. "You did? When?"

"About an hour ago," replied Sadie. "After work. I remembered what you said about taking a chance. And I took one."

"Without knowing what really happened in that bar?" Jazz challenged. Surely Carl must have told her.

"That's right. I guess I didn't need to know the details. Just like I don't need to know what you did."

The fight went out of Jazz. "Not everybody is that open-minded."

"Then shame on them." Sadie tilted her head to the side. "So don't you want to know why I'm here?"

"You said you were here about Carl," Jazz reminded her.

"I am. Sort of," Sadie said. "I need a new outfit for the Lady Gaga concert on Saturday. Will you go shopping with me? The sooner, the better."

Jazz had never been shopping with another woman in her adult life. The prospect sounded like it would be—she could hardly believe the word that popped into her head—fun.

"I can go after work any day as long as we're finished by five," Jazz said. The weekday start time at her telemarketing job was still six o'clock.

"Let's go tomorrow! We can get you something new, too. Something that'll make Matt drool."

Just the mention of Matt's name caused Jazz to flinch.

"Matt and I aren't dating anymore." The words came out in a rush, surprising Jazz. She hadn't intended to tell the waitress about the breakup.

"I knew at work today that something was wrong!" Sadie put a hand on Jazz's arm, her brows drawing together, her eyes turning huge. "What happened?"

A lump formed in Jazz's throat. "I can't talk about it."

Sadie's entire focus was on Jazz, as though nothing was more important than Jazz's heartache. "Of course you can, honey."

That was all it took. The story poured from Jazz. She couldn't tell Sadie everything but she could relay part of it. The girl at the farmer's market who'd asked about her crime. The realization that everybody at Faircrest High was gossiping about Matt dating an ex-con. Her fear that she could cost Matt his chance to run the athletic department.

"Oh, sweetie." Sadie rubbed her arm. "And you think Matt was about to tell you he loved you?"

Jazz nodded sadly. Without another word, Sadie enveloped her in a hug, patting her gently on the back.

"You shouldn't hug me," Jazz said, sniffing. "I'm sweaty."

"Doesn't matter." Sadie continued to hold her. "You need some comfort before I tell you you're an idiot."

Jazz pulled back. "Excuse me?"

"You're an idiot, Jazz Lenox." Sadie balanced her hands on her hips in that feisty way of hers. "You don't give up the love of your life because people are gossiping about you."

"The gossip's true," Jazz countered.

"It most certainly is not true that you're the kiss of death because you've been in prison," Sadie said. "Isn't that what you just got through telling me about Carl?"

Jazz shook her head. "It's not the same. Nobody's job is in jeopardy if you date Carl."

"Shouldn't Matt get to decide whether you're more important to him than a job?" Sadie asked. "You're a good person, Jazz. It's time you realized that."

Matt had said something along those lines on more than one occasion. Were both Matt and Sadie right? Was it time Jazz forgave herself for her past and went after her future?

Her heart hammered. Could she go to Matt and apologize? Plead her case by telling him she loved him? Live happily ever after with the uncle of her biological twins?

Her hopes plummeted, and reality crashed over her like one of the ocean waves at Folly Beach. Yes, the impetus to breaking up with Matt had been the gossip. The underlying reason went far deeper.

Sadie was looking at her expectantly, waiting for an answer.

"You don't understand," Jazz said.

"Then explain it to me."

Jazz envisioned Brooke and Robbie's dear little faces. She remembered Matt telling her he'd advised his sister to insist on a closed adoption. She heard Bill Smith saying he wouldn't take a DNA test, insisting it was best to leave well enough alone.

"I can't."

No matter how much it hurt, the best thing Jazz could do for Matt and the twins was to stay out of their lives.

WITH KICKOFF STILL twenty minutes away, the stands at the Faircrest High football game were nearly full on Friday night, the crowd buzzing with anticipation. If the Falcons pulled off the victory, they'd clinch home-field advantage for the playoffs.

Matt scanned the faces in the stands from the sideline of the field, noticing his father and Principal Middleton next to each other, deep in conversation. He continued his perusal until he located what he thought was the right section.

Yes, there were Carl Rodriguez and Sadie's son, Benjy, with their heads angled together. Carl was pointing out something on the field, where the teams were going through warm-ups. Neither Sadie nor Jazz were with them.

"Matt!" It was a female voice, loud enough to be heard over the rumbling of the crowd. "Matt!"

Sadie stood on the other side of the fence that partitioned the field from the spectators' area. Matt looked to the right of Sadie, to the left of her and behind her. She was alone.

He masked his disappointment and joined her at the fence. She wore jeans with a Faircrest High sweatshirt and carried boxes of popcorn and bottled water.

"Hey, Sadie," he said. "Ready for the game?"

"Oh, yes! My son and I are here with Carl." She pointed to the area of the stands Matt had already scouted out. "We love watching Arthur play. He's so exciting!"

"Nobody will argue with you there." Danny had been one of the prime beneficiaries of Arthur Rodriguez's stellar play. Danny was averaging about three catches a game, a good number for a high school wide receiver.

"I asked Jazz to come along but she said no," Sadie announced. "I knew you were wondering."

No use in denying what Sadie had found so obvious. "Thanks."

"I probably shouldn't tell you this," Sadie began. "Okay, I definitely shouldn't tell you this, but Jazz is hurting. She misses you."

Hope leapt inside Matt before reality stomped it back down. "Jazz broke up with me."

"She told me," Sadie said, which was a surprise. Matt had seen firsthand how carefully Jazz guarded her privacy. "She was afraid she'd cost you your job."

"There's more to it than that." Matt couldn't stop wondering about the terrible secret Jazz claimed she could never tell him. "Jazz was very clear she didn't want to see me again."

"That doesn't make sense, Matt. Believe me, she's torn up about the whole thing. I can tell."

"Hey there, little brother." Terry appeared beside Sadie at the fence, carrying multiple soft-drink cans. She smiled at Sadie. "Sorry to interrupt but I need to tell Matt his niece's soccer game tomorrow morning was switched to eleven."

Matt did some quick mental calculations. He already knew he'd have to miss Robbie's game, which was scheduled for the same early morning hour as his own. He should be able to catch the end of Brooke's, though.

"Thanks, Terry," Matt said. "This is Sadie. She works at Pancake Palace with Jazz. Sadie, my sister, Terry."

"Oh! A friend of Jazz's! Nice to meet you," Terry said. "Isn't it just awful about her and Matt breaking up?"

"Yes! We were just talking about that." Sadie and Terry didn't resemble each other except in speech patterns, where they were eerily similar. They'd probably make great friends. "In fact, I was going to tell Matt if he wanted to run into Jazz accidentally on purpose he should come to the Harvest Festival tomorrow."

"I've heard about that festival! It's supposed to be wonderful," Terry said. "Don't three or four elementary schools get together and put it on?"

"Right," Sadie said. "It's gotten so big we're holding it at Ashley Greens Park this year. My son Benjy's so excited. I'm in charge of the apple pie bake-off, and I talked Jazz into being one of the judges."

"I make a terrific apple pie," Terry boasted.

The Faircrest High fight song blared from the stands behind Sadie and Terry, where the marching band had set up. Terry pointed to her ear, then waved at Matt. He got the message that more conversation was fruitless, although the two women managed to talk to each other as they headed toward the stands.

Sadie had already revealed the most pertinent piece of information, anyway. Jazz was upset over dumping him.

That welcome thought stayed with Matt throughout the entire game, a squeaker that Faircrest won in the last minute when Arthur Rodriguez broke free and outraced the defense for a thirty-five-yard touchdown.

Matt oversaw the celebration and helped supervise the exodus of fans until the stadium was empty except for the workers picking up trash and the parents closing up the concession stand. He ventured onto the field to retrieve a plastic bag blowing end-over-end in the wind, looked up and saw his father.

Matt waited where he was, plastic bag in hand, until his father reached him. "Dad. What are you still doing here?"

"I stayed to talk to my son."

"Danny?" Matt asked. His brother, who'd made a gorgeous over-the-shoulder catch for a touchdown in the first half, probably hadn't left the locker room yet.

"No, not Danny, although that was some fantastic catch." His father's chest puffed out the way it always did when he discussed Danny and football. "I need to talk to you."

"Where's Mom?" Matt asked. His mother made it a point not to miss any of the games her children played, whether it be football or soccer.

"She got a ride home with friends." His father gestured to the home team's bench. "These knees are aching. Mind if we sit?"

"Of course not." Matt was aware of the damage football had done to his father's knees, as was everybody with more than a passing acquaintance to Len Caminetti.

"Don't look so serious, son." His father's chest was

still sticking out. "Ray told me tonight he's going to offer you the A.D. job permanently."

Matt had the answer to what his father and Principal Ray Middleton had been discussing during the game.

"This is what we've worked for." His father slapped him on the back. "It's great news, isn't it?"

"Yes," Matt agreed.

"Then why don't you look happy about it?"

Because now that Matt was on the verge of achieving his goal of becoming the head of the athletic department, the reality of giving up coaching the high school soccer team sunk in. He'd have to surrender the head coaching job on the youth team, too. There simply weren't enough hours in his day to do everything.

But of course Matt had known all along he'd have to pay a price for success.

"I am happy," Matt said, not sure he believed that.

"Me, too," his father said. "I'm proud, too."

Matt's heart swelled. He'd been waiting to hear those words for a lifetime.

"It was a stroke of luck that I ran into Ray tonight," his father continued, seemingly unaware that he'd just told Matt he was proud of him for the first time in his life. "He didn't know you weren't dating Jazz anymore."

Everything inside Matt stilled. "How did you know about that?"

"Your sister," his father answered. "She called and asked you to double date and you told her you broke up."

"So you're saying I wouldn't be offered the job if I was still dating Jazz?" Matt asked.

His father nodded. "That's the impression I got."

"What if I got Jazz back?" Matt hadn't consciously realized he meant to try until this minute. The decision must have been percolating for some time. It went against Matt's nature to give up on the woman he loved, especially because he was almost positive she loved him in return. She'd done something she thought was unforgivable but he'd make her understand that nothing could make him stop loving her. "What then?"

His father's eyes narrowed. "Considering all the flak Ray has been getting, I expect he'd hire someone else and you'd go back to being assistant A.D."

"You wouldn't like that, would you, Dad?" Matt asked.

Deep furrows appeared in his father's forehead. "You wouldn't like it, either. You're a go-getter. I can't see you continuing to work under someone else."

"You're right," Matt said. "I don't want to be assistant A.D."

His father let out a deep breath. "Good, then it's settled."

"I think it is," Matt said slowly, "because I don't want to be the A.D., either."

"For cripes' sake, son! Is this about that woman? Now, don't get me wrong, I like Jazz. Everybody in the family does. But you don't even know if you can get her back!"

"I still don't want to be the A.D. at Faircrest," Matt said, surprising himself as much as his father. The sentiment had been brewing for months but this was the first time he'd admitted it to himself.

"What? Where's this coming from?"

Matt thumped the area over his heart. "Right here. I'm not cut out for school politics. I don't want to be, either."

"But…but what will you do?"

"I don't know yet, Dad. I need some time to think about it." Matt shrugged. "Who knows? I might coach soccer full-time. Would you be proud of me then?"

"I…I…" His father threw up his hands. "What does me being proud of you have to do with anything?"

"A lot." Matt rose and looked down at his father. "You should have told me you were proud of me before today, Dad."

"I did!" His father scratched his head. "Didn't I?"

"Not once," Matt said. "But you know what? I've come to realize something. I love you, Dad. But I've gotta stop thinking about what would make you happy and do what makes *me* happy."

Getting back together with Jazz was the first item on Matt's list. The prospect would have seemed unlikely a few short hours ago. It didn't anymore.

All that was left was to figure out how to go about it.

CHAPTER FIFTEEN

MATT CUPPED HIS HANDS around the sides of his mouth the following morning, enabling him to yell louder than anyone else watching the youth soccer game. He was even getting more volume than Terry.

One of his niece's teammates had just sent the ball squirting down the right side of the field with a pretty kick. If Brooke caught up to the rolling ball, she'd have a terrific scoring opportunity.

"Go, Brooke!" Matt shouted. "Dig deep!"

The game was tied at one goal apiece. Time had already been running short when Matt arrived after coaching his own team to a tie. There couldn't have been more than a minute left, probably even less.

"Run faster, Brooke!" Matt bellowed.

His niece had such exceptional speed that she could beat most boys her age in a footrace, one of the reasons the coach had moved her from goal to the field. Yet Brooke appeared to be out for a jog. Her red ponytail was barely swishing.

The opposing team's defender was an average mover at best. The defender outraced Brooke to the ball and booted it to midfield. The referee lifted his wrist and checked the time on his watch. He put the whistle hanging from a lanyard around his neck to his mouth and blew three times. The game was over.

"You'll get 'em next time, Brooke," Terry yelled.

Matt thought his niece could have gotten 'em *this* time. The girl didn't seem to realize that. Brooke slapped palms with opposing team members, grinning like she'd gotten the game winner. She skipped to the sidelines where one of the mothers was handing out juice boxes.

"Pacific cooler!" Brooke enthused. "My favorite flavor!"

She was clearly more excited about the juice than she had been the scoring opportunity. Matt couldn't relate. At Brooke's age, he'd been so in love with soccer he'd rejoiced after every win and taken losses hard. He still adored the game.

Did Brooke even like soccer? The possibility that she might not had never entered Matt's mind until Jazz raised the subject at the Coastal Carolina Fair. Matt had rejected the notion then but a seed of doubt had taken root. Now it sprouted.

Ask her, Jazz had advised.

He broke away from Terry, who was talking to some other parents, and sidled up to his niece. "Hey, Brooke."

The girl's smile disappeared. She hung her head.

Matt frowned. "What's the matter?"

"You're disappointed in me, aren't you?" Brooke spoke so softly he had to strain to hear her.

"No! Of course not! Why would you say that?"

"I heard you yelling," she said.

Matt patted her gently on the head. "I was only yelling because I wanted you to do your best."

She nodded, although she must have been aware she hadn't put forth her top effort.

"Do you like soccer, Brooke?" Matt voiced the question he should have asked before suggesting she take up the game.

She scuffed her feet in the grass before gazing up at him with troubled green eyes. "I like dancing."

"But not soccer?" he persisted.

Very slowly, Brooke shook her head back and forth. Matt got a sick feeling in his gut.

"I don't understand," he said. "Why didn't you ever tell me that before?"

"You never asked," Brooke said.

Matt's stomach heaved when he thought of all the times he'd taken the twins to the park to work on their soccer games. He'd assumed they wanted to go. That was probably true of Robbie. But had he pushed Brooke into taking up the game he loved?

Terry came toward them, carrying a small bag of pretzels another of the mothers had supplied for an after-game treat. Terry looked from Brooke to Matt. "Something wrong?"

Matt might as well admit he was the problem. "I just realized I'm kind of pushy."

"Well, duh," Terry said. "You *just* realized that?"

"Yeah." Matt hadn't accepted the label when Jazz pinned it on him. Now he couldn't avoid it. "That's not all. I think Brooke wants to quit soccer and take up dancing."

"Really?" Terry seemed as surprised as he'd been. "Is that true, honey?"

Brooke nodded solemnly.

"I never knew you wanted to dance," Terry said, frowning. "Why didn't you tell me?"

The little girl chewed on her lower lip before answering. "I thought everybody wanted me to be a soccer player."

"Oh, Brooke." Terry hugged her daughter to her. "Your dad and I want you to do what makes you happy. Uncle Matt, too. If that's dancing, that's fine with us."

"Really?" Brooke appeared not to trust her ears.

"Really." Terry smiled down at her daughter. "There's only two soccer games left. As soon as the season's over, we'll find a dance studio. How does that sound?"

"It sounds great!" Brooke jumped up and down with considerably more energy than she'd shown on the field. The field she wouldn't have been on if not for Matt.

Because Matt's father wasn't the only one in the family who could be overbearing.

"Wait 'til I tell Heather and Caroline." Brooke ran off toward a group of teammates.

"Well, that was unexpected." Terry spoke to Matt but her gaze followed her daughter. Brooke used expansive hand gestures as she talked to a cluster of other little girls, then executed a nearly perfect pirouette. Terry laughed. "How did you figure out Brooke wasn't happy playing soccer?"

"I didn't," Matt said. "Jazz did."

"Yet another reason to get her back." Terry's lightning-quick change of subjects might have confounded strangers, but Matt was family. He was used to it. "So what's your plan?"

Matt had intended to show up at Jazz's door with flowers—azaleas, like the ones stenciled on her bedroom wall. He was going to convince her no secret could change the way he felt about her by pulling her into his arms and kissing her until she believed him. But in light of what he'd accepted about himself, pushing his way back into her life seemed like a bad idea.

"What makes you think I have a plan?" Matt asked.

Terry snorted. "You're kidding me, right? I grew up with you, remember? You always figure out a way to come out a winner."

"Love isn't a competition, Terry," he said.

"Wow." Terry pronounced the exclamation as though it had two syllables. "I didn't think you knew that."

The lesson was a tough one for Matt to digest. During the drive home, he had to fight the urge to go to Jazz. Maybe if he had an inkling of what horrible thing she'd supposedly done, he could find a way to accept that she'd dumped him. But how could he discover her secret?

Matt kicked off his shoes and powered up his laptop as soon as he was inside his town house. Searching for answers about Jazz on the internet was a long shot, but it was his only idea.

The last time he'd typed *Jazz Lenox* into a search engine, he'd come up empty. He tried a new tactic, entering the name of the Graham Correctional Institution. At the very least, he could learn more about the women's prison where Jazz had spent five years of her life.

He clicked on the first result that appeared and learned that level-three facilities like Graham were designed to house violent offenders and inmates who exhibited behavioral problems.

So why had Jazz been incarcerated there?

Returning to the list of results, Matt scanned through a few screenfuls of hits before clicking on a link to a newspaper feature story about the facility.

The story focused on special-needs prisoners, touching on the mentally and physically disabled, but spending the most time on pregnant inmates. Matt skimmed through the narrative. He was about to click out of the story when his attention was snagged by an anecdote about a young woman who'd given birth in prison.

She couldn't stop crying even though she knew adoption was the right decision. The quote was from the doctor who'd performed the delivery. *It was heartbreaking. Imagine being eighteen and having to give up your twins.*

Twins? Matt backed up a few paragraphs. The unnamed young woman had no family outside the prison walls. She'd been serving a five-year sentence for an unspecified crime. Her twins were fraternal, a girl and a boy.

Matt's pulse beat so hard and heavy he could feel it reverberating inside him. He scrolled to the top of the story and checked the date. It had been published eight years ago.

Brooke and Robbie were eight years old.

He mentally replayed his relationship with Jazz, focusing on the time they'd spent with his niece and nephew. In his mind's eye, he pictured Jazz's long nose, her widow's peak, her lean build. The children shared those characteristics.

Could Jazz be the twins' birth mother? Was that the secret Jazz was so sure Matt couldn't forgive?

Matt's mind raced. If he were right, it would explain so many things. He jumped to his feet and headed out the door without bothering to turn off the computer.

His destination was the Harvest Festival.

IF JAZZ ATE ONE more bite of apple pie, she might go into sugar shock. That wouldn't be doing the organizer of the bake-off any favors. Sadie was flitting from judge to judge inside the tent where the entries had been arranged on a long table. Each of the four people Sadie had lined up to rate the pies held a scoresheet.

"Hey, girl." Sadie hovered near Jazz, reminding Jazz of a hummingbird who couldn't keep still. "Have I told you how great you look? That yellow top is super cute."

"Thanks." Jazz didn't point out that Sadie had chosen it on their shopping trip while insisting Jazz needed more color in her wardrobe. Jazz was too busy chewing a sample of apple pie that was heavy on the cinnamon.

"Have you picked a winner yet?" Sadie asked Jazz for the third time. "It's almost time to award the ribbons."

Jazz swallowed, gave the cinnamon-rich entry a semifavorable rating and handed Sadie her completed scoresheet. "Here you go. But you really need to relax. You're not announcing the winners for another thirty minutes."

"I know that. It's just that this is my first time in charge and I want everything to be perfect." Sadie sucked in a breath through her teeth. "You couldn't tell which pie Terry baked, right? Because that would be bad. Bias, you know?"

"Terry?" Jazz repeated. "Matt's sister?"

"Didn't I tell you Matt introduced us at the high school football game last night?" Sadie scrunched up her nose. "No, I guess I didn't. Anyway, Terry entered a pie. She's here somewhere with her husband and these adorable redheaded kids."

Brooke and Robbie.

Jazz fought the urge to rush from the tent and scour the festival, just to get another look at the twins. She closed her eyes briefly. Would this longing never go away? Not only for the children, but for their uncle, too?

"Speaking of Matt, there he is!" Sadie exclaimed.

"What?" Jazz whipped toward the direction Sadie was pointing.

Matt stood just inside the tent, looking tall and muscular in jeans and a T-shirt with his golden-brown hair appealingly disheveled. His eyes locked with hers, and Jazz fought a wave of love.

Without breaking eye contact, Matt walked past the other female judges directly to where Jazz stood at the end of the table. Her heart leaped and her stomach fluttered.

His gaze didn't waver from her face. "Hey, Jazz."

She fought to compose herself, praying he wouldn't notice the reaction he was having on her. She couldn't let him challenge her assertion that she wanted him out of her life. She cleared her throat. "Hey, Matt."

"Sadie, can I borrow your judge for a few minutes?" Matt addressed Sadie but kept looking at Jazz.

It didn't take many brain cells to figure out Sadie had been culpable in informing Matt that Jazz would be judging the apple pie bake-off. But why was Matt here after Jazz made it clear they were through?

"Sure can. Jazz's judging duties are done." Sadie held up the completed scoresheet, then winked at Jazz before heading off to check on another judge.

Jazz gazed at Matt, drinking in the sight of him. She yearned to tell him that just this morning she'd reevaluated what the restaurateur at Charles Towne Flair had told her and started researching culinary institutes. She wanted to say she was stronger for having known him, that she was ready to take some chances with her life and that, above all, she missed him.

Except she couldn't, not when she harbored the secret she could never reveal.

"We don't have anything to talk about, Matt."

"I think we do," he said. "I'm here about Brooke and Robbie."

Jazz's throat constricted and it felt like a strong hand clutched her heart. Could Matt know? Impossible. Nobody knew.

"Let's go outside where we'll have some privacy," he suggested in a quiet voice.

The other judges were milling about the tent, some still sampling pieces of apple pie, some talking to Sadie, others looking at Matt. Jazz nodded toward the back entrance of the tent. Every step Jazz took felt like an eternity, like she was walking a plank. She wondered if a plunge were coming.

Once they were outside they stood facing each other, with a few feet between them. The air smelled of freshly mowed grass and the sun was directly overhead, warming what would otherwise be a cool October day. Although they had relative privacy behind the tent, the area was within sight of arts-and-crafts booths, a pumpkin patch and a hoop-toss game that had been set up for kids.

Children shouted and laughter rang out but the sounds seemed muted, the silence between Jazz and Matt deafening. Jazz couldn't stand it another minute.

"What about Brooke and Robbie?" she blurted out.

Matt's gaze bore into her, as though he were trying to see inside her soul. Time seemed to stretch, although it was probably only a few seconds before his lips parted to speak. "Are you their birth mother?"

Jazz gasped, stunned that he obviously knew every last thing about her. "Why would you ask such a thing?"

"Just answer the question, Jazz."

Denying the truth would be pointless. Somehow he'd found out her secret. Jazz braced herself, but how can you prepare for the man you love to hate you?

"Yes," she said.

He continued to stare at her, his expression unreadable. Her mind reeled with memories, thoughts, questions of her own.

"How did you know?" she managed to ask on a strangled breath, although that hardly mattered. He *knew*.

"I wasn't sure until you confirmed it." His voice was a monotone.

"I can explain." Jazz shook her head at the absurdity of her claim. Nothing she said would justify the inexcusable. But she had to try. "I promised myself to never search for them. And I didn't. That day in the park was a fluke."

She cleared her throat, willing herself to continue. "Red hair runs in my family. Even at birth, my twins were redheads. But stumbling across them like that was such a long shot I convinced myself I was wrong, that they couldn't be who I thought they were."

"When did you know you weren't wrong?" Matt still spoke with no emotion. His handsome face looked chiseled, his expression giving away nothing.

"At the adoption-day party. When Robbie said his birthday was July twenty-fourth." Jazz wiped her damp palms on her slacks. If her heart beat any faster, it might give out. "I wasn't really sick that day. I left the party early because I was determined to stay out of their lives."

Matt gave no indication whether he believed her. If she were on the receiving end of the story, she might not believe it herself.

"Who's their father?" Matt asked softly.

"My ex-boyfriend, Luke. The guy who held up the convenience store."

"Did you tell him you found them?" Matt asked. A legitimate question.

"Luke never knew I was pregnant. He died in a prison knife fight before I could tell him." Jazz had never revealed the father's identity to anyone. It hadn't been necessary. "Luke was a foster child like me. He didn't have family, either."

Matt didn't reply. Jazz couldn't stand the thought that he was thinking ill of her.

"I know what you're going to say. That I used you to be around Brooke and Robbie." Jazz raised a hand so he wouldn't interrupt. "I don't blame you for believing that. They're great kids." She sniffed and blinked away the burning sensation behind her eyes. She would not cry. "No, they're terrific kids. But it's not true."

"I know." Matt took a step closer to her.

Jazz didn't understand. "That they're terrific kids?"

"No," Matt said, coming closer still. Delicate laugh lines rimmed his mouth and eyes but she'd never seen him more serious. "I know you didn't use me to be around the twins."

"You do?" Jazz had been so sure Matt would never forgive her for keeping her identity secret that it was almost too much to process.

He reached across the chasm between them and took her hand. She wondered if he felt hers shaking.

"You wouldn't have tried so hard to avoid my family if you were using me," Matt said. "It's clear to me now that you were avoiding the twins."

"Only because I didn't feel like I had the right to be around them." Jazz felt compelled to tell him everything no matter the cost to herself. "I never wanted them to find out about the criminals in their birth family."

"You were never a criminal, Jazz." Matt squeezed her hand. "You made some poor decisions, sure, but you were in the wrong place at the wrong time."

Matt was giving her an out, the way he'd done so many times before. The difference was that now Jazz believed him. The pressure in her chest lessened but didn't entirely abate.

"You were right about me. I wouldn't reach for the things I wanted because deep down I didn't believe I deserved them." Jazz took a deep breath. "I'm going to change that, Matt. Because of you."

"I'm glad," Matt said.

Silence reigned between them even though there was much more to say. Matt still held her hand in his warm grip. Jazz had the crazy wish that she could freeze this moment. Even though the impossible had happened and he'd forgiven her, the heartbreaking fact was that they still had no future together.

"Aren't you going to ask why I think you were with me?" Matt asked softly.

He was treading on perilous ground. Jazz shook her head, silently imploring him to leave it alone.

"I think you were with me because you love me." Matt's voice was a soft, sexy purr. "If I'm wrong, tell me now. Because if you don't, I'm going to kiss you."

Jazz slipped her hand from his and turned her head. She'd told him nothing but the truth up to this point. Could she bring herself to lie about her feelings for him?

"Jazz?" He sounded unsure of himself, which stabbed at her heart. Matt was meant to exude confidence, no matter how maddening that could sometimes be. Lying to him wasn't an option.

"I won't be the reason you get passed over for the A.D. job," Jazz said.

"Not going to happen," Matt replied. "I got offered the job yesterday, and I turned it down."

"What?" How was that possible? Since Jazz had met him, Matt had been working toward that goal. "Why would you do that? Please say it wasn't because of me."

"It was and it wasn't," he said. "It burned me up to be put in a position where I had to defend you. But more than that, I realized I didn't want the job. I just wanted to please my father."

If Jazz hadn't witnessed the dynamic between Matt and his father, she might have suspected Matt of spinning the truth. But Matt's explanation made sense.

"Good for you." Jazz hoped that Len Caminetti would appreciate how difficult it must have been for Matt to reach that decision. Matt's father should applaud his son for forging his own path. "But what will you do now?"

"I'll stay on as assistant A.D. until the new hire gets on track, but in the meantime I'll be looking for another job that will allow me to keep coaching youth soccer." Matt smiled. "Turns out I'm stubborn as well as pushy. I don't want to give up coaching. But I refuse to give up the woman I love."

Moisture filled her eyes. Jazz blinked to clear her vision, and the face of the man she wanted to spend the rest of her life with came into focus.

"I love you, too." The words seemed to burst straight from her heart, too insistent to hold back.

Matt hauled her into his arms, claiming her mouth with a sweet familiarity that sent the blood pulsing through her veins. Jazz kissed him back with all her pent-up longing, savoring the sensations because she'd thought she'd never feel them again.

"Wow," Matt said when they broke for air. "I might not be able to take things slow if you keep kissing me like that."

"Why would you go slow?" Jazz asked.

Matt pointed to his chest. "Pushy. Remember? If you don't keep me in check, I might even ask you to marry me."

Because he was a family man.

Jazz drew back from Matt's arms as a realization spread through her with sickening clarity. A quality she loved about Matt could very well keep them apart.

"What's wrong?" Matt asked.

"We've got to tell your family, Matt," she said. "We especially have to tell Kevin and Terry."

"Tell us what?" Terry asked.

MATT'S SISTER WAS within a few feet of them, approaching from the back of the tent. Jazz had been so intent on Matt she hadn't paid attention to anything but him. Her stomach felt like it was going into a free fall.

"You're back together, aren't you?" Terry grinned. Without waiting for an answer, she called over her shoulder to her trailing husband. "Kevin, didn't I tell you Matt and Jazz would get back together?"

Kevin stopped at his wife's side. "Terry did tell me that."

"We want to hear all the details," Terry said, oblivious to what they had been discussing. "But first I'm supposed to tell you it's almost time to announce the winner of the bake-off. Sadie sent me out here to give you a ten-minute warning."

"That's not why I'm here," Kevin said. "I came to

ask if Matt knew whether anybody at this festival was selling beer."

"Forget about beer," Terry admonished. "We should bring out champagne to celebrate!"

Jazz summoned the strength to break in to the one-sided conversation. "Champagne's premature. I was just about to tell Matt I won't be with him if it will cause problems with his family."

Terry stopped smiling and tilted her head quizzically. "What problems? We all like you, Jazz. Even Dad likes you."

The moment Jazz had been trying to avoid since Robbie had told her his birth date had arrived. But before she could come up with the words to answer Terry, Matt gathered Jazz to his side with one arm. Even the warmth of his body couldn't chase away the chill of anxiety running through Jazz.

"Before this goes any further, I want you both to know I love Jazz. I'd like to have your approval, but I don't need it." Matt sounded sure of his position but Jazz couldn't bear for it to come to that.

Terry placed her hands on her hips. "Why wouldn't we approve?"

Jazz could have let Matt answer for her, but she was the one who'd put them all into this situation. It was time she faced the consequences.

"Brooke and Robbie are my biological children." Jazz was surprised that her voice sounded strong and clear. Terry gasped and Kevin's mouth hung open. Matt's arm tightened around Jazz, empowering her to continue. She quickly and succinctly went over the circumstances that had led them to this point. By the end of her story, Terry and Kevin stood with their shoulders touching, a vivid reminder that they were united.

"Why didn't you tell us this before?" Terry's voice trembled but didn't crack. "Don't you think we had a right to know?"

"I never thought it would get this far," Jazz said.

"I can vouch for that." Matt's arm was still secure around Jazz. "I know it's a lot to swallow but everything Jazz told you is true. She put the children first every step of the way. That's why she dumped me."

"What about now?" Terry asked, her voice wavering more than before. "What's going to happen now?"

The realization struck Jazz that Terry was afraid Jazz would try to take the twins from her. Jazz left Matt's side and laid a hand on Terry's arm, which felt stiff.

"Please believe I'd never do anything to hurt the twins or you," Jazz implored. "You've given them a wonderful life, much better than I could have. If you don't want them to know who I am, I'll go along with that. I'll do whatever you want. I'll even leave Charleston."

"Then I'll leave, too," Matt said.

Abruptly, Jazz turned around. Matt was steely-eyed, his lips set in a flat line. He would really leave his beloved hometown to be with her, she realized.

"That is, if Jazz will have me," Matt amended.

"Wait a minute!" Terry exclaimed. "Who said we wanted either of you to move away?"

"What we want you to do, Jazz, is take a DNA test." Kevin spoke like the lawyer he was. "We want to control when and how we let the children know who you are. That could be next week, next month, next year or not until they're eighteen."

Jazz nodded. Since meeting with Bill Smith, Jazz had changed her stance about keeping her identity secret from the twins. One day Brooke and Robbie would be curious about their birth parents, just as Jazz longed to know if Smith was her father.

"Like I said, I'll go along with whatever you decide," Jazz stated with as much sincerity as she could muster.

Terry looked at Jazz long and hard. "I believe you."

Kevin nodded once, signifying his agreement.

"Thank you for believing me," Jazz said. "I swear, I'll never undermine your role as parents or get in the way of your family."

"But aren't you going to be part of our family?" Terry asked. "Didn't Matt ask for our approval because he just proposed to you?"

"I can't propose yet." Matt gave Jazz a wry smile. "I have to let enough time go by for Jazz to know I'm not pushing her."

Jazz didn't give herself time to reconsider the question that popped into her mind. "What if I proposed to you?"

Matt's eyes widened. Jazz wasn't sure why she glanced over at Terry until the other woman's head moved in a barely perceptible nod. Only then did Jazz let herself dare to believe that everything might work out.

Jazz took Matt's hand in hers and the certainty that she was doing the right thing grew. Nothing had ever felt so right.

Before Jazz could speak, joyful shouts rang out.

Two red-haired children wearing blue jeans and long-sleeved T-shirts rushed toward them at a frenetic pace, then stopped dead. Color stained their cheeks. As always, Brooke and Robbie appeared to be happy, well-adjusted children. They also seemed a little perplexed.

"Why is Jazz holding Uncle Matt's hand like that?" Robbie asked, slightly breathless.

"Shhhh," Matt told his nephew. "Jazz is about to ask me to marry her."

"That's not the way it's supposed to be!" Brooke shouted. "Boys propose to girls!"

"What are you going to say, Uncle Matt?" Robbie asked.

"You heard your uncle, children!" Terry put a finger to her lips. "Shhhh."

Jazz gazed from Matt to his sister, brother-in-law, niece and nephew. Brooke and Robbie were beaming, their small faces alive with excitement. Terry and Kevin wore smiles that were more reserved.

"I guess there's no chance we can do this without an audience?" Jazz asked.

"No chance," Brooke answered.

"No chance," Robbie echoed.

"Okay, then," Jazz said. "Here goes."

She gazed into Matt's eyes, which had turned soft and serious. She took a mental snapshot, aware this was an occasion that would live forever in her memory. "I love you, Matt Caminetti. Will you marry me?"

"Say yes, Uncle Matt!" Robbie said.

"Yes!" Brooke added.

It seemed incredible that the most wrenching decision Jazz had ever made had brought her to this wonderful man and this incredible moment.

"Yes," Matt said.

EPILOGUE

Twenty months later

THE BABY GIRL had red hair.

Wispy tufts of it that appeared brown until the sunlight streamed through the hospital window and showed her true color.

"She's as lovely as her mother." Matt sat on the edge of the bed where Jazz lay propped against the pillows, their newborn daughter cradled in his arms.

After just over a year of marriage, Jazz was used to flattering comments from Matt. This was the most lavish compliment yet because Jazz had never gazed upon anything more beautiful than Ashley Lenox Caminetti. They'd named her after Ashley Greens Park, the place they'd met.

"Ashley does look like my side of the family." Jazz should have felt exhausted after fourteen hours of labor, but nothing compared to the high of bringing a new life into the world with the man you loved. She ran a light hand over the sleeping baby's head and breathed in her new-baby smell. "When Brooke and Robbie were born, they had the same thin red hair."

Matt traced the curve of the baby's cheek with a forefinger that looked disproportionately huge. Ashley's pale eyelashes fluttered and her mouth puckered before she settled back into a deep sleep.

"She's their cousin *and* their sister." Matt spoke in a soft voice. "Brooke and Robbie are two lucky kids."

"I'm the lucky one, marrying into a family as wonderful as yours," Jazz said.

Terry and Kevin had never restricted Jazz from spending time with the twins, even arranging for Jazz to take Brooke to dance class Monday nights and to pick Robbie up from soccer practice Tuesday afternoons.

By the time they'd sat the twins down a few months ago and told them Jazz was their birth mother, Brooke and Robbie had treated the revelation as no big deal. They already considered Jazz to be part of the family.

"You think my father is wonderful?" Matt asked with a raised eyebrow.

Jazz smothered her laugh so she wouldn't wake Ashley. Len Caminetti had more rough spots than an emery board.

"Your dad came to a Charleston Kicks game last month, didn't he?" Jazz didn't mention that it was the first game Len had attended since the pro soccer organization hired Matt two seasons ago. Matt's job was mainly administrative but he also trained the Kicks goalkeepers and still had time to coach youth soccer on the side. "I think Len is really trying to support you."

"He's trying to get us to invite him over to dinner more often." Matt winked at her. "My mom told me he brags to all his friends that his daughter-in-law is going to be a famous chef one day."

"I need to finish culinary arts school first." With another nine months left before she earned her associate's degree, enrolling in the program had already netted Jazz fabulous rewards. So far it didn't even matter that she was an ex-con. One of her professors had vouched for her at a downtown restaurant, helping Jazz get a part-time job as a kitchen's helper where she had gained valuable experience.

Jazz had no plans to do anything in the immediate future except care for Ashley and go to class, but her professional future looked bright. Everything, it seemed, was finally going her way. But only because she'd taken some chances. Maybe it was time to take another one, she decided.

"I'm going to call Bill Smith and ask him to reconsider taking the DNA test," Jazz announced. Voicing her plans cemented the fact that it was the right move. "You remember that Bill's a twin, right? When we talked to him in Beaufort, I never mentioned I'd given birth to twins. That might make a difference to him."

"It might not," Matt pointed out.

Jazz cocked an eyebrow at him. "Are you advising me not to take a chance?"

Matt shook his head. "Never. I'm the guy who goes after what he wants. That's why I have a gorgeous wife and a beautiful baby."

Ashley shifted in her sleep and let out a soft, sweet sigh. Matt and Jazz smiled at each other.

"Is it almost time for visiting hours?" Jazz asked him.

Matt checked his watch. "Only a few minutes until the invasion."

"I told you Sadie and Carl were coming, right?" Jazz

asked. "Sadie's dying to see the baby but she reminded me you haven't seen her engagement ring yet."

"I'll ooh and aah," Matt promised. "And did I tell *you* that Danny's coming with my mom and dad? And that Terry and Kevin are bringing Brooke and Robbie?"

As if on cue, laughter and loud conversation drifted down the hall. A whoop sounded followed by what sounded like two pairs of pounding footsteps.

"Brooke! Robbie!" Len Caminetti's voice carried into the room. "No running in the hospital!"

"Are you ready?" Matt asked in a singsong voice. "Because the gang's almost here."

Before Jazz had fallen in love with Matt and he convinced her to forgive herself for the past, Jazz had been alone. No more. In the crook of Matt's arms, their infant daughter opened green eyes that went well with her red hair.

I've come a long way, baby, Jazz thought.

"I'm ready," she said aloud.

* * * * *

COMING NEXT MONTH

Available July 12, 2011

REQUEST YOUR FREE BOOKS!
2 FREE NOVELS PLUS 2 FREE GIFTS!

Harlequin

Super Romance

Exciting, emotional, unexpected!

YES! Please send me 2 FREE Harlequin® Superromance® novels and my 2 FREE gifts (gifts are worth about $10). After receiving them, if I don't wish to receive any more books, I can return the shipping statement marked "cancel." If I don't cancel, I will receive 6 brand-new novels every month and be billed just $4.69 per book in the U.S. or $5.24 per book in Canada. That's a saving of at least 15% off the cover price! It's quite a bargain! Shipping and handling is just 50¢ per book in the U.S. and 75¢ per book in Canada.* I understand that accepting the 2 free books and gifts places me under no obligation to buy anything. I can always return a shipment and cancel at any time. Even if I never buy another book, the two free books and gifts are mine to keep forever.

135/336 HDN FC6T

Name	(PLEASE PRINT)	
Address		Apt. #
City	State/Prov.	Zip/Postal Code

Signature (if under 18, a parent or guardian must sign)

Mail to the Reader Service:
IN U.S.A.: P.O. Box 1867, Buffalo, NY 14240-1867
IN CANADA: P.O. Box 609, Fort Erie, Ontario L2A 5X3

Not valid for current subscribers to Harlequin Superromance books.

Are you a current subscriber to Harlequin Superromance books and want to receive the larger-print edition? Call 1-800-873-8635 or visit www.ReaderService.com.

* Terms and prices subject to change without notice. Prices do not include applicable taxes. Sales tax applicable in N.Y. Canadian residents will be charged applicable taxes. Offer not valid in Quebec. This offer is limited to one order per household. All orders subject to credit approval. Credit or debit balances in a customer's account(s) may be offset by any other outstanding balance owed by or to the customer. Please allow 4 to 6 weeks for delivery. Offer available while quantities last.

Your Privacy—The Reader Service is committed to protecting your privacy. Our Privacy Policy is available online at www.ReaderService.com or upon request from the Reader Service.

We make a portion of our mailing list available to reputable third parties that offer products we believe may interest you. If you prefer that we not exchange your name with third parties, or if you wish to clarify or modify your communication preferences, please visit us at www.ReaderService.com/consumerschoice or write to us at Reader Service Preference Service, P.O. Box 9062, Buffalo, NY 14269. Include your complete name and address.

HSR11

USA TODAY *bestselling author B.J. Daniels*
takes you on a trip to Whitehorse, Montana,
and the Chisholm Cattle Company.

RUSTLED

Available July 2011 from Harlequin Intrigue.

As the dust settled, Dawson got his first good look at the rustler. A pair of big Montana sky-blue eyes glared up at him from a face framed by blond curls.

A woman rustler?

"You have to let me go," she hollered as the roar of the stampeding cattle died off in the distance.

"So you can finish stealing my cattle? I don't think so." Dawson jerked the woman to her feet.

She reached for the gun strapped to her hip hidden under her long barn jacket.

He grabbed the weapon before she could, his eyes narrowing as he assessed her. "How many others are there?" he demanded, grabbing a fistful of her jacket. "I think you'd better start talking before I tear into you."

She tried to fight him off, but he was on to her tricks and pinned her to the ground. He was suddenly aware of the soft curves beneath the jean jacket she wore under her coat.

"You have to listen to me." She ground out the words from between her gritted teeth. "You have to let me go. If you don't they will come back for me and they will kill you. There are too many of them for you to fight off alone. You won't stand a chance and I don't want your blood on my hands."

"I'm touched by your concern for me. Especially after you just tried to pull a gun on me."

"I wasn't going to shoot you."

Dawson hauled her to her feet and walked her the rest of the way to his horse. Reaching into his saddlebag, he pulled out a length of rope.

"You can't tie me up."

He pulled her hands behind her back and began to tie her wrists together.

"If you let me go, I can keep them from coming back," she said. "You have my word." She let out an unladylike curse. "I'm just trying to save your sorry neck."

"And I'm just going after my cattle."

"Don't you mean your boss's cattle?"

"Those cattle are mine."

"*You're* a Chisholm?"

"Dawson Chisholm. And you are…?"

"Everyone calls me Jinx."

He chuckled. "I can see why."

*Bronco busting, falling in love…it's all in a day's work.
Look for the rest of their story in*

RUSTLED

*Available July 2011 from Harlequin Intrigue
wherever books are sold.*

SPECIAL EDITION

Life, Love and Family

THE TEXANS ARE COMING!

Reader-favorite miniseries Montana Mavericks
is back in Special Edition with new loves,
adventures and more.

July 2011 features *USA TODAY* bestselling author
CHRISTINE RIMMER
with
RESISTING MR. TALL, DARK & TEXAN.

A Texas oil mogul arrives in Thunder Canyon on
business and soon falls for his personal assistant. Only
one problem—she's just resigned to open a bakery!
Can he convince her to stay on—as his bride?

Find out in July!

Look for a new
Montana Mavericks: The Texans Are Coming title
in each of these months

| August | September | October |
| November | December | |

Available wherever books are sold.

www.Harlequin.com

SEMM0711

Harlequin®

ROMANTIC
SUSPENSE

Secrets and scandal ignite in a danger-filled,
passion-fuelled new miniseries.

**Family. Lies.
Full exposure.**

When scandal erupts, threatening California Senator
Hank Kelley's career and his life, there's only one place he can
turn—the family ranch in Maple Cove, Montana. But he'll need
the help of his estranged sons and their friends to pull the family
together despite attempts on his life and pressure from a sinister
secret society, and to prevent an unthinkable tragedy that would
shake the country to its core.

Collect all 6 heart-racing tales starting July 2011 with
Private Justice
by *USA TODAY* bestselling author
MARIE FERRARELLA

Special Ops Bodyguard by **BETH CORNELISON** (August 2011)
Cowboy Under Siege by **GAIL BARRETT** (September 2011)
Rancher Under Cover by **CARLA CASSIDY** (October 2011)
Missing Mother-To-Be by **ELLE KENNEDY** (November 2011)
Captain's Call of Duty by **CINDY DEES** (December 2011)
